TRESSED TO KILL

TRESSED TO KILL

LILA DARE

WHEELER
CHIVERS

DARE LILA

This Large Print edition is published by Wheeler Publishing, Waterville, Maine, USA and by BBC Audiobooks Ltd, Bath, England.
Wheeler Publishing, a part of Gale, Cengage Learning.

A Southern Beauty Shop Mystery.

The text of this Large Print edition is unabridged.
Other aspects of the book may vary from the original edition.
Set in 16 pt. Plantin.

LIBRARY OF CONGRESS CATALOGING-IN-PUBLICATION DATA

Dare, Lila.
  Tressed to kill / by Lila Dare.
     p. cm. — (A Southern beauty shop mystery) (Wheeler Publishing large print cozy mystery)
  ISBN-13: 978-1-4104-2949-0 (softcover)
  ISBN-10: 1-4104-2949-0 (softcover)
  1. Beauty operators—Fiction. 2. Beauty shops—Fiction. 3. Women—Southern States—Fiction. 4. City and town life—Georgia—Fiction. 5. Murder—Investigation—Fiction. 6. Large type books. I. Title.
  PS3604.A735T74 2010
  813'.6—dc22   2010016640

BRITISH LIBRARY CATALOGUING-IN-PUBLICATION DATA AVAILABLE

Published in 2010 in the U.S. by arrangement with The Berkley Publishing Group, a member of Penguin Group (USA) Inc.
Published in 2010 in the U.K. by arrangement with The Berkley Publishing Group, a division of Penguin Group (USA) Inc.

U.K. Hardcover: 978 1 408 49213 0 (Chivers Large Print)
U.K. Softcover: 978 1 408 49214 7 (Camden Large Print)

Printed in the United States of America
1 2 3 4 5 6 7 14 13 12 11 10

To my daughters,
Lily and Ellen,
who bring such joy just by being.

ACKNOWLEDGMENTS

On the expert knowledge front, my deepest gratitude to Patrol Officer Tim Pippio of the Warner-Robbins, Georgia, police department for all things law enforcement and to Dylan Campbell of Toni & Guy for all things beauty salon. All errors — intentional or otherwise — are mine.

On the writing front, thanks to my critique group for their insightful comments that helped bring the women of Violetta's salon and the town of St. Elizabeth to life: Marie Layton, Lin Poyer, and Amy Tracy. And many thanks to my other early readers, including my mother (my beloved editor-in-chief) and Don Jordahl. I owe a huge debt of gratitude to the writing instructors and mentors who have inspired and encouraged me over the years and into the present: Coleen Grissom, Bob Flynn, Win and Meredith Blevins, Cornelia Read, and David Liss. Thank you all!

I am grateful to my wonderful agent, Paige Wheeler, for believing in me and my books and for working tirelessly and creatively to find my novels a home. Thanks also to Peggy Garry at Folio for keeping track of all contract details. I also thank Michelle Vega of Berkley Prime Crime for her editing expertise and Rebecca Chastain for her copyediting. I thought I was competent with commas until she got ahold of the manuscript. Annette Fiore DeFex designed a beautiful cover, and the artist, Brandon Dorman, did a splendid job capturing the feel of the book. Many thanks also to my Berkley Prime Crime publicist, Megan Swartz, and the rest of the Berkley Prime Crime team.

Most important, I thank my beloved husband, Tom, for his infinite patience and his unwavering belief that I'd be a published mystery novelist one day. Ditto for my mom, Joan Hankins, who has always believed I could do anything I set my mind to. What a gift it is to have people in your life who encourage and support you.

CHAPTER ONE

[Wednesday]

A half-moon curl of platinum hair sprang from my scissors to join the growing pile on the floor.

"Don't take too much off, Grace," Vonda Jamison cautioned, craning her neck to check my progress. I'd been cutting her hair since we were in high school — you'd think she'd trust me by now.

"Sit still." I tapped her head with my comb. Snip, snip. More curls drifted down. "You said you wanted it short."

"Short, not shorn." She slouched back against the black leatherette chair. "Maybe I should go red."

I swiveled the chair so she faced me instead of the mirror. The usual salon noises — customers chatting, water running in the shampoo basin, the phone ringing — washed around us, but I tuned them out from long practice.

"How's Ricky?" I asked. When Von started talking about changing her hair color, it usually meant she and Ricky were on the outs.

Her huge sigh was all the answer I needed. After fifteen years of best-friend-hood — we'd met as high school sophomores — we were pretty good at reading each other's eye rolls, shrugs, and sighs. "Over again?"

"Over *forever*."

Not likely. Vonda and Ricky Warren had been on-again, off-again as long as I'd known her. One particularly long stretch of "on" had resulted in a six-year marriage, twice as long as my ill-fated attempt at matrimony. When they divorced, I thought the "off" might be permanent, but they'd hooked up again before they'd paid off the lawyers' fees. So I laughed, earning myself a glare. I deliberately changed the subject. "Are you going to the meeting tonight?"

"Absolutely. Constance DuBois and her crowd are primed to snag all the funding for their 'Preserve the Rothmere Antebellum Mansion' initiative. PRAM." She wrinkled her nose. "How can people vote to pay for historically accurate nineteenth-century wallpaper rather than new PCs for the schools? I swear, RJ's using the computer equivalent of an abacus at Jefferson

10

Davis Elementary. I'm going to make damned sure the vote goes in favor of funding the school's technology center."

Nothing got Vonda riled up faster than issues involving her eight-year-old, Richard James Warren IV. I agreed with her that the school needed to update its technology, but I also knew historical homes like the Rothmere mansion brought a lot of tourists to St. Elizabeth, Georgia. And tourists meant money for local businesses like my mom's salon, my place of employment.

Choosing not to disagree with Von, I started to texturize the hair on her crown. "And what about the Morestuf Mart? Do you think we should approve that at the town hall meeting?"

"Hell, no." Vonda's answer was swift and sure. "A big box store like that will eat into the profits of the downtown shops and places like Violetta's." Her gesture took in the whole salon. "The historic district is the primary reason tourists come to St. Elizabeth. They can get Morestufs and Home Fix-Its and what have you back in Detroit or Philly or Kalamazoo — they come to St. Elizabeth for our charm and quaintness and Southern hospitality." She let her voice lapse into an exaggerated drawl. "Right, sugah?"

"Right," I agreed, laughing. Vonda and

11

Ricky owned a bed and breakfast on Peachtree Street, and tourists were their lifeblood, as they were for most of the town since the paper mill shut down about ten years back. Pulling out my hair dryer, I cut off further conversation as I finished Vonda's hair. "There." I turned the chair so she could see.

"Grace, honey, you're a genius." She beamed at her reflection. Wispy bangs hung slightly over her brown eyes, giving her gamine face with its pointy chin a mysterious look. She looked great, if I did say so myself.

"You're just figuring that out?" I returned her exuberant hug and walked her to the door.

"See you at the meeting tonight?" she asked, slipping on Jackie O sunglasses.

"Wouldn't miss it," I assured her.

And neither would anyone else in town, I thought as she left, surveying the bustle in the salon. Normally, Wednesday afternoons were a bit slow, but the salon, the front half of my mom's Victorian home, was packed. Mom, the Violetta the shop is named for, was doing a cut at her station near the front windows with the blinds lowered to cut the glare. Stella Michaelson, our manicurist, tackled two manicures at a time in the Nail

Nook, an alcove behind the register, with her white Persian, Beauty, curled on a cushion at her feet. Althea Jenkins, my mom's best friend and our part-time aesthetician, waxed and tinted brows in the small room that used to be the formal parlor but which my mom had co-opted for the salon when she decided Violetta's should offer spa services. Rachel Whitley, a high-schooler and aspiring beautician, shampooed our clients in the sink of the former powder room. We'd removed all the walls (and the toilet) and replaced some of them with waist-high barriers of glass bricks, and it really opened the place up.

In addition to our regular clientele, I noticed several of what I called the *haute ton* — a term for high-society women I stole from my favorite Georgette Heyer Regencies — waiting for trims and mani-pedis. Not only was the town hall meeting an important budget forum, it was this week's best opportunity to be photographed for the *St. Elizabeth Gazette,* our weekly newspaper more concerned with society events and the results of local gardening contests than the Iraq war or Wall Street projections. And that wasn't a bad thing. Living in Atlanta with Hank, I'd endured enough stories of child abuse, gang violence, and

13

political skullduggery to last me a lifetime. The upbeat stories in the *Gazette* exactly suited my current mood.

Lucy Mortimer, the curator of the Rothmere mansion and museum, was my next client, and Rachel was just finishing up her shampoo. Rachel gave me a "two minutes" signal and I got a diet root beer from the small fridge we kept behind the counter and relaxed for a moment, enjoying the way the sun slanted through the wooden blinds and striped the broad pine floorboards.

I tuned in to the conversation Mom was having with the teenage client in her chair. My mother, Violetta Terhune, leaned in over the girl's shoulder. The violet tunic Mom wore contrasted nicely with her gray-white hair and her still-lovely complexion, softened with a few wrinkles. Her blue eyes, framed by rimless glasses, smiled into the girl's eyes in the mirror, like they shared a secret. Her soft bosom and twenty extra pounds made her look sweet and accommodating and motherly, but I'd seen that determined smile on her face more times than I could count when I was a teenager. Come to think of it, I still saw it on occasion.

"Now, Mindy, honey, you know your mama's not going to like it if you come home with your beautiful hair in a Mohawk" — she stroked the girl's bright head — "and magenta stripes." Mindy started to protest, but Mom overrode her with, "Let me show you what I think would look just darling on you. I saw it on that actress, you know, the one in that movie about teenage vampires living in Dallas — such twaddle! — and you're way cuter than she is." And she began snipping at the girl's hair, talking all the while. Mindy's face went from rebellious to resigned to tentatively pleased as I watched.

And that, I thought, suppressing a smile, summed up both the delights and the irritations of living in a small Southern town. Everybody knew everybody, which created a warm sense of community. On the other hand, nothing was private and everybody thought they ought to have a say in your life, which annoyed the heck out of me. Slotting the soda can into the recycle bin — my idea — I returned to my station, stopping to tell Mindy she looked fabulous and earning a smile of approval from my mom.

I was finishing up Lucy's blow-out when the front door banged open, jingling the bells and clattering the blinds. A man entered, dressed in full Civil War regalia.

15

Confederate gray, of course, complete with a sword. That might have seemed strange or out of place in most salons, but Walter Highsmith owned the Civil War memorabilia shop two storefronts down from Violetta's and he stopped in frequently. I'd long suspected he was sweet on my mom, but as far as I knew their relationship had never progressed beyond dinners, conversation, and friendship. A short, plump man with a full goatee and a mustache that he waxed into rigid loops, Walter was, I thought, a bit barmy on the whole Civil War thing. He participated in reenactments and came running over to tell Mom whenever he acquired a particularly interesting piece of memorabilia. Today, though, his chubby cheeks were flushed an angry red, and he was almost sputtering as he sought out my mother.

"Hello, Walter," she greeted him, putting her combs into a jar of blue germicide. Mindy had left, eager to show off her new hair to her friends.

"Do you know what this is, Miss Violetta?" he asked, flapping an envelope. "It's an eviction notice. That . . . that woman is throwing me out at the end of the month. Right as tourist season starts!" The ends of his mustache quivered.

"Oh, no," Mom said. "Why would she do that?"

I knew the "she" my mom referred to was Constance DuBois, owner of several properties on the downtown square, including the building Walter rented for Confederate Artefacts. It originally housed the DuBois Bank and Trust, which had relocated to a bigger building on the west side of town in the mid-1980s.

"I've been there nineteen years, Miss Violetta. Nineteen years!" He stopped to take a deep breath. "Never have I been late with the rent. And now she evicts me without so much as the courtesy of a conversation, just because she has a friend — a Yankee from New York — who wants to open a scrapbooking shop. Frilly ribbons and precious papers and furbelows. Fah!" He threw up his hands and the letter wafted to the floor. He stamped on it. Then he pulled the sword from the scabbard at his side and ran the envelope through. "I'm not going to stand for it! She can't do this."

"Calm down, Walter," Mom said. All eyes in the shop were on the furious Confederate colonel waving his sword around with the envelope impaled on the tip.

Despite his fussy mannerisms and mid-nineteenth-century diction, I sympathized

17

with him. Losing his storefront on the square and relocating to some hole-in-the-wall tourists would never find would probably force him out of business.

The door opened again. A woman entered, talking nonstop into the cell phone glued to her ear. Uh-oh. Constance DuBois herself, grande dame of St. Elizabeth society; former Peach Festival Princess; president or former president of the Junior League, the PTA, the Historical Preservation Society, and Save Our Shoreline; chairwoman of the Seafarer's Spring Festival committee and PRAM; and evictor of Walter Highsmith. She sat on the boards of more local businesses than I could count, including her deceased husband's bank, now run by her son. I hadn't seen her since returning to St. Elizabeth from Atlanta four months ago, but a quick glance told me she hadn't changed. Same champagne-colored page-boy cut, same prominent cheekbones, same sleek body garbed in designer resort wear. Now sixty, my mom's age, she could probably still fit into the debutante dress she wore at eighteen.

Lucy Mortimer stiffened in my chair, and I looked at her curiously.

"Later. I said later!" Constance DuBois snapped into the cell phone before closing it. She greeted my mom with a smile that hardly moved the corners of her mouth and didn't touch her eyes. Botox.

"You!" Walter said, his eyes bugging. "What is the meaning of this?" He flourished the sword in her face. The envelope jarred loose and drifted sadly to the floor.

"Which words didn't you understand?" Constance asked, facing him. "Out. By. June."

"You won't get away with this."

"Cut the histrionics, Walter." She flipped a dismissive hand and turned back to my mother. Walter took a couple of heaving breaths, his gaze darting wildly around the salon, then slammed out the door without his usual polite leave-taking.

"Violetta. I simply must get my highlights freshened before the town hall meeting, and my usual stylist at Chez Pierre is out with the flu. So inconvenient. So, do be a dear and squeeze me in, won't you?"

Walter's dramatic departure hadn't fazed Constance one bit. Her words were a command, not a plea, and I ground my teeth, watching Mom for her reaction. A muscle jumped in her jaw, but she kept a polite smile on her face.

"I'm sure your little place here could use the business," Constance continued. She cast a patronizing glance at the chintz-covered chairs in the waiting area, the lush ferns hanging in wire baskets from the ceiling, and the restored wooden figurehead that came from the prow of a Spanish galleon, the *Santa Elisabeta*, sunk off our coast in the 1500s. Adventure divers showed up every year, trying to retrieve a gold coin or emerald ring. Constance flared her nostrils at the womanly figure, as if it were vaguely offensive, and sailed over to my mother's station, seating herself in the chair. "The town hall meeting starts in just over an hour, so you'd better —"

An orchestra started playing Vivaldi, and Constance flipped open her cell. "Speak. It's got to be tomorrow. No, Friday's too late. I —"

I stopped listening as Mom ran her hands through Constance's hair, getting a feel for it. I knew what she was thinking because I'd heard it a thousand times: A paying customer is a paying customer. Let's be grateful when anyone gives us their business. It's a blessing.

I had trouble seeing Constance DuBois as a blessing, but I finished off Lucy's hair with a spritz of hairspray and whisked the cape — violet, of course — from around her shoulders. "Thanks, Grace," she said, rising

20

from the chair.

"Hello, Constance," Lucy said as we passed the newcomer on our way to the register. Her voice trembled, and I wondered why she sounded so tentative.

"Good afternoon, Lucy," Constance said distantly. "Shouldn't you be at the mansion, clearing out?"

Lucy's face blanched, but she didn't say anything. What was that all about, I wondered, running her credit card. She barely lingered to sign before dashing out the door.

"What's she doing here?" a voice said in my ear.

I turned to see that Althea Jenkins had come up behind me and was gazing with undisguised disdain at Constance DuBois. Althea managed to look regal even in polyester knit pantsuits, J.C. Penney's dresses, or her aesthetician's smock. She had full lips and a broad nose, and a headband held her jaw-length afro, threaded with gray, back from her high forehead. Althea had a trick of thrusting her chin up just a hair, like she was inviting the world to take a swing. Just now, her chin tilted even higher than usual.

"Highlights," I said. "She needs to spiff up for the town hall meeting, and her snooty salon outside of town couldn't work her in. So, she's taking advantage of Mom's good nature."

"And not for the first time," Althea observed.

As if she heard us, Constance DuBois looked over. She seemed to hesitate at sight of Althea, but she nodded and said, "Hello, Althea."

"Connie," Althea acknowledged her.

"Don't call me —" A ping indicated an incoming message and she broke off to read it.

"Constance," my mom said, trying to pry her client's attention from her electronic gadget. "I've been trying to tell you. Your hair is overprocessed, and I'm not sure —"

"When I want your opinion, I'll ask for it," Constance said without looking up from her BlackBerry. "Just do the highlights, Violetta. God knows that shouldn't be too difficult, even for you. Or, if you're not up to it, let Grace take care of it. At least she has a license."

Anger made the palms of my hands itch. My mother was the best stylist east of the Mississippi, even if she'd never had any formal training. Did Van Gogh have a license to practice his art? Did Shakespeare? The fact that I had logged the fifteen hundred hours in a beauty school per Georgia state law and earned my cosmetology license didn't mean I was half the beautician my mom was. Althea's hand on my shoulder restrained me from giving Mrs. High-and-Mighty DuBois what for.

"Violetta can handle this," she whispered.

"On your head be it, Constance," Mom said mildly. "So to speak."

Punching numbers into her phone, Constance let herself be led to the shampoo area. Rachel massaged her head while Violetta mixed the highlights. When Constance interrupted the shampoo for the third time to take a phone call, Rachel gave me a speaking look. I gave her a thumb's up for her restraint, and she grinned, showing braces with black bands to match her goth hair and makeup. Wrapping a towel around Constance's head, she held her hand to her ear like she was making a phone call. I nodded. Cell phone in hand, Rachel slipped out the side door.

Constance settled in at Mom's station, looking frailer with wet hair outlining her skull and her thin neck exposed. "Let's get on with it," she said. "I cannot be late for the town hall meeting. There is critical business to conduct this evening."

"And the town would up and disappear from the map if she wasn't there," Althea whispered. In a normal voice she said,

"Come on back, Willa. I'm ready to do your facial now. My, have you found a new night cream? You look fresh as a magnolia blossom."

Since Willa Catherton was eighty-three if she was a day, likening her complexion to a flower petal was a bit over the top, but it made Miss Willa beam as she nudged her walker toward the spa room. "It's very kind of you to say so, Althea," she said.

I busied myself with end-of-day activities at the counter, inventorying supplies, checking the cash register receipts, and reviewing the next day's appointments. Mom finished applying Constance's highlights and was tucking her under the heat lamp when Vivaldi played again. Constance glanced at the number, and her brows twitched together. She took the call, sounding less autocratic than usual. "Hello? But I'm — You're here? Well, okay." She cinched the tie belt of her cape more firmly about her waist and headed for the door.

"Constance," my mom objected. "Those highlights are very time-sensitive. You can't —"

"I'll be right back," Constance said. "Surely a minute or two can't make that much difference." And as she stepped out the door, shutting it firmly behind her, a man's footsteps could be heard on the porch. Everyone left in the shop, including Stella and her nail clients and two women in the waiting area, edged a couple of steps closer to the front windows, trying to hear Constance's conversation on the veranda. The sun was setting at such an angle that Constance and her companion — it was clearly a man of above-average height — were nothing but silhouettes against the wooden blinds. His unintelligible voice came through as a dark grumble, while hers was higher, tinged with anger and maybe a bit of fear. That seemed completely out of character, so I dismissed the idea.

Constance slipped back in so suddenly she caught us by surprise. She marched back to her seat, twisting the pearl ring on her pinkie.

"You know, at Chez Pierre they offer the clients beverages," she said, looking around as if expecting a mint julep to appear, or at least a tall iced tea loaded with sugar.

My mom gripped her lips together and began sliding the foils from Constance's hair.

"And their décor is so modern and clean," she added. "You should take a run out there, Violetta, and take notes on their decorating scheme. It's got an Asian feel to it that's very twenty-first century. This place feels more like . . . like a frumpy hotel lobby."

"Now just a cotton-picking minute —" my mom started.

I interrupted her before she could assault a paying client, no matter how obnoxious. "Our customers like the homey feel, Constance," I said.

"Homey," she sneered. "What would you know about homemaking, Grace Ann? You couldn't hold your marriage together long enough to save for a house, never mind have children and turn it into a home. My mother, may she rest in peace, always said that when a man strays, you know that he's not getting his needs met at home." She ended with a pious sniff.

My face burned like she'd slapped me. "Why you —"

"Ow!" Constance yelped as my mom started rinsing her hair.

"Oh, pardon me, Constance, was that too warm?" Mom asked sweetly.

Yay, Mom!

Constance glared at her through narrowed eyes but settled back against the sink without saying anything more.

I stalked to the counter, and a frozen silence pervaded the usually cheerful salon as Mom trimmed Constance's hair and pulled out her dryer. The silence was broken by a collective gasp. I cut my eyes toward the women and stifled my own gasp as the first dried strands floated to Constance's shoulders.

"Oh, Constance, I am so sorry," my mother said, barely able to control her distress.

"Sorry? About what?" Constance looked up from her BlackBerry and stared at her reflection for one frozen minute. "Orange! My hair has orange stripes. You did this on purpose, Violetta Terhune." She surged to her feet.

"No! I'm sure it's because you spent that time on the veranda —"

"It is not *my* fault that you are an incompetent beautician, Violetta," Constance said, tearing the cape from around her neck with the ripping sound of outraged Velcro.

"I can fix it —"

"Fix it! The town hall meeting starts in twenty minutes. Besides, I wouldn't let you touch my hair again if you were the last beautician between here and Richmond. My gardener could do a better job with his pruning shears." Tears of rage glinted in her eyes.

"I like the orange," Rachel said, offering a

thumb's up from near the sink. "It's got a cool vibe."

A new voice sounded above the babble. "What's going on? Mother, what's the matter?"

The small crowd parted to let the newcomer through. Simone DuBois, a younger, dark-haired version of Constance who'd gone to high school with Vonda and me, let out a small shriek. "Mother! Oh my God, your hair is orange!"

"I noticed that, thank you, Simone." Constance's tone had gone from near hysterical to frigid.

"I'm sure we can sue," Simone offered, setting down her burgundy tote to pull out a notebook. I spotted the pointy nose and silky topknot of a Yorkshire terrier, tucked in with her wallet and keys and Kotex, no doubt. Dog as accessory — must be some fashion habit she'd picked up while working in New York, along with the black pencil skirt and stiletto heels. The dog glared at me with its pop eyes. "Mental distress, negligence . . ."

Just like a lawyer: when in doubt, sue somebody.

"I've got a better idea," Constance said. "Give me that." She grabbed the notebook. "I'm going to make sure this place is shut

down and stays that way. My Chi O sorority sister, Barbara Mayhew, is a member of
the State Board of Cosmetology licensing, if
I'm not mistaken. I'm sure she'd be appalled to hear about the violations that
abound in this . . . this collection of misfits
masquerading as a legitimate salon. First
and foremost, the 'proprietor' " — she
sneered — "doesn't have a cosmetology license."

She scribbled on the pad and moved
farther into the room, Simone trailing
behind her. "That cord is a hazard," she
noted, "and I'm sure those toxic chemicals
should be secured in some way." She gestured with her pen at the hair-coloring supplies peeking from an overhead cabinet. "No
illuminated emergency exit sign. And —"

A *rrrrowf* interrupted her as the Yorkie
struggled out of Simone's tote and beelined
for Beauty, who was observing the proceed-
ings with a total lack of interest from
beneath Stella's table. As the tiny dog approached, yapping in what it no doubt
thought was a menacing way, Beauty sat up,
licked a paw, and smoothed the whiskers to
one side of her pushed-in Persian nose. The
bundle of black and tan fur launched itself
at her, and Beauty dispatched it with one
swipe of her paw. Then she leaped grace-

fully onto Stella's lap and looked down her nose at the Yorkie, who was yipping and whining, a single drop of blood on its nose.

"— and a cat!" Constance wrote triumphantly as Simone wailed, "Peaches!"

She did her best to squat in the tight skirt, and the dog scooted toward her, whimpering. She gathered it into her arms and found a tissue to blot its nose. "Are you okay, my little dumpling?" She nuzzled the dog to her cheek. Apparently deciding her little dumpling would survive, she spun on her heel. "Come on, Mother. We're going to be late to the meeting."

"Your salon is done for, Violetta," Constance spat, reluctantly following her daughter. "Just wait —"

"Wait for what?" Althea appeared in the door of the spa room, Miss Willa hovering behind her.

Constance narrowed her eyes at the sight of Althea's still figure and the calmness in her deep voice. Then, catching a glimpse of her orange-striped hair in a mirror, passion overcame caution and she said, "Wait for what's coming to her. She's going to get her just desserts!"

"I don't think you want to be talking about 'just desserts,' Connie," Althea said.

Something in her voice glued my eyes to

her face. It revealed nothing.

A line of tension connected the two women, and I don't know what would have happened if my mother hadn't said with dignity, "Violetta's is closed. It's time for the town hall meeting." She made a shooing motion, and everyone drifted toward the doors.

The customers left first, twittering with excitement, and I knew the whole of St. Elizabeth would have the garbled details of Constance Dubois's visit to Violetta's before the town hall meeting was over. Althea helped Miss Willa down the stairs and returned to hug my mom.

"Don't you fret, Vi," she said, studying my mom's face. "Things'll work out. Have faith."

"I do," Mom said with a real smile.

Stella left next, moaning and apologizing that Beauty's presence had gotten Violetta in trouble. "I wouldn't have had it happen for the world, you know I wouldn't," she said, Beauty cradled in her arms.

"I know. Don't worry about it. We like having Beauty around," Violetta comforted her. "She adds a note of class."

With a glance at her watch and another mumbled apology, Stella took off down the stairs, anxious to pick up her daughter from

31

band practice.

"Well, I think that woman was a real . . . witch," Rachel announced, changing her word choice at the last moment when she felt my mom's eyes on her. The multiple piercings in the seventeen-year-old's ears glinted against the unrelieved black of her tee shirt and jeans. Even her high-top sneakers kept with the goth theme. "All that fuss over an orange stripe or two in her hair. Why, I know kids who would pay to have you do their hair like that."

"You okay, Mom?" I asked, helping her lock up after Rachel disappeared down the stairs, hopped on her pink scooter, and motored away.

She smiled wearily. "I've been better, but this, too, shall pass."

"Not if Constance DuBois has anything to say about it," I said, punching a throw pillow into shape on one of the waiting-room chairs.

"We can talk about this in the morning, Grace. Let's get over to the hall."

"Wouldn't want to miss the fireworks," I agreed.

CHAPTER TWO

Fireworks didn't come close to describing the town hall meeting. Vesuvian explosion, maybe. Constance DuBois sat on the stage with the mayor and a few other key players, including a Morestuf vice president. She wore a beigey blond wig in a shag style that would have been right at home in a 1980s disco. Heaven knows where she dug it up at such short notice, but I seemed to remember that her mother had died of lung cancer. After one searing glare at my mom and me when we took our seats, she avoided looking in our direction.

The evening started with a knock-down-drag-out between Vonda's vociferous group supporting funding for school computers and Constance and her cronies lobbying for PRAM monies. After the vote, Vonda sat with her arms crossed over her chest, scowling. Next on the evening's fight card — I mean agenda — was a face-off between the

Morestuf contingent and the Save Our Downtown Supporters (SODS). The crowd seemed to be about fifty-fifty on the issue, with the Morestuf lobbyists touting the cheap price of goods and the convenience of everything-in-one-place shopping, and the SODS citing statistics about how much money tourism brought into St. Elizabeth and holding up the idol of tradition.

The Morestuf VP turned puce when Constance DuBois informed him that "St. Elizabeth doesn't need or want the cheap goods made in some sweat shop that you sell to the undiscriminating." He retaliated with something about "elitist snob" and "foe of capitalist competition" and "out of touch with the reality of most of the area's demographic." I think he meant we had some poor people in town who couldn't afford the downtown shops. He was right about that; my budget was more in line with Morestuf prices than those in Filomena's Fashion Cove across the square from Violetta's.

The town voted to postpone a decision on the Morestuf store until a committee could generate a report about potential impacts to the environment and the economy. When my mom jabbed me with her elbow, I raised my hand to volunteer for the committee, noticing that Simone was waving her hand, too, like the spring-butt she had been in high-school. I hoped she wouldn't bring the rabid Yorkie to committee meetings.

The crowd started dispersing shortly afterward, even though a few agenda items remained. Mom insisted on staying because she wanted to chat with a couple of the SODS and set up a strategy-planning meeting. I told her I'd wait and walk back with her. My apartment was only two blocks past her house. With the crowd having dwindled to a handful of people, and my mom in the center of a cluster of agitated business owners near the stage, I ducked out to find the restroom.

I took the stairs to the third floor in an attempt to get a little exercise. I never quite seem to make it to the gym, but I do leg lifts while waiting in line and triceps presses with cans of tomato sauce during commercial breaks on *Desperate Housewives,* and that keeps me in reasonable shape. The stairwells were vaguely depressing in the way of uncared-for spaces, and smelled faintly of cigarette smoke. Was it new, illicit smoke, I wondered, or had it permeated the walls in the 1950s and '60s when every town employee probably had a pack-a-day habit?

Stepping out of the stairwell into a narrow

side corridor, I heard arguing. I slowed, caught by the tension in the raised voices coming from one of the small offices across from the restrooms. A line of light snuck out from between the not-quite-closed door and the jamb.

"Your opposition is costing us time and money," a man said.

I recognized the Texas accent: Mr. Morestuf.

"Our shareholders want profits, not lawsuits. We can make it worth your while if you persuade these Save Our Downtown loonies to pipe down. A bank can turn a huge profit with a project of this size."

"You can stuff your profit. This town values its heritage and will never vote to approve a Morestuf Mart. I'll see to it."

The woman's voice was even more familiar. It had the same steely edge as when she told Violetta the salon was done for. I wondered if her enmity rattled Mr. Morestuf the way it did me. Apparently not.

He said meaningfully, "You'd be smarter to throw in with us. You might not like the consequences if you don't."

"Is that a threat?" Constance's voice was incredulous.

I heard a smile in the man's reply. "Why Mrs. DuBois, we are the largest and most powerful retailer in the United States. We don't need to threaten anyone."

His words said one thing, but his tone of voice said another.

"I don't like being threatened, Mr. Richardson, and I make you a solemn promise here and now that you will never build a Morestuf in St. Elizabeth."

Footsteps approached the door, and I hastily ducked into the nearest bathroom, missing his last words and Constance's retort. My heart hammered at having nearly been caught eavesdropping, and I leaned against the door for a moment until Mr. Morestuf's heavy tread receded. Turning, I was momentarily confused by the bank of gleaming urinals on the wall. Oops. The room smelled strongly of disinfectant. I jerked open the door and hustled out, walking smash into Constance coming out of the ladies' room. I put out a hand to steady her, and she wrenched away.

"Watch where you're —" She broke off as she recognized me. "Oh, it's you."

Her eyes seemed puffy, and foundation had rubbed off the tip of her nose. Had she been crying? "I'm sorry —" I started.

Not even pausing to say something scathing about my presence in the men's room, she wheeled and tip-tapped down the hall in her tan pumps. The ladies' room door swung open again, and Cathy Finnegan, a local judge I knew slightly from church, emerged, wiping her hands down the side of her jeans to dry them.

"What was that all about?" she asked, staring after Constance.

"Heck if I know," I said.

We chatted for ten minutes or so about her upcoming trip to do missionary work in Haiti before she said her farewells and I finally made it into the ladies' room.

When I returned to the auditorium, my mom was alone and ready to leave.

"Thanks for waiting," she said. She draped a white cardigan around her shoulders and gathered up her tote, stuffed with her knitting and files for the SODS project.

We left as a janitor with string mop in hand waved at us from the stage and shut off the lights in the auditorium. Eerie exit lighting illuminated the hall as we made our way to the front entrance. The stone floors glistened wetly, so rather than dirty the clean floor, we headed for the back door that opened to the parking lot. Night air, fragrant with gardenia and jasmine, washed over us in a warm gust.

"We're in for a storm," Violetta announced, massaging her left shoulder, famous town-wide as a predictor of bad weather.

I caught a hint of ozone in the air and breathed deeply, feeling like I'd been holding my breath ever since Constance DuBois entered the salon. "We need the rain." Browning lawns and wilting shrubs testified to an unusually dry spring. The town's gardeners — and they were legion — had probably gotten together for a quick rain dance ceremony.

We started across the parking lot, the rising wind pushing us. Even though it was after nine, the asphalt still retained the heat of a sultry May day, and its tackiness grabbed at our shoes. Yuck. Only a handful of cars remained.

"You doing okay?" I asked Mom, giving her a sideways look.

The sodium-vapor lights in the parking lot cast an orangey glow that softened her outline. Her glasses had settled halfway down her nose, and her cardigan sat askew on her shoulders. With her hair worked into tufty spikes with styling product, she looked like a cozy Beatrix Potter hedgehog.

"I think we can beat Morestuf," she said, dodging the real issue. "The SODS are going to circulate a petition, and we're all going to review our pricing policies. Something that Morestuf man said stuck with me. We shouldn't be setting our prices to earn as much as we can from the tourists. We've got to remember the people who live here year-round, especially the ones less fortunate than we are."

"Mom, you already —" A sound that was half-groan, half-gargle caught my attention. I looked around. We had reached the far edge of the parking lot where it butted up against Carver Square, a small plot of grass and shrubs with ornamental benches. A lone car, a dark Jaguar, was parked across two spaces in an attempt, I guessed, to avoid door dings. The sound seemed to come from the driver's side of the car.

Mom and I glanced at each other and, with one accord, leaned to see around the trunk. The first thing I noticed was a shoe, a pump, lying by the rear tire. As my eyes scanned the ground, I picked out a bare foot and then a glimmer of paleness that must be a leg.

"Someone's hurt," Mom said. She started toward the supine figure, dropped to her knees, and put a hand on its shoulder. "Are you okay? Can you hear me? Ooh!"

A crack of thunder made me jump as lightning illuminated the waxy face of

Constance DuBois and my mother kneeling beside the body, staring at her uplifted hand coated with blood. Before my vision returned to normal, I had my cell phone out and was dialing 911.

Mom insisted on draping her cardigan over Constance's face once I ascertained that she was gone by feeling for a pulse on her neck. Then, she let me put an arm around her shoulders and lead her to the closest bench in Carver Square while we waited for the police to arrive. She was shivering. When she couldn't find a tissue in her tote, she wiped her bloodied hand on the grass, dragging it back and forth numerous times. Lightning came more often now, although the rain held off, and the look of confusion and sadness on her face made me ache.

"Poor Constance," she said.

"Poor Simone." I thought how devastated I'd be if something happened to Mom and conjured up real sympathy for Constance's daughter.

"I wonder what happened? It wasn't a heart attack."

Not with all that blood. "Maybe she tripped and banged her head."

"Mmm."

A brief silence fell, broken only by the barrage of thunder, and then Mom said what we'd both been thinking. "If only we'd been a few minutes earlier."

If only. Two of the saddest words in the English language. What if we'd come out five minutes earlier? I watched the wind dance an empty plastic bag across the park until my ears picked up the sound of sirens drawing closer. I stood and waved my arm as a police car skidded into the town hall parking lot, followed by a second car driving more cautiously. The first fat raindrops plopped onto my head as the blue and red lights swirled around me and then the skies opened up. Within seconds, before the policeman even opened his door, I was drenched.

Just great. Could this day get any worse?

Apparently it could.

"Grace, darlin'," a deep voice drawled as a tall figure stepped out of the police car. "You know I'm always happy to get together for dinner, shug. Or breakfast." The voice leered. "You don't have to make 911 calls to have an excuse to see me."

Hank. My ex-husband. One of St. Elizabeth's finest.

CHAPTER THREE

[Thursday]

"They scraped blood out from under my fingernails and put it in a little baggie," Mom said, pouring our breakfast tea the next morning. After the coroner's team had zipped Constance's body into a bag and hefted her into a hearse, and a Detective Washington finally gave us permission to go home, I'd spent the night in my girlhood bedroom in Mom's house, not wanting to leave her alone.

I choked on a mouthful of Earl Grey. "What? Why?"

Her shrug lifted the hem of her nightgown so her scuffed blue slippers showed. "Probably because they think I did it."

"Did what?" But I knew.

"Killed Constance."

"That's absurd. You couldn't have." I poured some Cap'n Crunch into my bowl with hands that shook. In my apartment,

I'd have breakfasted on microwave oatmeal sprinkled with berries and a handful of walnuts, but returning to my childhood home also meant adopting childhood habits. Especially comforting ones like sugary cereal. The cheery yellow kitchen with the brick wall and appliances from when I was a teenager felt like a cocoon. The oven dinged and Mom opened it, letting the delicious scent of cinnamon buns drift into the room.

"For later," she said, divining my thoughts. "When the ladies get here. We'll close the salon today, in Constance's memory, but I know Althea and Stella will be here. And probably Rachel, too, when school lets out." She settled into the ladder-back chair across from me with the pan of cinnamon buns in front of her and began to ice them with little swirls of her knife.

In the early days, after my dad died and she and Althea, also newly widowed, had turned their skills at hair cutting and facials into a business, she used to put out cinnamon buns or cookies or brownies for her customers. Back then, she did the cutting right here in the kitchen and I swept the clippings up in a little dust pan from the time I was five. Eventually, as word of her expertise grew, she turned the front of the old Victorian into a salon and quadrupled her business. The family — Mom, me, and my younger sister Alice Rose — had lived above the shop, falling asleep each night to the lingering odor of permanent solution.

I'd grown up loving the smells of the salon. Although I'd tried college — two years at the University of Georgia — I'd missed doing hair and left to attend beauty school. I'd worked for Vidal Sassoon in Atlanta after Hank finished with the police academy and we got married. Three years later, we got divorced. I stayed in Atlanta for another six months but felt lost and lonely on my own. Atlanta might be less than five hours away by car, but it felt like a separate universe. Now I was back and not too sure I fit in here anymore, either. Small-town life felt confining after almost four years in a metro area of five million. But it had its compensations . . . like homemade cinnamon rolls.

"Why'd you stop making goodies for the salon?" I asked, scooping up a blob of icing on my finger and licking it.

Mom shot me an incredulous look. "No time. It was one thing to do some baking when it was just a friend or two dropping by now and then for a trim and a little gossip. But now —"

"Now it's a lot of friends dropping in for cuts and color and more gossip than you'd find in *People* magazine," I finished for her.

"Now it's a bona fide business," she said with an emphatic nod. "No matter what Constance DuBois might think."

The dead woman's name hung in the air. "Maybe," I said tentatively, "this cloud might have a silver lining. I mean, she probably didn't have time to get in touch with the licensing board before —"

The back door, the one that led to the small yard and alley behind the house, burst open. "Violetta, did you hear what happened?"

Althea Jenkins stood on the threshold, brilliant poppy shirt tucked into matching broomstick skirt, vibrating with an air of uncharacteristic excitement. "Constance DuBois —"

"We found her," I said before she could finish.

"You what?" She put a hand to her heart and looked from me to Mom.

We both nodded. "It was horrible," Mom said. "The blood . . ." She poured Althea a cup of tea as her friend sank into a chair.

"We found her on our way home from the town hall meeting," I said. A thought crossed my mind. "I didn't see you there,

Althea. I thought you were planning to go."

"I wasn't feeling well," Althea said shortly. "Indigestion." She blew on her tea, letting the fragrant steam drift into her face. "Tell me what happened."

Mom and I took turns filling her in on the events from the meeting.

"I'm so very sorry, Vi," she said when Mom's voice trailed off describing how she tried to help Constance. "I can see that finding her was a real shock for you. But good riddance to bad rubbish."

"Althea!" My mom's voice was shocked. "You shouldn't speak ill of the dead."

"I never hesitated to say what I thought about Constance Wells DuBois when she was alive; I don't know why I should stop now that she's dead," Althea said, a stubborn look on her face. Sunlight skimmed the prominent angles of her jaw and cheekbones, pooling her deep-set eyes in shadow.

"What did she ever do to you?" I asked, surprised by the venom in her voice.

A knock sounded at the door before she could answer. With the familiarity of long friendship, she rose to answer it.

"You ain't welcome here, Hank Parker," Althea said when she saw the figure standing in the doorway.

"Official business," he said with a half

smile, pushing open the screen door. "Morning, Grace," he said, the smile growing broader as he took in the long red University of Georgia tee shirt I'd slept in and the tousled hair tumbling about my shoulders. I tried to tuck my bare legs under the chair.

The smile left me cold. Arctic. I could remember the time when it turned my insides to mush, but that was before I caught him with Melissa Littleton and realized she was one in a string. I wasn't sure what I'd ever seen in Hank, beyond the smile and the hot bod, now sporting a small potbelly under the khaki of his uniform shirt. He'd been a lineman on the football team but a lazy student, and it had taken him several years of flipping burgers and selling vacuums after high school to find his niche as a cop. With my twenty-twenty hindsight, I saw his passion for the law had more to do with cop groupies and guns than with protecting the public. At the time, I thought it was noble. Was I an idiot, or what? Once he signed on with the Atlanta PD, we got married, and it was all downhill from there. Down a steep, icy hill on a toboggan with greased runners.

"What do you want?" I asked with as much dignity as possible, given my state of semi-dress.

"I could tell you what I really want if we were alone," he said. He tucked his thumbs into his belt and slouched against the door jamb.

I flushed with fury and embarrassment.

"I won't have that kind of talk in my kitchen," Mom snapped. "You keep a respectful tongue in your head."

"Yes'm," he mumbled. His expression grew sullen. "I want my NASCAR memorabilia back, Grace."

I avoided my mom's gaze. When I'd caught Hank cheating, I'd boxed up his NASCAR stuff, his greatest treasures, and hidden them from him in a fit of anger and hurt. It wasn't one of my finer moments. I hadn't gotten around to giving them back before I left Atlanta, and they were stored in a closet upstairs. "Later, Hank," I said. "It was a long night. Mom and I have stuff to do."

"I'd say so," he said meaningfully. "I'm here to escort you to the GBI. That's the Georgia Bureau of Investigation."

He was still looking at my mom, a glimmer of satisfaction in his eyes.

"What?" all three of us chorused.

"You're wanted for questioning pertaining to the murder of Constance DuBois. Come on now." He straightened and let his hand rest suggestively by the handcuffs clipped to his utility belt. "You, too, Grace."

"Not until we get dressed," Mom said calmly, taking the air out of him. "You just run along and tell that nice Detective Washington we met last night we'll be by in about an hour."

"But —" Hank gaped at her.

Mom started up the staircase, and I quickly followed, holding the hem of the tee shirt down over my fanny. As we reached the second floor I heard Althea say, "If you so much as touch one of those cinnamon buns, I'll have to cut your hand off."

The night's storm had washed the sky clear of pollen and haze, and the temperature and humidity both lingered at reasonable levels — under ninety. That would change as the day went on. Right now, though, it was refreshing, and I kept the window down as I drove Mom to the GBI office in Kingsland via State Road 42. St. Elizabeth inhabits a point on the southeast coast of Georgia, bounded by the Satilla River to the north and the Cumberland Sound to the east, a little closer to Jacksonville, Florida than Savannah. SR 42 is the umbilical cord tying us to I-95 and the rest of the Eastern seaboard. Once west of I-95, we quickly reached US 17 and turned south. I parked my aging Ford Fiesta in the lot fronting the GBI Region 14 building and got out to the smell of warm tarmac and newly mown grass.

Sternly clipped boxwoods of different heights stood out against the pinky tan brick of the single-story building, like felons assembled for a lineup. Long vertical windows brought to mind arrow slits as we headed up the short sidewalk. The grass on either side was a dusty moss color, rather than emerald, and I knew the GBI must be adhering to the watering restrictions imposed in the drought.

I felt a bit unnerved at the prospect of the coming interview, but I squared my shoulders and walked beside my mom to the simple gray door and opened it. A uniformed policeman — Officer Kent, according to his nametag — who looked young enough to still be memorizing the Pythagorean theorem or diagramming sentences, sat behind a long counter and phoned someone when we told him why we were there. "It'll be a minute, ma'am, if you'd like to have a seat," he said when he hung up. Jug ears stuck out from a head shaved to a quarter-inch of stubble, and he

51

looked almost embarrassingly earnest.

Mom settled onto one of a rank of molded blue chairs, her purse on her lap, and pulled out the knitting that accompanied her everywhere. I elected to stand and let my eyes flit from the dusty corn plant in the corner to the photograph of the governor grinning from the wall. I wasn't going to vote for him next time around; he was too cozy with developers for my taste. Just as I was eyeing an ancient *Field & Stream,* the door beside the counter opened and a man stood on the threshold. He was six feet tall, I'd guess, and fortyish, with a nose that had been broken at least once. He wore a navy blazer over a white shirt and charcoal slacks, not a uniform, but every inch of him shouted "cop" or maybe "soldier." From the steely eyes that seemed to miss nothing to the trim waist and close-cropped hair going gray at the temples, he crackled with energy and alertness. My gaze fell on Officer Kent behind the desk, and I caught him looking at the newcomer with something akin to hero worship.

"Mrs. Terhune?" the man said, looking at Mom. His voice was a surprise, deep and crisp without a hint of a drawl. He wasn't from south of the Mason-Dixon, that was for sure. I wondered how he'd ended up in

Georgia.

"Where's Detective Washington?" Mom asked, stowing her knitting.

"I'm Special Agent Dillon," he said. "The St. Elizabeth Police Department asked us to take over the DuBois case."

"Do you go by Marshal?" I asked with the hint of a smile.

His gaze flicked to me, and he didn't deign to answer. I got the feeling it wasn't the first time he'd heard a Marshal Dillon joke. Officer Kent at the desk glared at me, as if I were making fun of his hero. He was probably too young for *Gunsmoke.*

I moved to join my mom and the detective, but he stopped me with a glance. "I'll be back for you in a while, Miss Terhune. I hope you don't mind waiting." His tone said he didn't give a flip if I minded or not. And he ushered Mom through the door, which closed with a definitive snick of the lock.

Well! I'd assumed we'd be interviewed together, but apparently Special Agent Dillon didn't want to give us a chance to sync up our stories. Although we'd had all night to do that, if we'd had a mind to. I circled the small waiting area twice, then asked Officer Kent if there was some place to get a cup of tea. He accepted a dollar bill from me and returned with vending machine mystery liquid that was, at least, hot. I sipped at it and settled down with the *Field & Stream,* preferring it to the most recent issue of *Chopper Underground,* which was my only other reading choice.

I knew a lot more about backyard butchering than I was ever likely to put to use by the time Special Agent Dillon appeared with Mom. She didn't look like he'd been pulling out her fingernails or blinding her with klieg lights. In fact, they seemed to be on good terms. She was offering to email him her recipe for barbecue rub, and he was saying he might stop in some time for a haircut.

"It's about time for a trim," he added, running a hand across the top of his head.

"Anytime," Mom beamed.

I snorted softly. The man's hair would meet Marine standards; if he showed up at Violetta's it would be only to glean more information about Constance DuBois's murder. I'd have to warn Mom to be careful around him.

He turned to me, and the smile died out of his eyes. And they weren't really steel colored, I noted. More a navy blue with a darker rim. Striking.

"Okay, Miss Terhune. Let's chat." At least he held the door open for me.

"I'm going to run down to the Perk-Up

for a cup of coffee," my mom called as the door closed. "I'll be back in half an hour."

Now why hadn't I thought of that?

Expecting a dingy interrogation room complete with table bolted to the floor and one-way mirror, I was surprised when he led me to an office. A comfortable office with sunlight streaming through a large window, a coffee pot emitting a tempting odor from a credenza behind the desk, and a triptych of photos featuring a woman in jodhpurs putting a handsome black horse over a series of jumps in an arena.

"Your wife?" I asked with a nod at the photos.

"My horse," he replied. He settled himself in the desk chair, and I sank into one of two ladder-back chairs that faced the desk. At least it was padded, unlike the unyielding molded plastic in the reception room.

"Let's get right to the point, Miss Terhune," Dillon said, resting his forearms on the desk and leaning toward me. "I think you or your mother — and right now I'm leaning toward you because I liked your mother — stabbed Mrs. DuBois last night to keep her from shutting down your beauty shop."

Wham. His words socked me back into the chair, and I took a moment to catch my

55

breath. "That's ridiculous," I sputtered.

"Is it? Let's review." He held up his forefinger. "One. Your mother sabotages Mrs. DuBois's hair —"

"My mother did no such thi—"

"— and Mrs. DuBois threatens to shut down Violetta's, depriving you and your mother of your source of income. Don't even try to tell me that didn't happen because I've talked with several witnesses who described the scene to me. And I've seen the orange stripes in the victim's hair."

I wondered which of our "friends" and clients had been so quick to tell the police about yesterday's run-in.

"Two." He held up another finger. "Neither you nor your mother have an alibi for the time of Mrs. DuBois's death."

"We were at the town hall meeting."

He shook his head. "Uh-uh. The meeting was over. You wandered off. Your mother met briefly with a group dedicated to preserving the downtown area, but they left twenty minutes before you called 911 to report finding a body. What happened in that twenty minutes, Miss Terhune? Did you do it together?"

His accusations battered me, and I wondered why he was so hostile. Was this just his interviewing technique? Did he hope to jolt a confession from me? Well, he could think again. I hadn't been married to a cop for three years for nothing. I took a deep breath and kept my voice even. "You don't really suspect me, Special Agent. You haven't read me my rights." I sat on my hands to keep them from trembling.

He kept his face impassive, but I caught a glimpse of something in his eyes. Surprise? Maybe even respect. "You're strangely knowledgeable for a civilian. Have you been arrested before?"

I was onto his style, and the new attack didn't faze me. "My ex was a police officer."

"I know."

Ah-ha. Here was the source of his hostility. Who knew what Hank had been saying about me? Whatever it was, I wasn't going to degrade myself by trying to offer a defense.

I met his gaze levelly. "Maybe we should start over. Would you like to hear what happened last night?"

This time I caught a glimpse of a smile, quickly suppressed. "Please."

"Let's start with my alibi." I told him about chatting with Judge Cathy Finnegan outside the restroom.

He made a note. "We'll check with her."

The look he gave me said he thought I'd made the whole thing up.

Then I told him about the meeting and the conversation I overheard between Constance and Mr. Morestuf.

"Del Richardson," he said, checking his notes. "I understand they had a heated exchange during the meeting."

I nodded. "And he tried to intimidate her afterward." I repeated his words, as close as I could remember them. "Constance accused him of threatening her, but he laughed it off. It sounded like a threat to me, though."

"Could she really have put the brakes on the Morestuf going up?" Dillon asked.

I gave it some thought, cocking my head to one side. "Maybe. Constance is — was — a powerful woman with a lot of connections, not just in town but up to the governor. He's her cousin-in-law."

Special Agent Dillon looked dubious. "Cousin-*in-law?* That's not a relative. Back in Wisconsin I knew my barber better than I knew any of my cousins, never mind their spouses."

"I think you'll find we here in the South take family a bit more seriously," I said. It was my turn to smile. "Including the governor. He's known to take an active interest in family matters. He and Constance were like this." I twined two fingers together. "At least, that's what Constance says. Said."

"Great," Dillon muttered under his breath.

I offered him a pseudo-sympathetic smile. "I'm sure it's hard to detect with someone like the governor breathing over your shoulder."

"So I'd better wrap this up quickly," Dillon said. He raised one strong brow. "Can you think of anyone, besides yourself and your mother, of course, who would want to kill Constance DuBois?" An image of Vonda flashed into my head. She might have hated Constance and been enraged by how the vote went, but no way would she stab the woman. And Walter Highsmith, railing about his eviction and waving his sword, certainly had reason to hate Constance. "Wanting to and actually doing it are two different things," I said. "Constance pissed off a lot of people in her day, Agent Dillon. Right up to yesterday, in fact. And her husband did, too, when he was alive. Their bank foreclosed on a lot of folks over the years. And I hear their son, Philip, is carrying on the family tradition."

"So you're suggesting someone offed her to get revenge for a foreclosure that might have happened years ago?" He arched his brows skeptically.

Put like that, it sounded pretty unlikely. I shrugged.

"So what was your mother doing while you were eavesdropping on the victim?" He changed tack as easily as a sailboat in a brisk wind.

I folded my lips together to keep from blurting anything out. Truth was, I didn't know what my mother had been doing and I didn't know what she'd told him earlier. "She was meeting with the Save Our Downtown crew," I said.

"After that," he pushed.

"I don't know," I had to admit. "Probably reading through her notes, waiting for me to return from the ladies' room."

"But you don't know that," he said. "You weren't with her."

Before I was forced to concede his point, a rap on the door brought my head around. A young woman with frizzy, ginger-colored hair stood in the doorway, twisting the gumball-sized pink beads on her necklace. "Special Agent? There's a phone call for you."

"Take a message, Shasta," he said impatiently.

Her brown eyes widened, and she shook her head. "It's the governor."

CHAPTER FOUR

Back at Violetta's a sign on the door proclaimed "Closed out of respect for the passing of Constance DuBois." I wondered who had put it there; it sounded like Stella. Inside, Mom and I found Stella painting burgundy polish onto Althea's nails. Stella looked up and smiled as the door closed, but the smile didn't dim the worry in her green eyes. The forty-year-old mother of a tween daughter, she had a lot to worry about, including a husband who worked only sporadically and a home moving into foreclosure. She didn't need the added aggravation of wondering whether her place of employment was going to be shut down. Rachel watched from her perch on the counter, crunching on an apple.

"Shouldn't you be in school, young lady?" Mom asked the teen.

"Half day today." She tossed her head to get her black bangs out of her eyes. "Teacher development or something. I heard you got arrested, Miss Violetta." She took another bite of apple and looked at us expectantly.

"What?" The word came out too loud, and I lowered my voice. "Who told you that?"

She shrugged slim shoulders under a black tee shirt with the name of some band stenciled under a silver and white skull with vampire teeth. "I heard it at school. They said Miss Violetta killed that bi— that woman who threw a hissy in here yesterday. Did you?"

Her voice contained no fear or criticism, only curiosity. Youth. Or maybe just Rachel.

"Of course not," Mom said. "You should know better than to listen to gossip."

"Much less repeat it," Althea said meaningfully. She spread the fingers of one hand to admire her nails.

"I didn't think you had," Rachel said, unrepentant. "Not when I heard she was stabbed, like, a dozen times. That didn't sound like you."

I wondered what form of murder Rachel thought *did* sound like Mom.

"Mrs. DuBois died of a single stab wound," Mom said, tucking her purse behind the counter. "And she was not . . . interfered with. The special agent was kind enough to tell me that much. I'm sure it's a comfort to her family to know that she died almost instantly."

Hmph. Special Agent Dillon hadn't told me squat all. Of course, our conversation had been interrupted by the governor's call. I suppressed a laugh, remembering the look on his face as he picked up the phone and I left.

"Well, if you didn't do it, who did?" Rachel asked the question on all our minds. She arced the apple core toward a trash can, and it swished in.

"Coulda been most anybody," Althea said, "except Vi."

"Oh, my goodness, it couldn't have been any of us," Stella said, screwing the top back on the nail polish bottle. "I can't believe anybody did it on purpose, not anybody from St. Elizabeth."

"It's hard to stab someone through the heart in a parking lot by accident, Stel," I pointed out.

"Maybe it was a robbery," she suggested.

I didn't remember seeing Constance's purse near her body, so maybe it *had* been a robbery. But . . . "Why would a thief leave the car?" I asked. "That Jag must be worth a lot."

"Maybe you scared him off before he could get the keys," Stella said.

The thought gave me the heebie-jeebies. Had the murderer still been there when Mom and I started across the parking lot? Had he seen us? Mom's eyes met mine, and I knew she was thinking the same thing.

"We don't need to worry about it," Mom said in her "the subject's closed" voice. "It's the police's job to figure out what happened to Constance."

"They already figured out *what,* Mom. Now they need to figure out *who.* And since they seem to think it might have been one of us, I think we'd be smart to do a little poking around."

"I agree," Stella said in a surprisingly firm voice. "It's just horrid that people think you had something to do with it, Violetta."

"Like, yeah," said Rachel. "I vote we investigate. I can be Veronica Mars."

"Who?" I asked.

"She's this sixteen-year-old detective on the CW. She totally rocks. I was really bummed when the show got cancelled, but I've got a DVD set with all the episodes and I watch it, like, all the time."

Mom shot me a "look what you've done now" look.

"I say definitely not." Althea rose from the manicure chair to pace the width of the salon. "When you go poking around in old

65

secrets, you don't know what's going to jump out." She blew on her nails, avoiding everyone's eyes.

"Old secrets? I don't think we'll have to go back further than a week or two to find someone with a grudge against Constance," I said.

"Well, count me out," Althea said. She marched toward the door and jerked it open, just as Simone DuBois raised her hand to knock.

Both Althea and Simone fell back a step, Althea still holding the door. Then, Althea said, "Losing your mama must be real hard on you, Simone. When are the services going to be?"

I noticed she wasn't hypocritical enough to say she was sorry about Constance's death.

Simone, dressed in head-to-toe black, including a little pillbox hat that screamed Jackie Kennedy, said, "Oh, come off it." Her dark eyes looked sunken in her pale face. The night's grieving had aged her. "None of you care that my mother is dead. In fact, I came over here to tell you that I know you murdered her" — she looked directly at Mom — "and I'm going to move heaven and earth to make sure you're held responsible. You knew she was going to close down this . . . *salon*" — she said the word as if it were *bordello* — "and you killed her to keep it from happening. Well, you won't get away with it, I can promise you that."

"*Rowf,*" echoed the Yorkie, poking its head out of Simone's tote.

From her spot under Stella's table, Beauty swished her tail, not even bothering to open her eyes.

"Oh, shut up, Peaches," Simone said. "Don't think I can't put you out of business. I'm not my mother's daughter for nothing. When I'm through, you won't have enough paying customers to buy kitty kibble." She glared at Beauty as if it were all her fault.

My natural tendency to feel sorry for any woman who had lost her mom in such a horrible way was dissipating under the lash of Simone's tongue. "Come on, Simone. You know my mom didn't have anything to do with Constance's death. It's ridic—"

"Grace." Mom stopped me and stepped forward, holding her hands out to the angry woman. Simone whipped her own hands behind her back, as if fearing contamination. Mom's arms dropped to her sides. She smiled sadly. "I never wished Constance ill and I certainly didn't harm her, Simone. We might have had our differences, but I respect how much she cared about St. Elizabeth. She worked hard to preserve —"

"I don't need to hear about my mother from you, Violetta," Simone said, tears trickling down her face. She plucked the Yorkie out of her tote and cuddled him to her cheek. He licked at the tears. "You might as well put up a 'Closed' sign now, because I'm going to see to it that you pay. I'm going to see this place closed and see *you* in jail." She spun on her high heel, lost her balance, and tripped down two steps, catching herself before hitting the ground. Peaches yelped.

"My ankle!" Simone bent to rub her leg, no mean feat in a skirt tight enough to cut off circulation, and set Peaches down. She hobbled down the last two stairs, the dog frisking at her feet, and I thought I heard her mutter, ". . . sue them for . . ."

Althea, who had stood holding the door open throughout the exchange, said, "I'm out of here," and bolted down the stairs.

"Althea, wait." Mom caught the door before it banged shut and followed her friend, leaving the three of us to stare after them in astonishment.

"Well!" Stella said.

I was definitely asking Mom what that was all about as soon as she came back. For now, though, I pretended nothing was wrong. Filling Stella and Rachel in on my interview with Special Agent Dillon, I also told them about overhearing Del Richardson, the Morestuf VP, and Constance after the town hall meeting.

"Well, he must have done it," Stella said with relief. "He's not even from around here."

I didn't share Stella's belief in the virtue of all St. Elizabeth's citizens, but I let it go. "Well, he certainly had a good motive," I said. "When Constance decided to do something, it got done. Look at how she got the town to vote for restoring the Rothmere home. And she told him flat out that she was going to make sure he didn't get permission to build a Morestuf."

"What about that guy she was arguing with on the veranda? They were really going at it," Rachel said. "It looked like he was going to hit her."

"You saw them?"

"Yeah, I went out to call Bethany about practice, remember? I don't think they saw me, though, because I was, like, on the side of the house."

And she'd taken good care not to draw their attention, I was sure. Not that I cared. The mystery man — the angry and potentially violent mystery man — might be a good suspect for the police to look into. The more the merrier. "Who was it?"

Rachel twiddled with the cauldron-shaped earring that dangled halfway to her shoulder. "I never saw him before. They were talking about business stuff, I think. About the Sea Mist Plantation and foreclosures and statues of limitations."

"Statutes," I said, thinking hard. The Sea Mist Plantation was a swanky golf resort with private homes and an upscale shopping center that Philip DuBois and some partners had developed in the early 1980s. I couldn't believe it was in danger of foreclosure. Why, they were hosting a prestigious pro-am golf tournament next week; it always brought in boatloads of tourists and buckets of money.

"There's Philip, too," Stella said into the silence.

"Her son?"

Stella nodded. "They've been having huge fights about the bank. I heard it from my friend Janelle, the head teller. Something about loans. He says the bank can make more profit if they loosen up on their loan policies, and she refused. I don't really understand it, but I know Constance threatened to have the board fire him as president."

"She'd fire her own son?"

"Yeah, he was really worried about it," Rachel said.

Stella and I stared at her. How did a seventeen-year-old know anything about banking?

She grinned at our expressions, showing a mouthful of braces. "His son Trey is in my biology class. He said his dad interviewed with a bank in New York City. Trey, like, really doesn't want to move to New York. Or anywhere. Especially not with senior year coming up. He's on the basketball team, you know, and he's pretty sure he can get a scholarship to UGA."

I couldn't care less about Philip the Third's sports aspirations, but it was interesting to hear that Philip Junior took his mother's threats seriously enough to look for another job. "Why don't you see what else Janelle knows about the situation, Stella? See if she can give you details. I'll track down Mr. Morestuf and try to find out what he was up to after the meeting."

"How will you get him to meet with you?" Stella asked.

"I don't know. Maybe I'll tell him I'm representing the SODS and want to see if we can come to a compromise. Or, better yet, I'll tell him that committee Mom made me volunteer for at the town hall meeting — about a Morestuf's impact on the environment and economy — needs some data from him."

"That's good," she said, carefully aligning her polish bottles so the labels faced front.

"And I'll get onto Trey and see what he knows," Rachel put in.

"No," Stella and I said simultaneously. We looked at each other, and I nodded for Stella, the mother of a young daughter, to continue. "This is adult stuff, Rachel," she said gently. "If Mr. DuBois is involved in anything . . . iffy, we wouldn't want him hearing from Trey that you were asking strange questions. It might make things . . . awkward for you."

Rachel swung her legs and pushed off from the counter. She landed with a thud. "Give me some credit. Like, he'll never know what I'm getting at."

"But —" Stella tried again.

Rachel slung her heavy backpack over her shoulders. "Besides, I have as much right to help Miss Violetta as you do." The level look she gave us was strangely grown-up, despite the braces and goth garb. Without waiting for an answer, she opened the

door and slipped through, closing it softly
behind her.

CHAPTER FIVE

Stella left shortly after Rachel. I waited almost an hour for my mom, but she foiled my plan to ask about Althea's outburst by not coming back. For all I knew, they had gone to a matinee or were having an early dinner at the Lucky Manatee tavern. After mopping the salon's floor, watering the ferns, and grouting a loose tile by the sink, I was suddenly more tired than a hound after a day's hunting. Locking up, I noticed a coating of pollen and dust on the veranda and promised myself I'd sweep it in the morning. I drove the couple of blocks to the apartment I rented from Genevieve Jones, an octogenarian whose only son had died of pancreatic cancer at sixty. She had converted her garage into an apartment for him — he'd never married — and she agreed to rent it to me when I moved back.

My mom, of course, assumed I would move back in with her, but I couldn't. I'd lived with her until I married Hank and then I'd lived with him. I'd even had roommates for my two years at UGA and at beauty school. Now, at thirty, I needed my own place, needed to see what it was like to live on my own, to come and go as I pleased, to answer to no one. I knew if I moved back into my old bedroom, I'd wiggle into my old habits like putting on a comfy slipper. And so would Mom. Mrs. Jones showed no tendency to monitor my comings and goings. She kept busy with tai chi and bridge and visiting shut-ins, and I spent long hours at the salon. I checked in on her a couple of times a week and helped with the gardening in exchange for a reduction on the rent. Other than that, we pretty much left each other alone.

Today, however, she popped out onto her porch as soon as I pulled up to the curb. She was a tall, thin woman with the fragility of an origami crane. Her skin was tissue-paper thin, and I sometimes fancied I could see the bone glowing through. Snow white and thinning, her hair stood up in a pouf around her scalp, heightening her resemblance to a crowned crane. Blue eyes still snapped with life, though the pigment had faded to a pale periwinkle.

She waved an arthritis-gnarled hand.

"Yoo-hoo! Grace! I just poured myself some lemonade . . . would you like some?"

"Sure," I said, resigned. I knew she'd been lying in wait for me, hoping to pump me for details about Constance DuBois's murder. By now, word must be all over town that Mom and I had found the body. Still, her lemonade was homemade, tart, and refreshing, so I accepted a glass with pleasure and sank into one of the wicker chairs on her porch. A honey bee buzzed among the honeysuckle that twined up the porch slats, and I made a mental note to cut it back one day soon.

She let me take precisely two sips before leaning forward and asking, "Is it true your mama got arrested for the murder?"

"Mrs. Jones!"

"That's what I heard at the Piggly Wiggly when I went to pick up lemons and white vinegar. It works a treat on mildew in my shower stall, especially in the door track. I pour it in there and — shazam! — no more mildew." She nodded brightly.

I set my lemonade down with a click on the glass-topped table beside my chair. "Mom and I found Constance DuBois's body. We went down to police headquarters today to help them with their investigation. Neither of us was arrested." Of course, if

Special Agent Dillon had his way, we still might be.

"I knew Ethel Spillman was wrong," Mrs. Jones said with satisfaction. "And I told her so. 'Why,' I said, 'Violetta Terhune wouldn't hurt a fly, Ethel, and you should think shame on yourself for repeating such a rumor. The Good Book tells us in the Psalms to keep our tongues from evil and our lips from spreading lies.' Ethel went off in a huff after that, I'll tell you."

The small-town gossip mill was enough to make me miss the anonymity of Atlanta. But not the traffic and gangs and crowds. "Thank you, Mrs. Jones," I said. "You're absolutely right — my mom would never hurt anyone." Not even an arrogant, know-it-all, trouble-making shrew like Constance DuBois.

"You can count on me to spread the truth, my dear," she said, patting my hand. "I already called the police to tell them that they got the wrong woman."

Great, I groaned inwardly. Now Dillon would think we were trying to throw dust in his eyes by having friends and neighbors give character testimonials. "Thank you," I said again, weakly. "But it's probably better if you let the police get on with it and don't make any more phone calls."

"Oh, no," she said, shaking her head so the crown of hair quivered around her face. "I learned long ago that you can't just let things take their natural course. That's the lazy person's answer. Not that I'm saying you're lazy, Grace. But one must be proactive to get things done in this life. That's the word my great-nephew uses — proactive. He's an architect, you know, and a very handsome boy."

I did know. She'd been trying to fix me up with the thirty-five-year-old "boy" since I moved into the garage apartment. I had no interest in dating. Zero, zilch, none. The wounds from my divorce were still too raw. But Mrs. Jones didn't get the hint. "Thank you for the lemonade," I said, standing.

"Anytime, dear. And you tell Violetta that I'll help any way I can with her defense. If the police are foolish enough to arrest her, of course. We could put those collection jars at some of the businesses around town. You know, with a picture of Violetta and a sign saying 'Violetta Terhune Defense Fund,' or something like that so she can afford a really good lawyer. Did you know I have a great-nephew who's a lawyer? But he lives in Richmond. And two of my great-nieces are lawyers, too."

Waving a hand in farewell, I escaped

78

before she could think of any more schemes to "help" my mom or any more great-nephews to fix me up with. The heavy scent of the honeysuckle followed me down the stone path to my apartment. It sat back a little ways from the house and gleamed with the same pale yellow paint. Azaleas, hibiscus, and oleander flourished along the sides and back, and a huge pecan tree shaded the apartment and screened it from the house and street. Unlocking the door, I let myself in and immediately punched on the window air-conditioning unit. After my absence of more than twenty-four hours, the apartment — single bedroom, old-fashioned bathroom, and kitchenette with a two-burner stove — smelled musty. The answering machine's blinking light caught my eye, and I listened to the messages while standing in front of the air conditioner, letting the cool stream play over me.

The messages were evenly split between those who wanted to know if Violetta was in jail and those who proclaimed their faith in her innocence. Vonda was among the latter. She ended her call with a brisk, "Call me."

I picked up the phone to call my best friend, but then thought better of it. Right now, people were behind Mom, sure of her innocence. But I'd lived in St. Elizabeth long enough to know that if the police didn't arrest someone else pretty soon, people would begin to talk. The mere association of the words "Violetta Terhune" and "murder" would make people think twice. Business at the salon would drop off. Friends would call less often. I'd seen it happen to a high school teacher, Tim Moore, who coached the girls' softball team. The police had questioned him when Debbie MacArthur disappeared; he'd apparently been the last one to see her after practice one Friday. Everyone protested his innocence at the beginning, but as the weeks went by and Debbie remained missing, the rumors turned ugly. Someone egged his house. He moved away before the start of the next school year — to Biloxi, I think — and got a job with a Catholic school. Debbie turned up a year after that with a baby boy. She'd run away when she'd found out she was pregnant by her boyfriend. Then, everyone said they knew all along Tim hadn't done anything, was a great guy, but it was too late. I wasn't going to let something similar happen to my mom. Reaching for the phone book, I started calling hotels.

I figured Del Richardson, Mr. Morestuf, as

a room service and valet parking kind of guy, and I was right. The clerk at the Sea Mist Plantation Inn, the largest and swankiest hotel in St. Elizabeth, immediately connected me to Richardson's room when I asked for him. After I fed him the story about needing some data from him about a Morestuf's impact on the local economy, he agreed to meet with me. I assumed we'd meet in the hotel lobby or café, but he had other ideas.

"Meet me at the Morestuf site. You know where it is, darlin'? Just north of the intersection of SR 42 and Forest Boulevard. You need to see the land to get a feel for what we can accomplish in your community. Say, in an hour?"

I took some care dressing for the meeting, wanting to strike an appropriate note between businesslike and casual enough for a building site. I finally settled on a sea green linen pantsuit that brought out the green in my hazel eyes and that I hadn't worn since leaving Atlanta. A cream shell went under the three-quarter-sleeve jacket, and low-heeled pumps finished the look. I pulled my light brown hair into a quick French twist and even applied a little mascara and lip gloss. There. No one would mistake me for a high-powered Wall Street executive, but I looked professional enough that Richardson would take me seriously. I hoped.

The building site was a field bounded on one side by the road and on two sides by scrub pines and kudzu, the imported Japanese vine that smothered everything that couldn't outrun it. I was pretty sure that campers who spent the night outdoors would awaken to find their tents overgrown by kudzu. A boggy area sulked to the east of the site, studded with cat tails and scummed with algae. It looked like prime alligator territory, although the only wildlife I saw was a pair of redwing blackbirds. The area was also deserted, which I hadn't anticipated. I guess I'd thought there'd be a housing tract within a stone's throw or surveyors taking measurements or a gas station on the corner. But there was nothing except an occasional car speeding past on SR 42 and a dark blue Cadillac Escalade parked on the side of the road. Richardson stood beside the driver's door, a brawny figure with a bull neck and a white Stetson hat. A leather sports coat added to his bulk, and cowboy boots made of some exotic hide encased his feet. The hint of jowl at his jaw line and the mesh of lines around his eyes put him in his mid-fifties. I got out and we shook hands. A large school ring glinted on his finger, and his grip nearly crushed my hand. The swamp smells of mud and rotten eggs filtered my way as the wind kicked up.

"A pleasure to meet you, Grace," he said, the Texas twang as bright as his smile. "I can call you Grace, right?"

"Sure, Del," I agreed. This "let's be buddies" approach told me he was fairly desperate to find some allies in St. Elizabeth. Maybe I could make use of that.

He handed me an inch-thick manila envelope. "I think you'll find all the stats and data you need in there," he said. "Environmental impact statements, reports on the boost to local economies when a Morestuf goes up in the community, et cetera, et cetera. But numbers only tell part of the story, right?"

I nodded. He strode toward the middle of the field, and I followed, walking on tiptoe to keep the heels of my pumps from sinking into the sandy soil. The humidity had increased, and moisture quickly slicked my skin. Great drops of perspiration beaded Richardson's forehead, and he swiped at them with the back of his hand.

"People are the real story. You saw that mobile home park we passed on the way out here, darlin'?" He flung his hand in the direction of town. "Well, when this Morestuf gets built, those people will have jobs, good jobs, with benefits. And they'll be able to walk to work. What do you think about that?"

I thought it sounded good, in theory. "But what about the business owners in St. Elizabeth proper?" I asked. "What will happen to their livelihoods?"

"They'll adapt, Grace, they'll adapt. That's how business works. The tourists will still buy the pricey clothes and local paintings in the downtown area because it's so 'charming and Southern.' Real people like you and me, we'll have options when the Morestuf opens. Options that better fit our budgets."

He was good . . . I had to give him that. Linking us together as if my income weren't a light-year away from his. He probably got his boots at Neiman Marcus and bought Christmas gifts at Tiffany's. My shoes came from Payless, and I made my Christmas presents by hand, more often than not.

"It sounds good, Del," I said, putting all the open-eyed innocence I could into my voice, "but I know Constance DuBois was dead set against it, and her opinion carried a lot of weight in St. Elizabeth."

"She came 'round to our side before she died, God rest her soul," he said. "She was a reasonable woman — a businesswoman — and those facts convinced her." He nodded at the envelope in my hand.

I gaped at his bold-faced lie. "So, you were able to talk her around after the town hall meeting? I thought I saw you escorting her to her car. That was very gentlemanly of you." If he could lie, so could I.

A tide of red seeped from his neck, over his jaw, and flushed his cheeks. "Cut the crap," he said, all trace of friendliness gone from his voice. "I didn't lay eyes on her after I left the building. If you're implying —"

"I heard you threaten her," I said, my voice cold. "And I heard her say she'd make damned sure you didn't get to build your store." A mosquito whined in my ear, and I shook my head. The sun was drifting down the horizon, and the lengthening shadows had brought out the little bloodsuckers.

Richardson's large hand slapped at my arm. I gasped and jerked away from his grasp, almost falling. My twenty-twenty hindsight told me I should have insisted on meeting at the hotel when I saw how isolated this place was. I half turned to run.

"Mosquito," he said, holding up his palm to show a spot of blood. His thin smile told me he had read my thoughts and was enjoying my fear. I rubbed at the welt on my arm.

"Thanks," I muttered.

"You are in way over your head, Miss Terhune," he said, smoothing the sleeve of his jacket. "Go back to your shampooing and hair-cutting. Oh, yes, I made a few calls after we talked," he said, correctly interpreting my expression. "Take a look at the information in there." He tapped at the envelope, and I had to keep myself from jumping back. "And then convince your Save Our Downtown friends to get on board. Or maybe I'll remember seeing you walk the DuBois woman to her car. Or your mother . . . aren't the cops already talking to her?"

With a final flash of his big teeth, he headed toward the SUV. I stayed put, shivering despite the heat, until the Escalade was out of sight. Then I hurried toward my car, slapping at mosquitoes as I jogged. Once inside with the doors closed, I sat for a moment, catching my breath and scratching at the bites on my arms and face. That went well, I told my wide-eyed reflection in the rearview mirror. The flushed face looking back at me didn't agree. I'm sure I saw the glint of red eyes at water level in the bog as I turned on my headlights, reversed, and sped toward the welcoming lights of St. Elizabeth.

[Friday]

I'm no fonder of total honesty in self-analysis than the next person, but the episode with Richardson forced me to admit I was stupid and cowardly. Stupid for meeting Richardson in the middle of nowhere. I couldn't believe I confronted him without proof of any kind, with no more than the suspicion raised by overhearing his confrontation with Constance. But I so wanted to find Constance's murderer quickly, to clear Mom's name. And cowardly because I had no intention of telling my mom or the ladies at Violetta's about the encounter. As it turns out, the next morning was so busy — we had a bride and her bridesmaids in for mani-pedis and updos — that I barely had time to draw breath. Mom was securing curls atop the maid of honor's head, and the bride and two bridesmaids were giggling in the Nail Nook when the door swung open.

Special Agent Dillon stood on the threshold. Conversation stopped for a moment as all the women stared. One of the bridesmaids whispered "hottie" as conversation resumed. Apparently unaware of the interest his masculine presence excited, Special Agent Dillon looked around and stepped toward the counter. His glance might seem casual, but I was sure he could describe everyone in the room, list the magazines in the waiting area, and had probably noticed the dead fronds on one of the ferns and the chip in the shampoo sink's enamel. Or maybe I'm paranoid. I said neutrally, "May I help you?"

"I need a hair cut," he said. His navy eyes studied me, and I wondered if he were really here looking for probable cause for a search warrant. Although I didn't know what he could possibly find that would relate to Constance's murder.

"Do you have an appointment?" I asked, pretending to thumb through our scheduling book.

"Do I need one?"

"Of course not, Agent Dillon," Mom intervened before I could tell him to try Chez Pierre. She gave me a "mind your manners" look and actually smiled at him. "Grace has an opening right now. I'd do you myself, but I've got to finish up with the girls in Lacey's wedding party." She turned to smile at Lacey, who waved the hand Stella wasn't working on.

"Congratulations," Special Agent Dillon said with a genuine smile.

I rolled my eyes, but the smile made it hard to catch my breath. It cut creases into

his lean cheeks and showed a deep cleft —
I'm sure he hated having it called a dimple
— in his chin. Even his eyes lightened, tran-
sitioning from a somber navy to the marine
blue of a sunlit sea, like a mood ring. His
effect on me took me by surprise, and I said
more coldly than I intended, "This way. I'll
get a smock."

He handed me his navy blazer and I hung
it in the closet where we kept the smocks. I
helped him into the violet garment, privately
awarding him points for not balking at the
color. Settling into the chair by the sink, he
tipped his head back. I wished Rachel were
here and not sitting in a history class or
chem lab so I wouldn't have to wash his
hair. Conscious of my mother's eyes flicking
my way, I adjusted the water temperature
and squirted shampoo into my hand. Feeling strangely tentative, I began to work it
into his scalp. His hair was bristly under my
fingers, his skull hard. He closed his eyes as
I massaged his temples, and I felt him relax
infinitesimally. I got the feeling he didn't
relax often and I took it as a challenge. The
pads of my fingers dug into his scalp, and I
worked them in small circles from the crown
of his head to his nape. The bracing scent
of eucalyptus and honeydew floated up
from the lather. Dillon's head weighed

heavy in my hands as he finally let the taut muscles in his neck relax. Suddenly aware of a strange sense of intimacy that made me as uncomfortable as a hamster at a cat show — did he feel it, too? — I began to rinse his hair, deliberately keeping the water on the cool side. Giving his hair a perfunctory toweling, I led him to my station and adjusted the chair down as he sat.

"What did you have in mind?" I asked. Not that he had a lot of options with less than an inch of growth.

"The truth?" he suggested, his eyes meeting mine in the mirror.

"Well, if you let it grow another six months or so, we could do a Brad Pitt sort of fringe —"

His brows drew together, and his eyes were a dark navy again. "Just a trim, Miss Terhune."

"Oh, call me Grace," I said, impatient with the formality. "And I'll call you Marsh, okay?" I knew I was picking a fight because the intimacy of shampooing his hair had unsettled me, but I couldn't help myself. I snipped at the hair just over his right ear.

"Miss. Terhune." He emphasized each word. "I got a call from Del Richardson this morning."

I hesitated a moment, trying to still my

trembling fingers, before saying, "Really? Did he confess to stabbing Constance?" I pressed Dillon's head down so he couldn't read my face as I trimmed the hair at his nape.

"Not hardly. He said he remembered seeing a woman walking with the victim in the parking lot. The description he gave sounded a lot like your mother."

"That . . . that lying swine!" I gritted between my teeth. Anger rose in me with such force I accidentally nipped Dillon's ear with the scissors.

"Ow!"

I inspected his ear, rubbing it between my thumb and forefinger. "It's not even bleeding . . . don't be a baby."

"Maybe this wasn't such a good idea," he muttered. His hand fumbled with the smock's Velcro closure at his neck.

"You can't leave with your hair like that," I said, visions of the salon's reputation taking a nose-dive if he told anyone where he got his cut. I put my hands on his shoulders to hold him in place, then jerked them away as the heat of him warmed my palms. "The cut's on the house," I said.

He gave me a considering look, then leaned back in the chair. "At least put the scissors away," he said.

I decided to tell him the truth — I had nothing to lose and maybe something to gain if he believed me instead of Richardson. "Look, I'm sorry . . ." And as I shaved his neckline, I told him about meeting the Morestuf VP the night before. Not wanting anyone to overhear, I leaned in close to tell the story, my voice barely above a whisper. The warm scent of him, a mix of soap and clean sweat and a spicy aftershave tickled my nose, but I ignored it. Mostly.

When I finished, he was silent for a long moment. He shut his eyes as if in pain and then opened them to glare at me in the mirror. "You seriously met a man you think is a murderer in a field in the middle of nowhere."

"Ssssh," I hissed as my mom turned to stare at us. "I guess it wasn't the brightest thing I've ever done."

"That's one way to put it," he said. "The word stupid comes to mind. And idiotic. And foolhardy."

"Fine," I said, jerking the smock off him with a ripping sound. "Don't believe me."

"I didn't say I didn't believe you." He rose to his feet in a leisurely way. "I only said you were stu—"

"I heard you the first time!"

He continued as if I hadn't spoken. "I

didn't say I *did* believe you, either. We haven't been able to verify your so-called alibi yet. Judge Finnegan hasn't returned my calls. I find that suspicious."

"She's in Haiti!"

"Convenient for you. At any rate, the investigation is ongoing. I suggest you let us do our jobs and not muddy the waters any more with your Miss Marple amateur hour." His voice was stern.

"Veronica Mars, actually," I said, then clapped a hand to my mouth.

"What?"

"Nothing." The door jangled open, and I looked over with relief to see Patricia Farnsworth enter, her blond hair two weeks past due for a touch-up. "My client's here."

"We're done for now," Special Agent Dillon said, retrieving his blazer from the closet and shrugging into it. "Let Mrs. Terhune know I'd like to chat with her again when she has a chance. Just routine."

Yeah, right.

He handed me his card. "She can call my cell." And with a generalized wave to the salon's occupants, he left.

Relief slumped my shoulders, and I took a deep breath, holding it for a moment before blowing it out. I hadn't been aware of the tension building up in my muscles. "I'll be with you in a minute, Patricia," I said. I handed the man's card to Mom and gave her his message.

"What was that all about?" She gestured with her comb toward my station.

"Nothing much. What do you think about trying to attract more male clients?" I asked in an effort to distract her. "Of course, we'd have to get smocks in a more . . . neutral color. Say, black. Or dark green."

She pursed her lips with interest. "It's a thought. Let's see what Stella and Althea think."

"More men get their nails done these days and have facials, too." I kept an earnest expression on my face, but inside I was celebrating. I'd done it — successfully led her away from the explosive topic.

"Why not? Skin care is for everybody," she said. She peered at me over the top of her glasses. "And don't think you're putting one past me, missy. You can fill me in when this place clears out."

My distraction techniques never worked when I was in high school, either. Well, two could play that game. "Fine. And you can tell me why Althea ran out of here in a lather yesterday." I turned on my heel to shepherd Patricia to the sink.

CHAPTER SIX

Mom and I rocked on her veranda at seven thirty that evening, enjoying the cooling air and the chirrup of crickets as the sun lazed its way down the horizon. Citronella candles kept the mosquitoes at bay and their scent mingled with the perfume of gardenias and camellias floating up from bushes planted at the base of the house. I love summer nights, where twilight lasts longest and the world seems peaceful, suspended in time by the magical gloaming. I sipped my Budweiser and rocked, unwilling to shatter the serenity to interrogate my mom.

She showed no such reluctance. Setting her beer can on the ceramic elephant plant stand we use as a table, she said, "So. What were you telling Special Agent Dillon about meeting someone in a field last evening?"

The woman had a bat's hearing. I swear, when I was a teenager, she could hear Vonda and me plotting mischief even if we were in my bedroom with the door closed and she was cooking dinner. I sighed and took another sip of beer. Mom watched me, not pushing, her hair spikier than usual, wearing a touristy St. Elizabeth tee shirt with a beach scene silk-screened on the front, and cropped pants. Freeing my ponytail from its elastic, I shook my hair so it fell around my face. It was a trick I'd learned in middle school when I didn't want too much scrutiny from a teacher. I combed it with my fingers. With another deep breath, I told Mom about meeting Richardson and about the threat he'd made good on by calling Special Agent Dillon.

"I'm sorry," I finished. "It was stupid."

"Oh, Grace," Mom said. "If he really killed Constance, he could have hurt you. Made you disappear. Whatever possessed you?"

"If we don't figure out who killed Constance DuBois, the police are going to keep harassing us. It's going to hurt the business. I just want it cleared up."

"It's not worth putting yourself at risk for. Losing the salon wouldn't be the end of the world." The tightness in her voice communicated her unspoken thought: Losing you would be.

I leaned over and held her hand. She

squeezed mine hard and released it to reach for her beer. "Besides," she said with determined cheerfulness, "the women of St. Elizabeth couldn't survive without Violetta's. Can you see Miss Willa or Cassie Beaumont sashaying into Chez Pierre? Why, the women around here come to Violetta's as much for the socializing as for the haircuts and facials."

"They do indeed," I said, helping her lighten the mood. And it was true. Sometimes women stopped into the salon even if they weren't having their hair done, just to catch up on gossip or chat with friends. I finished my beer. It had grown darker as we talked, and I couldn't see Mom's face clearly anymore. I didn't want to upset her again, but I forced myself to say, "What about Althea?"

"What about Althea?" came a voice from the foot of the steps.

I jumped, knocking over my beer can. It rolled to the top of the stairs where Althea picked it up. She straightened, a dark figure in a tunic top and jeans.

"I asked Althea to come over," Mom said. "It didn't feel right to tell you her story without her permission."

Of course not. Mom was totally discreet and sensitive to her friends' confidences, despite what she did for a living. The gossip swirling around Violetta's did not originate with her.

"So, you want to go poking around in my past, Grace?"

"I want to keep my mom from getting arrested," I said, keeping my tone neutral despite the edge of anger in her voice. "I don't want her to lose Violetta's because clients stop coming, afraid of guilt by association, sure there's 'no smoke without fire.' "

"Well, hell, baby girl, I don't want that to happen, either," Althea said with a sharp laugh. "You may have noticed that I get my paycheck from Violetta's. Let's take a walk. Your mama doesn't want to hear my story again."

Mom looked from Althea to me but said nothing. I couldn't read her expression, but her voice was calm as she said, "I'm going to lock up and read for a while before bed. See you in the morning. Althea, don't forget Sissie Lingenfelder is coming at seven thirty for her facial. I booked her before we open so she can catch a plane out of Jacksonville. She's off to California for her daughter's graduation."

"I know, Vi. I'll be there."

"Good night, Mom." I bent to kiss her cheek.

Althea and I clomped down the stairs together and turned right. The sidewalks in the older section of town buckled up from the thrusting of tree roots, mostly big live oaks that had probably watched Sherman march across Georgia. Wearing only flip-flops, I kept my eyes on the ground, not wanting to stub a toe.

"You don't remember my William, Grace, because you were knee high to a grasshopper when he died. But he was a good man. A very good man," Althea began.

"I've seen pictures. He was handsome, too."

"Yes, he was."

I heard the smile in her voice and wondered what memories she was reliving.

"But that's neither here nor there. Fact is, he was a sweet man, but he wasn't much of a judge of character. Some of the men he called friends . . . lordy. There was one in particular, a skunk named Carl Rowan. He was white — not that I hold that against him — but this was back in the early '80s when it was still unusual to see a white man hanging with a black man, at least in small-town Georgia. William always held to it that Carl was a real friend because he didn't pay any mind to the threats he got sometimes for hanging with a black man. The Ku Klux Klan even burned a cross in his yard once. Me, I think Carl took up with William because he's the only one who would tolerate him.

"William worked in the paper mill in those days, and I did facials sometimes to make ends meet, with your mama. Your daddy was still alive then, so there wasn't really a salon, but we had friend who wanted us to cut their hair and do their facials — they said we were as good as any of the stylists in the high-class beauty parlors. Carl, he didn't work. He'd inherited some property from an uncle or something and he spent his time drinking and smoking and playing cards."

"Sounds like a real bum."

"You got that right."

We walked in silence for a few minutes, turning east, and the smell of the ocean grew stronger. It wasn't a happy smell tonight, like it usually is; it smelled mournful. But maybe that was just me reacting to something I heard in Althea's voice.

"Anyway," Althea resumed, kicking at a pinecone on the sidewalk, "something happened between Carl and the DuBoises — they were the only bank in town then, in that building Walter Highsmith has now.

Carl said they stole property from him, that Philip DuBois convinced him to put it up as collateral to buy into a development Philip and his partners were undertaking. Something went wrong — they were denied the licenses or permits they needed, or something — and the project never got off the ground. Everyone involved lost a lot of money. Carl had to forfeit the land. Carl would have it that Philip deliberately sabotaged the project so he could get his hands on the property. He ran off at the mouth, saying he was going to contact the attorney general, go to the newspapers, tell what he knew about Philip DuBois and his business dealings. Only he was killed before he got the chance. And my William with him."

We had reached the boardwalk that ran along the St. Elizabeth beachfront. Reggae music filtered from a bar down the block, and lights from restaurants and bistros spilled into the night. The Intracoastal Waterway was a dark presence on our right, separating the mainland from the offshore islands and the Atlantic beyond. Its gentle waves welled up and subsided with a shushing both monotonous and vaguely ominous, like jungle drums throbbing. I shivered and made myself remember the beach on a sunny day when Alice Rose and I splashed in the surf and built sand castles or when Vonda and I lay on our towels and scoped out the boys playing Frisbee or bodysurfing.

"Did they catch who did it?" I asked. By mutual accord we stopped walking, and the beach breeze flapped at Althea's loose shirt.

"They never found the bodies," Althea said, her voice cracking. "The police said there was no evidence that the men hadn't gone off on their own, so I don't know how hard they tried to get at the truth. I don't think they ever even interviewed Philip DuBois about it."

"You think —"

"I *know* Philip DuBois either killed Carl Rowan or paid to have it done. And William died because he was in the wrong place at the wrong time with the wrong sorry-ass friend." Althea spat the words with a bitterness that almost thirty years hadn't sweetened. "I never heard from my William again after he left that February evening to meet up with Carl and play some poker. He wouldn't walk out on me, just disappear. And with Carl?" She snorted.

"I tried to get someone to believe me, make 'em keep investigating, but Rowan's widow packed up her stuff and moved north with their kids not a month after Carl disappeared, and there wasn't anybody else, with the exception of your mama, who was interested. And your daddy was sick by then. Violetta had her hands full taking care of him and you and Alice Rose, who was just a baby. She did what she could, though, and after your daddy passed, well, we got together and started Violetta's, which kept the wolf from the door."

I wanted to ask for more details, but I couldn't force Althea to relive the horror of that night, those weeks. Maybe I could find something in back issues of the *Gazette* about the disappearances. Instead, I asked, "Is that why you and Constance DuBois didn't get along? Because you think her husband was mixed up in William's death?"

Althea took a deep breath in through her nose and didn't speak for a long minute. I thought she wasn't going to answer.

"When I got to thinking about that time more clearly, a year after William died, about what happened with Rowan's property and all, I realized Constance must know something. She was as much a part of the bank's business as Philip was. Hell, some people thought she was the one who called the shots. Anyway, I went to talk to her. At the house, not at the bank. To give her her due, she agreed to see me."

"What did you say?" I found myself caught up in Althea's story, envisioning a younger Althea, maybe wearing gloves and a hat, calling on the wealthy Mrs. DuBois at her mansion.

"She offered me lemonade. I asked her if she'd had my husband killed."

"You didn't!"

Althea nodded grimly. "Yes, ma'am, I did."

"What'd she say?"

"She got all icy — like she did with Walter at the salon the other day — and told me I was getting uppity and that I'd better learn my place."

I gasped.

Althea seemed pleased with my reaction. "And this was in 1984, not 1954. Anyway, I stared her down and told her she should think shame on herself. Then I said I knew something hinky had happened with Carl Rowan's property and that he and my William had been murdered because they knew. Well, at that, she got all quiet for a moment, and then she pulled out her checkbook. She said she could see that the strain of making it on my own was telling on me and she wanted to help out. She wrote me out a check for fifty thousand dollars."

"Wow," I breathed. That seemed very un-

Constance-like to me.

"I tore it into shreds and let them fall on her antique carpet," Althea said with satisfaction. "It was blood money, I told her, and you can't try to make yourself sleep better at night by buying me off. I was shaking with fury, Grace, shaking, and I think I scared her. She's given me a wide berth ever since because she knows I know."

Even in the dim light, I could see the grim set of her mouth and chin. A silence fell between us, broken only by a burst of laughter and music as The Roving Pirate's door opened, spilling light and partiers onto the boardwalk.

"What happened with the property, Rowan's property?"

"A couple of years after the murders, why, the DuBoises developed that property and made themselves millions in the process. It was the last stretch of undeveloped coastline in these parts. Sea Mist Plantation. No more problems with building permits or what have you once the DuBoises owned the land." Weary cynicism weighted her voice. "Of course, Beau Lansky was on the zoning commission back then, Constance's cousin's husband."

And our current governor.

CHAPTER SEVEN

[Saturday]

I had a lot to think about the next morning as I got ready for Constance's viewing. Not owning anything black, I donned a forest green shirtwaist dress in a fluid cotton-rayon blend. Big gold buttons marched from collar to hem, which might have been too festive for a viewing, but it was my best option. I cinched it at the waist with the wide, black belt Vonda gave me two Christmases back and slipped on matching sandals. No hose. It was just too hot. Taking a little extra time with my hair, I French-braided it, tucking the ends under. Off my neck, it would be cooler.

Mom was waiting on the veranda when I arrived. Wearing a navy pantsuit with a black shell underneath, she was appropriately funereal, although the suit's boxy cut made her look stockier than usual. She greeted me with a hug, and we set off on foot for the Fagin-Jones mortuary, around the corner from Bedford Square. We walked in silence and stepped into the ultracool lobby of the funeral home with a sigh of relief. Even at nine, the humidity was building, and angry clouds promised a storm before day's end. A somberly dressed man, Aaron Fagin, who had given an oral report on embalming techniques when we were in the eighth grade, ushered us to the room where Constance DuBois reclined in a coffin surrounded by banks of flowers. The cloying scent of lilies pervaded the room, and I sneezed, drawing several people's heads around.

While my mom signed the guest book, I took in the crowd. Simone stood near the coffin, a slim figure in a black suit with a peplum and a small hat with a wisp of veil. Her brother Philip, who I always thought looked like a praying mantis with his biggish head and stick-thin limbs, stood beside her, his arm around a petite blonde I recognized as his wife, Susan. A handsome man I didn't know stood on Simone's left, a proprietary hand at the small of her back. He was tall, about six-two, and had bronzy gold hair that had been razor cut by an excellent stylist. His black suit seemed equally expensive, draping across his broad shoulders and chest with a fluidity you didn't find in cheap wools. I wondered who he was . . . maybe a boyfriend of Simone's from New York?

I spotted many of the town's leading citizens and members of the various committees Constance had served on. The bank's board of directors and employees were there in force, as well, the former wearing expensive dark suits and a collective air of consequence, the latter huddled together by the coffee urn, ill at ease and sneaking glances at their watches. Althea wasn't there — she'd said she wasn't a hypocrite — and I knew Rachel had a family commitment, but I spotted Stella as she came through the door behind two older women. She wore a black chiffon dress with a black straw picture hat and looked willowy and elegant with her auburn hair pulled into a chignon.

"You look nice," I greeted her.

She smiled her thanks and scanned the room. "Everyone who is anyone in St. Elizabeth is here, aren't they? Well, Constance was one of the town's most prominent citizens."

Even if not the most beloved. We made our way to the front of the room to pay our respects to Simone and Philip as Mom joined a knot of people I recognized as

108

SODS. She had told me earlier that she was going to keep a low profile, not wanting to upset Simone after the scene at Violetta's on Thursday, so I wasn't surprised when she didn't join us in the receiving line. Stella murmured, "So sorry," as we shook hands with Simone and her escort. Simone thanked her and shot me a dagger glance.

"I'm praying for you and your family in your time of grief," I told her. I was. I could see I'd startled her because she opened her mouth to say something, then closed it again. Finally, she said, "This is Greg Hutchinson, my fiancé." She patted the blond man's arm and looked up at him adoringly.

Only then did I notice the large diamond solitaire on her ring finger. Had it been there when she was at the salon on Wednesday or Thursday? I didn't remember seeing it, and I think I would have noticed because it was at least a carat and a half and sparkled like a Fourth of July fireworks display was trapped in the gem.

"Pleased to meet you," he said, shaking my hand. His grip was firm and his nails buffed. "I'm looking forward to getting to know all of Simone's friends."

Simone almost gagged but had the grace not to point out that we were hardly friends.

"Are you from around here?" I asked.

"I met Simone in New York," he said, squeezing her waist.

"Well, I wish you both happiness," I said, letting myself be pushed along by the press of people waiting to offer Simone their condolences. I felt weird offering condolences one minute and congratulations the next. Telling Philip how sorry I was about his mother, I found myself alongside the coffin. Clad in an oyster-colored silk suit, her personality air-brushed away, and her hair a deeper blonde than usual and stiffly coiffed, Constance didn't look like she was sleeping or at peace; she looked fake, a macabre Funeral Barbie. I didn't envy the mortuary assistant who'd had to dye her hair to get rid of the orange. Or maybe they'd used some kind of spray-on product. I leaned over the gleaming casket to get a better look.

"Lose something, darlin'?" a familiar voice drawled in my ear.

I jumped. "My sense of humor."

I sidled away from Del Richardson, who was pressing in close, breathing coffee breath on me. He followed me toward the refreshment table. Today's Stetson was black, for the funeral maybe, or possibly because it fit his villainous personality.

"I can't believe you told the police you saw my mother with Constance," I said, facing him.

"Just wanted to let you know we were playing hardball," he returned. He smiled, showing a lot of white teeth, but it didn't lighten his eyes. "Consider that a free lesson."

"In what? Lying?"

"A lesson in the Del Richardson Philosophy of Business. I don't lose. Ever. And certainly not to a two-bit beautician. At least Miz DuBois was a worthy opponent. I'll bet she had a trick or two up her sleeve." He sounded almost admiring. "You, on the other hand," he shrugged, "wouldn't be any more challenge than shooting a pit bull in a pen." He made a gun of his thumb and forefinger. "Pow."

"Don't you mean stabbing?" I asked sweetly.

"Are you threatening my daughter?" My mother was suddenly at my side, her eyes snapping with anger.

"Mom, this is Del Richardson, from Morestuf," I introduced them, good manners winning out over anger and fear, as they frequently do in the South. Etiquette trumped emotion every time.

"I know who he is," she said. "What I

111

don't know is why he's bothering you."

"Why, I hope I wasn't bothering Miss Ter-hune," he said. "We were discussing what a boon a Morestuf would be to the St. Eliza-beth economy. Right?" And with a tip of his hat, he faded into the crowd.

"What a high-handed —"

"Mom, did you know Simone is engaged?"

That distracted her. "No! Really? To who?"

"Him." I pointed discreetly. "His name is Greg Hutchinson."

She studied the pair as they greeted more mourners. "Handsome. Something about him looks familiar . . ."

"He looks kind of like that actor from the Batman movie, the one who played the DA who loses half his face."

"Mm." She put two cookies on a plate. "The engagement must be recent. I can't believe Constance didn't mention it. Re-member how she went around when Philip got engaged, telling everyone what he spent on the ring and how many people were invited to the wedding and that they were honeymooning in Fiji?"

"Tahiti."

"Remember how mad all the local busi-nesspeople got when she and Susan's mom went to Savannah for the cake and the flow-

112

ers? And they hired a photographer from Atlanta. My, my!" She shook her head.

A commotion near the door brought our heads around. Several people entered. A buzz of whispered comments swept through the room. One of the newcomers was Governor Lansky. Half a head taller than most of the men in the room, he had the kind of presence that takes a politician far, even without much in the way of academic credentials or real public service. He looked like a game show host. Thick, dark hair waved naturally across his brow. His perfect teeth probably put his dentist's son through college, and his smooth tan had an orangey undertone that told me it came from a bottle. His suit was perfection: black wool crepe, pale gray shirt, somber tie. His manner, though, seemed more fit for a political rally than a funeral as he glad-handed everyone who greeted him while making his way to Simone and Philip by the casket. His entourage of wife, chief of staff, and aides surged around him like remora fish cleaning a shark.

"Time for me to bug out," Mom said, giving my arm a squeeze. "I told Althea I'd get to the shop no later than ten. We're booked up clear through 'til six this evening."

"I'll get there soon," I promised. "I just

113

want to say hi to Vonda first." I waved a hand to signal my friend, who had come through the door on the governor's heels.

Mom wove her way through the crowd and ducked out as Vonda reached my side.

"Hi, girlfriend," she said. She'd slicked her bangs back with gel and wore a fitted suit that emphasized her lean build.

"I didn't expect to see you here," I said. "Not after what happened at the town hall meeting."

"Constance DuBois really cared about St. Elizabeth," she said, hugging me. "The least I can do is pay my respects."

"How adult of you," I said admiringly.

"Isn't it?" She looked around at the crowd. "I see the gov is here."

"Yeah, treating the occasion like a photo op." As I watched, Del Richardson approached Lansky, and the two shook hands and stepped away from the grieving siblings to engage in a brief conversation. Lansky clapped Richardson on the back, and they both chuckled before remembering the occasion and pasting sober expressions back on their faces.

"I'm going to chat him up about computers for the school. He *does* call himself the 'education governor,' after all. I'll give you a shout at Vi's this afternoon." And she faded into the crowd. I watched until I saw her claim the governor's attention, then I turned away. A quick stop in the ladies' room and I'd head over to the salon.

I wound my way through a labyrinth of plushly carpeted halls looking for the restroom. I heard voices from around the corner ahead of me and recognized Simone's. I couldn't place the man's voice. Memories of the last time I'd inadvertently eavesdropped on a conversation plagued me, and I almost turned around. But the need to discover something that would clear my mother glued me in place.

"I'm not selling," Simone said, keeping her voice low.

"You have to. I can't sell the bank."

Ah, the other voice must be Philip's. I'd stumbled on a brother-sister spat.

"Well, I won't. Greg and I have plans for Sea Mist."

"Greg! He's nothing but a fortune hunter. Even Mom said so."

"Greg and I love each other. Just because we haven't known each other from high school, like you and Susan —"

"Sea Mist should have been mine."

"Oh, get over it. You got the bank shares and the house. That's fair."

"It's not about fair, it's about liquidity. I

need cash."

"Sell the house."

I almost gasped. Selling the DuBois family mansion would be like Jefferson putting Monticello on the market. Apparently, Philip thought as I did.

"I can't do that!"

"Sounds like a personal problem." A hint of glee in Simone's voice told me she was paying off dozens of childhood slights from her older brother.

Desperation tinged Philip's voice. "There's more to this than you know —"

Something cold and wet poked my ankle. I smothered a scream and jumped back. Bright black eyes peered up at me.

"Shoo, Peaches," I whispered.

The Yorkie wagged her tail.

I backed up a step. She followed. *"Rrurf."*

"Peaches!" Simone called.

The dog looked over her shoulder, then turned back to me. "Go to Mommy," I urged her. Simone was going to come around the corner looking for the darn mutt and find me. She'd know I'd overheard everything and be furious. It would fuel her desire to destroy my mom. A thought came to me.

Before Peaches could gauge my intentions, I leaned over and scooped her up.

She growled deep in her throat.

"Play along," I told her. "Or I'll feed you to Beauty." I raised my voice. "Simone? Simo-one." I hurried around the corner, clutching the dog under one arm. Simone and Philip sprang apart like illicit lovers caught by a spouse.

"There you are!" I said, as if I'd been looking all over for her. "I found Peaches wandering around and knew you would be worried." With a smile, I handed the dog over.

"Thanks, Grace," Simone said grudgingly. "Are you Mommy's naughty doggy?" she cooed to Peaches.

Philip looked at me from under his brows. An awkward silence fell. "Well —" I started.

A huge woman sailed around the corner and put a hand to her heart at the sight of us. "Oh, Simone, Philip!" Tears started to her eyes, and she dabbed at them with a lace hankie. "I haven't had a chance to tell you how terribly, *terribly* sorry I am about your mother's tragic demise. I was shocked, absolutely *shocked* when I heard. Oh, what a cute little doggy. And you *poor* children . . ."

As the newcomer bathed Constance's children in condolences, I muttered, "Good-bye," and backed away, willing to sacrifice the restroom for an easy escape. I'd hold it until I got to the salon. I stepped from the cool of the funeral parlor to the increasing humidity outside and took a deep breath to rinse away the scent of lilies.

"Grace!" A voice stopped me before I walked two steps. I turned to see Stella and a fortyish African American woman hurrying to catch up with me.

"This is my friend Janelle Stevens," Stella said. Janelle was gorgeous, with skin the color of a Hershey's kiss, high cheekbones, and heavy-lidded eyes with curling lashes. She wore a mulberry-colored suit that showed off her tall, slim figure. "She's the head teller at the DuBois's bank."

"Nice to meet you, Janelle," I said.

"Likewise." Her tone was businesslike, but she glanced over her shoulder as if afraid of being observed.

"Look," Stella said, "Janelle's willing to talk to us, but let's go somewhere where Philip won't stumble over us."

"And I've got to be back at work in twenty minutes," Janelle said.

"How about Filomena's?" I suggested. "There's no reason why three women couldn't run into each other at a boutique, right?" And it was nearby and had a powder room I could use. We walked the half block to the store and I disappeared into the restroom while the other women riffled through the racks. When I came out, Stella was holding an emerald silk blouse up to her neck.

"That color is gorgeous on you," I said.

She turned over the price tag and winced. "Maybe, but I can't blow the month's food budget on one blouse." She hung it up.

"Just let me know if you need any help, ladies," Filomena, a willowy blonde about my mom's age, called from behind the counter as we moved toward a sale rack at the back of the store.

Stella took charge. "Tell Grace what you told me about Philip and Constance fighting," she suggested.

Janelle took a deep breath. "I want you to know I wouldn't be talking behind my employer's back if it weren't so important to Stella," she said.

"We've been best friends since third grade," Stella put in, squeezing her friend's hand.

"I understand," I said. "I really appreciate it, Janelle."

She nodded. "Well, like I told Stella, Philip was authorizing a lot of risky loans. The bank almost went under with the subprime mortgage crash, and his mama caught on to what he was doing. She read him the riot act, I'll tell you. My office is next door to his, and the walls aren't but a couple of layers of drywall — they don't exactly soak up much sound, not like in the old building when my dad used to work there."

I pulled a pair of lemon capris off the rack, trying to make it look like we were shopping and not conspiring. "So what happened then?"

Janelle lowered her voice even more. "I'm not sure, but I think Philip may have been using the bank's money to cover some of his own investments."

"Isn't that illegal?" Stella asked, wrinkling her brow.

"Very," Janelle said dryly. "I think his mama suspected because she told him she was going to have the auditors in."

"When was this?" I found a striped blouse that matched the capris and held it up.

Stella nodded approvingly. "That'd be cute on you, Grace."

"Last Tuesday," Janelle said, fiddling with the gold stud in her ear.

Stella and I exchanged a look. "The day before Constance died," Stella breathed. "So with his mother out of the way, he can sell the bank and have all the money he needs. Or hang on to it and not worry about getting caught?"

"I heard him tell Simone he can't sell the bank," I said. I handed Janelle a flowered scarf from a jumble in a sale basket. Its burgundy, purple, and cream pansies added pizzazz to her suit when she draped it absently around her neck.

"Of course not," Janelle said, shaking her head at our ignorance. "They'd have to have an audit before a sale could take place, and an audit is the one thing in the world Philip DuBois wants to avoid right now."

"So he's no better off than when Constance was alive?" Stella asked.

"I didn't say that. This gives him time to come up with the cash somewhere else," Janelle said.

"But to murder his own mother?" Stella looked doubtful. "Is he capable of that?" She looked from me to Janelle, her face troubled.

"I think very few people on this planet are incapable of killing," Janelle said matter-of-factly. "It's just a matter of what pushes each of us to the point where killing seems like the only choice. For you, Stel, it might be someone threatening Jessica. For Philip, maybe it's the fear of prison." She glanced at the dainty gold watch on her wrist. "Look, I've got to go. *Please* don't tell anyone I talked to you. It could mean my job." She unwrapped the scarf from around her neck and let it slither into the basket.

"We won't," Stella and I promised. "Thanks," I added. "I'm going to get this outfit" — I held up the capri set — "so you go on without me."

Both women were out of sight by the time Filomena rang up my purchase and accepted my check. Walking quickly, I pondered what I'd overheard and what Janelle had said. It sounded like trouble in Siblingville. Apparently, Constance had left the bank and house to Philip even though she wasn't happy with how he was running the bank — perhaps she hadn't had time to change her will — and Sea Mist Plantation to Simone. And Janelle intimated that Philip was desperate for money to make up investment losses and replace what he might have "borrowed" from bank deposits. Speaking of money . . . I wondered if there were any other interesting bequests in the will? Maybe someone besides Philip or Simone had been anxious to inherit and had killed Constance to speed things up. Wills were public record, weren't they? I needed to find out who all benefited from Constance's death. The old saw might suggest "cherchez la femme," but my version was more useful in modern times: cherchez la moola.

Vonda came by as promised when my mom and I were locking up for the day. Mom greeted Vonda, asked her when Ricky was going to make an honest woman of her again (like she did at least once a month), and shooed us out of the salon. "I'll finish up here," she said. "You two scoot."

So we scooted to a trendy, beach-front bar Vonda liked to troll in when she was on the outs with Ricky. I divide people into two groups depending on whether they prefer the ocean side of town or the river end. River people prefer the subtle beauty of the Satilla and the marshes to the flashy beauty and frenetic activity of the beach. Vonda's an ocean person. I'm a river person. I didn't mind the beach, though, especially when unsettled weather kept the tourists away. With a storm clearly imminent — the sky boiled with angry clouds over the water — The Roving Pirate, known to locals as The Pirate, had few patrons. We snagged a window table and ordered: a glass of house white for me and a mojito for Vonda. I asked her how it went with the governor.

She shrugged. "Oh, you know politicians. He promised to push for better technology for RJ's school — for all elementary schools in 'the great state of Georgia,' but you know how that goes. Politicians are like Alzheimer's patients: their long-term memory is great — who contributed to their first campaign, who tried to sabotage their bill in 1990 — but their short-term memory is nonexistent. I'll bet if you asked him right now who Vonda Jamison was, or what I talked to him about, all you'd get was a blank stare." She stabbed at a cocktail napkin with the little plastic sword that skewered a lime in her drink.

"I'm sure he remembers you," I said. Men always remembered Vonda.

A rumble of thunder drew our attention to the window. As I watched, a fat drop of rain splatted against the glass. Others quickly followed.

"More rain," Vonda said, her voice as dreary as the weather.

"We need it," I reminded her. "Think how happy the town's gardeners will be."

She spun her forefinger in circles. "Whoop-de-doo."

As if the rain had washed the last remnants of sun from the sky, darkness fell and opaqued the window so I could no longer see the heaving water. I could still hear it, though. A busboy meandered around the bar, lighting the candles in round amber-colored holders that squatted on each table.

The server arrived with refills. "That gentlemen over there wants to buy you a drink," she said, nodding her head at a suited man watching us hopefully from the bar.

Vonda looked him over. "Salesman," she said disparagingly. "Office products or restaurant supplies. Something boring." Nevertheless, she sent a thank-you smile his way. The moment of flirtation seemed to have chased away her doleful mood. "Hey, I saw Minnie Parker at the car wash yesterday."

"So?" I was totally uninterested in the whereabouts of my former mother-in-law. She'd suggested I have a boob job before Hank and I got married so I could "fill out the wedding gown a bit more." She'd had her breasts augmented for her fiftieth birthday, and she "just knew" that every woman short of Dolly Parton would have a more fulfilling life if they upped their cup size. When I told her I was perfectly happy with my 34Bs, she asked archly, "But is my Hank?"

"So, she looked fit as a fiddle, healthy as a horse . . . didn't Hank say he moved back here because she was ill?"

"Yeah." I didn't much want to ruin the

125

evening by talking about Hank.

"I think that was only an excuse," Vonda said, leaning across the table to peer into my face. "He moved back here because he wants you back."

"Well, as the old saying goes, 'wantin' don't make it so,' or something like that." I finished the wine in my glass and eyed the replacement sent over by Mr. Salesman. I didn't want to encourage him by drinking it. Vonda had no such hesitations and was halfway through her second mojito.

"You wouldn't get back together with him, would you?"

She tried to sound casual, but I heard the anxiety in her voice. Vonda had never thought Hank was good enough for me, as she put it, and she'd dragged me out to celebrate when the divorce became final.

"Vonda." I gave her a look.

"I knew you wouldn't," she smiled, "but I had to make sure. You haven't gotten laid in — What? A year? — and long stretches without sex can make any port look appealing in the storm."

I laughed, forcing the image of Special Agent Dillon out of my head. Where had he come from? "Believe me, I could be celibate for the next ten years and not get a hankering for Hank. I don't know why I stuck with

126

him so long, except he got to be a habit."

"A bad one. They should make a patch for getting over exes . . . you know, like a nicotine patch helps you go cold turkey with cigarettes."

I heard the wistfulness in her voice. "Missing Ricky?"

"Hell, no."

Her swift response and sidelong look at Mr. Salesman didn't convince me.

"Let's get out of here," I said, afraid that in her current mood she'd hook up with the guy and regret it in the morning. "I'll drop you and take the sitter home."

"No sitter. Ricky's got RJ for the weekend," she said. The fact that they still lived in the same house, albeit on opposite sides of the twelve-bedroom B&B, made joint custody easier. She pushed back from the table. "I miss him."

I didn't ask if she meant RJ or Ricky. "I know. C'mon."

The parking lot was only steps from the door, but we were drenched by the time we got to my car. The cold water pinging our skin and ozone-scented air jolted Vonda out of the doldrums, and she was laughing as we slammed the doors shut. "Thanks," she said, shaking her head like a blond spaniel and flinging water drops onto the windshield and dash. As frequently happens, the rain let up as soon as we were in the car.

"Timing," I said. "Everything in life is timing."

Her Magnolia House B&B was three blocks from my apartment. As I dropped her, a fire truck surged past, its siren shrieking. "See you at church tomorrow?" Vonda asked.

"Sure. Maybe we can do brunch afterward." The ladies from Violetta's — Mom, Althea, Stella, and sometimes Rachel — had a tradition of doing brunch after Sunday services at the First Baptist Church. I'd been joining them more often than not since I came back.

"It's a date," Vonda said. She looked out the side window at the darkening sky. The rain had tapered off to not much more than a drizzle. "Thanks, girlfriend."

"Anytime," I said as she leaned over to hug me. With a quick smile, she pushed open the door and dashed for her front porch, dodging the raindrops in a ridiculous serpentine we'd invented as teens. I laughed and waved as I put the car in gear.

Mom's house was on my way home, and I debated stopping in for a cup of herbal tea and a chat. As I turned onto her block, I spied the fire truck and a mass of firefighters, cops, and onlookers blocking the street. What the — ? Then I saw the flames leaping from the front of Mom's house.

CHAPTER EIGHT

I stomped on the accelerator, and the car shot down the street. I forgot to calculate the effect of wet streets, and the car slid, almost T-boning a police car, when I hit the brakes. I tumbled out. An ugly smell of gasoline and wet, burnt wood enveloped me.

"Mom!"

I dashed toward the house, heedless of the fire. My feet slipped on the wet grass and I sprawled flat on my stomach. I scrambled up again. A strong arm grabbed me around the waist and hauled me backward.

"My mom!" I struggled to free myself, clawing at the arm.

"Violetta's just fine, Grace," Hank's voice said in my ear. "Your mom's fine."

The words finally got through, and I stopped kicking back at his shins. His hands on my shoulders turned me forty-five degrees, and I could see Mom sitting between the open doors of an ambulance, a uniformed EMT doing something to her hands. She hadn't seen my arrival.

I wrenched myself out of Hank's grip and trotted toward her. "Mom! Are you all right?"

She looked at me over her shoulder. "I'm fine, dear, but this nice young man insists on putting ointment on my hands." She held up her hands, displaying pink palms.

The EMT smiled and said, "First degree. Not much worse than a sunburn." He tucked a tube of ointment and a roll of gauze into the box at his side.

"You're burned! What happened?"

"She very foolishly tried to put out the fire herself with a fire extinguisher." A stocky man of about sixty came around the far side of the ambulance. He had crew-cut hair and ruddy skin, and wore a fire hat that said "Chief."

"Roger MacDonald," he introduced himself, holding out a square hand. "Fire's out."

I shook it, liking the strength in his grip. I looked toward the house where, sure enough, the flames were gone and tendrils of smoke, slightly grayer than the night, wisped from the veranda. Two firemen were coiling a hose. "What happened, Chief?"

"It's not foolish to try to save your home,"

131

my mom interrupted. She glared at the chief from under her brows.

"What did you always teach your children, Mrs. Terhune?" MacDonald asked. "Get out in case of a fire, right? Don't go back in for *any*thing."

Boy, he had Mom's number. He even inflected his words like she had when she drilled me and Alice Rose about fire safety.

"Of course, but that's diff—"

I put a hand on her shoulder and leaned down to kiss her cheek. "I'm just glad you're okay," I said. "Now, would someone please tell me what happened?"

The ambulance driver indicated he needed to leave and eased Mom off the end of the vehicle. She avoided using her hands. Burned palms would make cutting hair difficult. But that was something to worry about another day.

"It was a Molotov cocktail," MacDonald said.

"A what?" I stared at him blankly, thinking I had misheard.

"Molotov cocktail," he repeated. "You fill a glass bottle with gasoline, stick a rag in the neck, light it, and throw it. Boom!" He flung his hands apart. "Drive by and toss it out the window. Piece of cake."

"That's absurd." Mom was shaking her

132

head. "Kids around here don't do that kind of thing. They might egg a house, or TP it, but not fire. Maybe in Atlanta." Sin city, as far as she was concerned.

"We don't know that it was kids," Mac-Donald observed. "Do you have any enemies?"

A vision of Simone shouting that she was going to put Violetta's out of business flashed into my head. I ignored it. "How much damage is there?"

"You were lucky," the chief said. "The bottle broke on the veranda. It didn't go through a window like it was probably supposed to. And the rain helped. All you've got is a little charring and some smoke damage on the siding."

"Thank God," Mom said. She gripped my hand, then winced and pulled away.

"Why don't you come home with me for the night, Mom? You can have the bed. I'll sleep on the sofa."

"Certainly not. I'm not going to let hooligans playing dangerous pranks chase me out of my home. But thank you for the offer."

"Then I'll stay here," I said, resigned. "We can call the insurance company in the morning."

"And I'll let the police know," MacDonald put in. "They'll probably have a detective out here first thing."

Great. Just what we needed. More face time with the police. Speaking of police, I looked around for Hank, to thank him for keeping me away from the fire, but he had left. Most of the crowd had drifted away now that the excitement was over, but a new figure came bustling down the sidewalk. When he got close enough, I recognized Walter Highsmith, incongruous in a plum-colored smoking jacket over striped pajama bottoms. His mustache drooped a little.

"Miss Violetta," he said in his reedy voice when he got close enough. "Are you all right?" He cast a suspicious look at Chief MacDonald.

I introduced them. They shook hands perfunctorily, giving off the vibes of rival tomcats.

"I've got to get going," the chief said. "I'll call around in the morning to finish up my report and make sure everything's okay."

"I can take care of Miss Violetta," Walter bristled.

With an ironic smile, Roger MacDonald turned away and strode to his red car.

"I don't need taking care of," Mom said. "I need sleep. Come on, Grace."

"I'll escort you," Walter said. He crooked a courtly elbow and offered it to Mom.

She took his arm willingly enough, and I realized she must be exhausted. I followed as they made their way carefully past the veranda to the rear door. The smell of gasoline and charred wood hung heavy on the air. Somehow, I didn't think I'd find it as restful as the familiar scents of permanent solution and hairspray.

[Sunday]
No attacks or break-ins marred our sleep, and Mom and I slept in, getting up barely in time to dress for church. I scrambled into my choir robe only minutes before the service started. I tried to lose myself in the rhythm of the service and our glorious anthem, but the night's events kept intruding. I'm afraid I heard only snatches of the sermon as I tried to puzzle out who could have thrown the Molotov cocktail. The crime didn't seem to fit anyone I knew. Simone was the only person I knew of who had a motive — she'd sworn to shut down Violetta's — but I couldn't visualize her siphoning gasoline into a bottle. Maybe she'd enlisted her brother's help? No, judging by the argument I'd overheard at Fagin-Jones, I didn't think Philip would give Simone fifty cents for a cup of coffee, never mind commit arson for her. Giving it up

with a sigh, I concentrated on singing the final hymn.

I caught up with Mom and Althea shaking hands with Reverend Kitchens after the service. He stood, as he always did, under the spreading arms of the huge magnolia tree that arched over the walkway leading to the sanctuary. A gentle wind whisked through the magnolia's shiny leaves and diffused their rich scent.

"Powerful sermon, Reverend," Mom told the smiling man.

"It's one of my favorite texts," he said. Of medium height, he had shiny black skin and the gentlest brown eyes I'd ever seen. I'd never heard him raise his voice in anger, even when Terrence, his youngest of five sons, brought a guinea pig to church one Sunday and let it loose in the choir loft. The choir hit some notes that Sunday that no composer ever intended.

I nodded my head, although I couldn't even have named the text the sermon was based on.

"Doralynn's?" Althea asked, hugging each of us.

"Sure," we agreed.

Mom filled Althea in on the night's excitements as we strolled the five blocks to Doralynn's Café and Bakery, home of the best biscuits in St. Elizabeth. And the stuffed waffles were to die for.

"I want you to move in with me, Vi," Althea said when Mom finished. "Just until things calm down. What's next? First, someone kills Constance and now someone's heaving bombs at your house. What is this town coming to?"

"It wasn't a bomb," Mom soothed. "Just a pop bottle with some gasoline. The fire chief said it was probably kids."

Hmmm. That wasn't how I remembered it, but I kept quiet. I knew nothing Althea could say would persuade Mom to leave her home.

We reached Doralynn's before Althea gave up. A St. Elizabeth's fixture, Doralynn's was hugely popular with tourists and residents alike. Lots of windows and comfortable décor in blue and white and yellow made it cheery even on the grayest day. This early in May it wasn't too crowded; anyway, Ruthie Steinmetz, the owner (who thought "Doralynn's" sounded more Southern than "Ruthie's"), always saved us a table on Sunday no matter how busy it got. Although the tourists celebrated Doralynn's as the quintessence of Southern cooking and hospitality, Ruthie was a self-described Jewish grandmother from Germany by way of

New Jersey. She'd opened Doralynn's over twenty years ago, and such was the power of suggestion and savvy marketing that many people believed the charming café on the river walk was a Southern institution. I didn't know what they made of the cheese blintzes on the menu.

Stella and Rachel waved at us from a table as we entered. I didn't see Vonda; she must've gotten stuck at home with her B&B customers.

"We waited for you to order," Stella said as we seated ourselves.

On the words, a waitress sailed up, order pad in hand. I didn't recognize her. Her name tag read "Amber." She looked to be in her early twenties and had blond hair, a pretty face, and a bosom that gapped the buttons of her blue and white checked blouse. When she asked, "Are you ready to order?" with a New York accent, I figured she must be one of Ruthie's grandkids, down for the summer break to earn some money and bake on the beach.

"Nah," she said when I asked. "I'm not related. Ruthie's been real nice to me, though, letting me wait tables here even when I told her I was looking for something temporary."

"Just until college starts up again, huh?"

Stella said. "I'll have the banana-nut pan-cakes."

Amber noted the order on her pad. She took the rest of our orders efficiently and returned with our iced teas in record time.

Stella reacted much as Althea had to Mom's news. "Come stay with me, at least until you get the damage repaired," she said. "You can have Jessie's room. She can bunk with me."

"All the damage is on the veranda," Mom said, awkwardly cutting her waffle with her bandaged hands. "I'm going to call Fred Wilkerson when I get home — I'll bet he can have it all fixed up by the end of the week."

"I don't think it was kids," Rachel announced through a mouthful of French toast. "The guys that do stuff like that, well, they're more into tagging than burning stuff up. And the paint fumes have, like, fried their brain cells. I can't see them coming up with the Molotov-cocktail idea. And if they had thought of it, they'd have made a bunch of 'em and thrown them at teachers' houses and stuff."

She had a point. As far as we knew, no other houses or businesses had been Molotov-cocktailed last night. Vandals and teens on a spree seemed to think more was

139

better, whether they were knocking down mailboxes, egging houses, or graffitiing overpasses. Why was my mom the only victim?

I asked her that question as we walked home from the café.

"How would I know, Grace?" she asked. "No one understands the working of a teenage mind. Even you and Alice Rose were a puzzlement to me."

"It didn't seem like that to us," I said, smiling. "Vonda swore you had ESP that time you showed up at her house just when she suggested we play spin the bottle with Trevor and Clay Spelkin."

"And her daddy grounded her for a month for having boys over when they were out," she said with a reminiscent smile.

"Well, I don't think it was kids and I don't think it was random," I said as we reached her house. The smell of charred wood was much fainter. The hammock just off the right side of the veranda was untouched and looked inviting. Maybe this afternoon I'd get a book and laze in it for an hour. Absently, I opened the mailbox beside me, its metal painted purple to match the house.

"It's Sunday," Mom reminded me.

I ignored her and plucked a folded piece of paper out of the box. No stamp. My name was written on it in capital letters. With suddenly shaking fingers, I unfolded it.

"This is a warning. Stop asking questions. MYOB." Not surprisingly, there was no signature.

"What's wrong, Grace?"

I handed her the note.

Just as she gasped, "Oh, good Lord!" a car pulled up and Special Agent Dillon got out. Dressed in jeans, a red knit shirt with a horse logo and "Ashmire Arabians" embroidered over the pocket, and work boots, his clothing looked Sunday-morning relaxed, although his expression was still Monday-morning grim.

"Good morning, ladies," he said. "First it's murder, now it's arson. Is there a felony in this town you're *not* involved in?"

I thought there might actually be a trace of humor in his voice, but the note bothered me too much for me to respond in kind. As he reached us, I handed it to him.

He read it. "When did you get this?"

"Just now." I gestured to the mailbox. "But I don't know when it was left."

Pulling a transparent baggie from his pocket, he slid the letter in, holding it by one corner. "Can I assume you both handled this," he asked in a put-upon voice,

141

"and messed up any fingerprints the perp might have left?"

"Excuse me for not expecting to find threats in my mom's mailbox," I snapped.

"Would you like to come in for some tea, Special Agent?" Mom asked.

"After I look around," he said. "That would be nice. Thank you."

Mom headed toward the house, taking the path around to the back door so she wouldn't have to walk on the burned veranda. I stuck with Dillon.

"What are you looking for?" I asked.

"Any idea who left that note?" He put his hands in his pocket and climbed the veranda steps.

"Well, it sounds kind of like Del Richardson." I explained about Richardson's "free lesson." "Maybe this is another lesson?"

"What about the MYOB for 'mind your own business'?" he asked, scuffing at a charred spot with the toe of his shoe. Bending, he took out a pocket knife, scraped at the wood, and used the knife blade to tip a sample into another baggie.

I considered his question. "That sounds more like a woman," I finally said. "Even a teenager. Simone? She's determined to shut us down."

"Wouldn't Simone DuBois know you

don't live here?"

It took me a moment to catch his meaning. "You mean since the note was addressed to me but left in my mom's mailbox?"

He nodded, then leaned to sniff at the siding where the fire had climbed up the side of the house.

"I don't know. She hasn't been back in St. Elizabeth too long. I used to live here . . . maybe she thinks I still do." I gave it some more thought. "I hate this!"

He turned to face me, and his navy eyes fixed on mine. "It is hateful," he agreed. "Murder's about the most hateful thing there is. I'm not surprised it bothers you to be mixed up in this."

His unexpected sympathy caught me off guard, and I sniffed back tears. "Ready for that tea?"

He followed me this time as I led the way to the side door. Before I could open it, he stopped me with a hand on my arm. The skin of his palm was work-toughened and warm against my arm. "By the way, Judge Finnegan called last night from Port-au-Prince. She verified your story."

"Of course she did. Because it wasn't a story."

He ignored my snippy tone. "I'll need a

143

list of everyone you've talked about the murder with."

"That's lots of people," I said, wondering if I could remember everyone. There were the ladies from the shop, various people at the viewing, Del Richardson, a few shop owners from the square, and some customers . . .

"Well, chances are one of them did this" — he nodded his head back toward the veranda — "so make sure you don't leave anybody out."

CHAPTER NINE

[Monday]

Mom's favorite handyman, Fred Wilkerson, came over Sunday afternoon and replaced the damaged boards on the veranda. The new boards looked like raw scars when I arrived for work on Monday morning, and I stared at them, deploring how they stood out against the weathered wood. He had also power-washed the siding; I thought it would look fine when he got it repainted the pale purple my mom chose ten years ago. Deliberately tromping on one of the new boards to break it in, I pushed through the salon door. Mom must be upstairs because the salon was empty, still dim with the blinds closed. Good. I wanted to phone a lawyer friend and see what I could find out about the contents of Constance's will before customers started arriving.

I had just picked up the phone when the door opened. "Miss Violetta?" a man's voice called. I whirled, dropping the phone. It bounced off my foot.

"Walter! You startled me."

Walter Highsmith stood just inside the door, dressed in his usual uniform. I swear, if he got a paper cut, his blood would be Confederate gray. His salt-and-pepper mustache was waxed and curled to perfection.

His full lips sagged into a pout when he recognized me. "Good morning, Miss Grace. I was looking for your mother. I hope she's all right after the incident Saturday night. It's disgraceful what the youth of today get up to. In my day, teenagers weren't allowed to roam loose at night, drinking and vandalizing and consorting."

How did Walter define "consorting"? I wondered.

"Young men and women were expected to dress modestly and wouldn't have been caught dead in the indecent garments kids wear today, to be respectful of their elders, and not speak unless spoken to. Why, when I —"

I cut into his pontificating. "You'll have to settle for me," I said. "Want some coffee? I was about to make some." Not true, but I realized I hadn't chatted with Walter since Constance's death, and he had argued with her mere hours before she died.

He accepted my offer, and I scooped Althea's Kona blend into the pot behind the register and added water. Walter sat in one of the chintz chairs in the waiting room, fussily smoothing his uniform pants where they creased across his thigh. As the scent of coffee permeated the air, I leaned across the counter on my forearms. "So, have you found a new home for Confederate Artefacts?"

A prim smile appeared on his face. "It is no longer necessary for me to find new premises."

"Really?"

"When Constance DuBois passed on so tragically and unexpectedly —"

"Was murdered, you mean." I had little patience for his euphemisms. He was surprisingly squeamish in his word choice for a man whose idea of fun was reenacting bloody Civil War battles.

"— I contacted the woman who was going to supplant me. The Yankee." He stroked his goatee. "She has decided not to open her scrapbooking store in St. Elizabeth now that Constance is not here to drum up business for her. I believe she's looking at Charleston instead." His face wore the satisfied look of a cat who has successfully filched a pork chop off the dinner table without being noticed.

"How fortuitous." Ye gods, he was infecting me with his speech patterns. "I mean, what a break for you."

"Indeed." He accepted the mug of coffee I passed him and blew on it.

"You know the police have talked to my mom about the murder. They think that she killed Constance because Constance threatened to shut down Violetta's."

"That is patently ridiculous," Walter said, shifting on the chair. If the cops had talked to him, too, he didn't own up to it. "Your mother would never think of taking such offensive action. It wouldn't be womanly." His concept of women appeared to have quit evolving about the time Scarlett O'Hara was saving Tara.

"You do know women can vote now?"

He looked at me blankly.

I sighed, trying to decide if his chauvinism was charming or exasperating. "So you don't think a woman could have killed Constance?"

"Not with a blade," he said. He puffed his chubby cheeks and let the air out explosively. "If she'd been poisoned, now . . ."

I didn't know where Walter got his rose-colored glasses, but I wanted a pair. The

Atlanta newspaper carried daily reports of women offing their family members, friends, coworkers, and assorted strangers with knives, blunt objects, guns, cars, knitting needles, scissors, and pencils. I was pretty sure Constance's manner of death didn't rule out either gender. I dragged the conversation back to my original point. "So you're going to stay where you are? The new owner is going to renew your lease?"

"Why, as to that, I haven't had any discussions with the new owner. That's probably not proper until after the will has been probated. But I'm sure she'll extend my lease. And I'm hoping she'll let me do some remodeling — knock out a wall to expand my display space. Mrs. DuBois never let me so much as change the paint color." He set his mug gently on the glass-topped end table and pushed himself to his feet. Looking over my shoulder, he pouted again, presumably because my mother hadn't appeared yet. "Please tell Miss Violetta I stopped by. I was planning to invite her to dine with me this evening at The Crab Trap, so if you'd give her the message and have her ring me?"

"Sure," I said. I walked around the counter to meet him at the door, forcing myself not to grab his arm so he couldn't escape before he told me. "But you know who inherits your building? You said 'she'?"

He raised his brows. "Of course. It's Miss Althea. Althea Jenkins."

I tackled Mom about it the minute she entered the salon. Her color was better than yesterday and she looked well rested. Her gray and white hair spiked up in a gentle halo around her head. I hated to disturb her serenity, but I had to know. "Mom, Walter Highsmith was here looking for you. He said Althea inherits the building he's in, that Constance DuBois willed it to her."

Her forehead wrinkled. "He must be mistaken."

"So you didn't know about it?" Relief trickled through me, and I drew in a long breath. I hadn't realized how tense I was.

"Why would Constance do that?" Mom asked, although it seemed like she was talking more to herself than to me. She pinched a dead leaf from one of the violets in the window.

Unease gripped me again. I remembered Althea's absence from the town hall meeting, her hatred of Constance. I didn't know the details of her financial situation, but I was pretty sure the building was worth at least half a million, and that would constitute motive in anyone's eyes. Special Agent Dillon's navy blue eyes came to mind.

"I don't know, Grace. And it's not our business. If it's true, Althea will tell us in her own good time." She sounded calm, but worry clouded her face.

"I'm going to ask her as soon as she gets here." I crossed to my station and began laying out my scissors and combs.

"You are not," Mom said sternly. "You will respect her privacy. Besides, she won't be here this morning."

"Why not?"

She pinched another leaf off the violet, not meeting my gaze as she said, "She had an appointment. With a lawyer," she added reluctantly.

"And you think it's about this inheritance," I said.

"I'm not thinking about it at all because it's none of my business."

"Mom, you and Althea are like sisters, closer than most sisters. She's been your best friend for decades. Of course it's your business."

"Even friends are allowed their privacy, Grace. Especially friends." She opened the wooden blinds, and sunlight flooded the salon.

From where I stood, I could see one of

the new planks on the veranda. "Althea didn't do that," I muttered. Appalled at the direction my thoughts had taken, I glanced at my mother, hoping she hadn't heard. No such luck.

Her eyes snapped with fury, and red mottled her neck. "Don't you even think it, Grace Ann Terhune," she said. "Don't think it. Althea Jenkins is not capable of that."

"I know," I said, holding up a placating hand. "I didn't really." Didn't really think that Althea could have stabbed Constance DuBois and then lobbed a Molotov cocktail at my mom's house. No way. It was just one of those thoughts that flit through your head before you can censor them. Even if I'd thought Althea might, in a moment of anger, kill Constance, I knew with one hundred percent certainty that she would never have put my mom at risk by trying to burn the salon. Besides, I remembered, Althea knew darn well I didn't live here. If she'd been trying to scare me away from investigating, she'd have left the note at my apartment.

"I'm sorry, Mom," I said as the first customer of the day came through the door.

"Hmph," she said. Turning away, she busied herself dusting blinds that didn't need dusting.

I greeted my client, hoping Mom's indignation would fade as the day wore on.

The salon was busy enough all day to keep me from brooding, and I was looking forward to a quiet evening working in Mrs. Jones's garden, when the phone rang and Stella picked it up.

"It's for you, Grace," Stella called.

I took the receiver disinterestedly but perked up when the voice on the other end identified herself as being from the mayor's office. She spoke her name so quickly I wasn't sure if she was Tina or Dina.

"You volunteered to be on the committee to assess the impact of a Morestuf on the local economy and environment, correct?" Tina-Dina asked.

"I suppose so," I admitted. I'm not sure raising one's hand while being poked in the ribs by one's mother should count as "volunteering."

"Great! The first meeting is this evening, in the conference room down from Mayor Faricy's office. Six o'clock sharp."

There went my relaxing evening. "I'll be there."

"Great!" Tina-Dina said again, and hung up before I could ask who else was on the committee. Hopefully, there'd be enough people that I wouldn't actually have to do anything. Not that I'm opposed to civic service, but I was more interested in clearing my mother's name, and Althea's if necessary, than analyzing statistics about Morestuf. Still, I knew Simone DuBois would be at the meeting, so maybe I could pump her, discreetly, for more details about her mother's will. My mom might not want me to ask Althea about it, but there was more than one way to skin a possum.

I hadn't been to the town hall since the murder and I couldn't help but look over at the spot where we'd found Constance's body. It was just an empty corner of the parking lot. A clutch of kids was tossing a foam football around in Carver Square, loosely supervised by a couple of women chatting on the bench where Mom and I had sat. As I watched, the ball sailed out of the park, landing about where we had found Constance. I winced.

Inside the town hall, the air-conditioning chilled my skin, damp from my walk. I shivered and hunted for the conference room. A copy machine thumped in one office as I passed and music drifted softly from another, proof that our city employees were earning their pay by staying late. The door to the conference room stood open and I walked in at 5:59 to find Simone DuBois seated at the table, facing a thin woman who hugged a stack of papers to her chest. Tina-Dina, perhaps?

"You must be Grace," the woman said, smiling. She had small white teeth, freckles, and light brown hair slightly darker than mine that did nothing to brighten her pale complexion.

Did my hair look that mousy? Maybe I should try some highlights like Mom kept suggesting.

"I'm Tina Sabol, the mayor's aide. He wanted me to thank you for agreeing to help St. Elizabeth make this important decision."

"Happy to help out," I said, seating myself across from Simone, who wore another black suit, this one with a short jacket and a ruffled white blouse. Was the black for mourning, or did she not own any colored clothes? I was betting on the latter. Maybe New Yorkers are all so busy rushing from place to place, talking at light speed, that they don't have time to coordinate outfits in the morning and rely on black because it's easy. I'd spent a week there at a hair color seminar, and it took me a month to slow myself back to a Southern pace. "Where's everybody else?"

"We're waiting for one more — oh, hi, Lucy," Tina said as Lucy Mortimer, a client of mine and the curator of the Rothmere mansion and museum scuttled in. Of average height, she carried a few extra pounds around her waist. In her mid-fifties, she wore a navy shirtwaist dress and tortoiseshell glasses. Between Simone's black and Lucy's navy, I felt like a macaw at a crow convention in the lemon-colored cropped pants and striped camp shirt I'd bought at Filomena's.

"Sorry I'm late," she murmured. "But with the new exhibit . . ."

"Not a problem," Tina assured her. "I was telling the others how pleased Mayor Faricy is that you all are going to examine this information from Morestuf" — she placed a two-inch-thick packet in front of each of us — "and figure out if one of their stores would be a boon for St. Elizabeth."

A "boon"? She sounded like one of the mayor's stump speeches. "Shouldn't we also look at data that isn't supplied by Morestuf?" I asked, flipping through the pages in front of me.

"Whatever you think necessary," Tina agreed. "Let me know if you need anything. Oh, and the mayor would appreciate it if you could have a presentation ready for the next town hall meeting, a week from today." With another smile, she disappeared.

"Next week?" Simone muttered, glaring at the packet. "Maybe next month."

Lucy looked at the papers with dismay, then glanced at her watch bracelet's small face. "I really don't have time for this. When I volunteered —"

"You were trying to impress my mother and persuade her to withdraw her recommendation from the Rothmere board of directors," Simone said coldly.

"Oh, no," Lucy said. "I was just . . . that is, I hoped . . ."

"What recommendation?" I asked when Lucy floundered to a halt. Good manners, of course, dictated that I politely pretend I hadn't heard Simone's comment. But curiosity, and the hope that I'd learn something that might help clear Mom's name, won out.

Simone said, "Some items disappeared from the Rothmere collection recently, valuable historical items. Jewelry that belonged to Amelia Rothmere, the sword Reginald Rothmere used during the War of Northern Aggression, some silver pieces. Mother held Lucy responsible."

Lucy fluttered with dismay. "I didn't steal —"

Simone waved an impatient hand. "I

157

didn't say you stole anything. I said mother held you responsible because you were in charge. It happened on your watch."

"You were going to lose your job?" I studied Lucy closely. She had been the Rothmere's curator for as long as I could remember. My second-grade class had gone on a field trip to the Rothmere, and a younger Lucy, with a brand-new PhD in history and a dress the clone of today's — or maybe it was the same dress — had guided us around, breathing life into the formal portraits of the Rothmere family as she skillfully wove their personalities into a tapestry of the Civil War and life on a Southern plantation.

"It wouldn't have come to that," Lucy said, glaring at Simone. "Constance would have listened to reason." She pushed her glasses up her sharp nose.

Not too likely, I thought but didn't say. Constance hadn't shown any inclination in that direction with the salon or with Walter Highsmith's store. Once she made up her mind, it tended to stay made up. "What will happen now?" I asked.

Both women stared at me, puzzled.

"Will the board still . . . let you go, now that . . ." Now that Constance is out of the picture? Now that Constance has kicked the bucket? Now that Constance has been conveniently murdered? I didn't know how to end the sentence with Simone sitting there, and so I let it fade.

Lucy shook her head. "No, the acting chairman talked to me yesterday and begged me to stay on. He said he didn't know what they'd do without me, that no other historian in the country has my expertise or knowledge of the Rothmere collection." She fell silent, basking in the glow of remembered praise.

"Quite a stroke of luck for you, then," Simone said nastily. "My mother getting murdered."

Lucy gasped and fluttered a hand to her cheek.

"I'm sure others benefited even more," I put in, hoping to draw Simone's fire from the hapless Lucy. "I mean, surely your mother was generous with her bequests?" Okay, it didn't qualify as subtle, but it was the best I could do.

"She was," Simone surprised me by saying. A wry smile twisted her face. "She left a boatload of special remembrances, nickel-and-diming the estate to death. Fifty thousand for the maid who worked for her since 1980, Dad's Rolex and his cufflink collection to Cousin Beau, her sapphire set to

Susan, a significant amount in trust for the Rothmere Foundation and more to some of her other charities, a painting for this friend, a piece of furniture for that friend, the old bank building to Althea Jenkins for some bizarre —" She glared at me, as if it were my fault. "What's it to you anyway?"

"Just curious." I shrugged. So it was true. Constance left Althea the property on Magnolia Street.

"Well, it's a pain in the ass," Simone said. "As her executrix, it'll take me weeks to sort through all the bequests and get them handed over. And just when I need the time to plan my wedding." She looked marginally happier at the thought of cake tastings, floral arrangements, and the opportunity to make her friends wear yards of pastel tulle, or so I assumed.

"Why didn't she appoint Philip?" I asked.

"Because she was mad at —" She cut herself off. "It's none of your business!"

"Maybe we should get started?" Lucy suggested timorously. "I do have to inventory a crate of artifacts that arrived today for the exhibition."

Simone took charge after that, divvying up tasks with an efficiency I envied. I drew the job of interviewing business owners to get their take on what a Morestuf would do to the town. Thirty minutes later we had come up with a plan and agreed to meet again in a couple of days, giving us time to conduct our interviews and review the data. Lucy suggested we have the next meeting at the Rothmere mansion, and Simone and I agreed. We left the conference room together and trooped silently to the front doors. A red BMW convertible idled out front, and Greg Hutchinson waved as Simone came through the door. She beamed and hurried to the car without so much as a good-bye to me and Lucy. As soon as she got in, the car shot off.

"Need a ride home, Grace?" Lucy asked, gesturing to an old station wagon.

"No, thanks," I said. "I'm going to stop by my mom's."

"It's awful about her being a suspect," Lucy said. She tucked a strand of hair behind her ear. "In Constance's murder, I mean. Not that she did it. And not that Constance DuBois wasn't . . . well, I mean, she could be a real bitch sometimes."

Hearing the word "bitch" from the usually genteel Lucy surprised me so much I didn't protest on my mom's behalf. "I guess she had a way of annoying people."

We descended the shallow stairs and strolled toward Lucy's car. It was parked on

Jackson Street on the east side of Bedford Square. The downtown square doesn't get much business in the evening — most of the nightlife is on the boardwalk — but we passed a couple walking a golden retriever and two girls roller skating hand-in-hand. The sounds of a distant lawn mower and birds twittering eased away some of the day's tension.

"She was selfish, through and through," Lucy said. "And even though she did a lot to raise funds for the Rothmere, it wasn't because she truly appreciated the mansion's significance or cared about the family. She just liked throwing fund-raising balls and getting her photo in the society section of *The Atlanta Journal-Constitution* sometimes. She didn't even try to get to know the Rothmeres. Why, did you know that Amelia Rothmere was an early advocate of voting rights for women? Or that Jeremy Rothmere, Reginald's youngest brother, conducted experiments with lights and mirrors that helped lead to the creation of the laser?"

Her voice throbbed with wonder, and she sounded like she was talking about her parents and siblings. "I'm sure they were fascinating," I said, halfway meaning it.

"Are," she insisted. "They *are* fascinating."

"I probably don't know as much about them as I should, considering they're part of St. Elizabeth's history."

A smile lit her face, transforming her from plain spinster to someone far more attractive. I wondered why she'd never married. Maybe because she couldn't find a man to measure up to Reginald or Jeremy, I thought. We stopped by her car and a squirrel scampered up the live oak overhanging it, scolding as he went.

"I'd be happy to give you a private tour anytime, Grace. And we could always use more docents for the museum." She took one of my hands between both of hers and peered earnestly into my eyes. "You have the aura of a nineteenth-century Southern woman — hard-working but gracious."

"Thank you." I think. I didn't see myself dressing up in period garb — those skirts and petticoats were hot. Hot as in suffocate from heat, not hot as in hottie. And shepherding flocks of bored school kids through the museum, explaining about funerary hair art and ice houses didn't light my fire, either. "I don't think I'm docent material, but I'll stop by sometime to go through the house."

"Why don't you come a little early on Wednesday, before the committee meeting, and I'll show you around," Lucy suggested. "You'll be amazed at the changes."

I agreed. "I don't think I've been there since I was nine or ten." I smiled at her, enjoying her enthusiasm. "You really love the place, don't you?"

"It's my life."

CHAPTER TEN

Mom wasn't home when I stopped by, and I figured she might be out with Althea, hopefully learning more about the surprise inheritance. I stopped to study the old bank building as I passed. It had a Greek look to it with a peaked roofline and lots of marble. Faint etching on a foundation stone said "Est. 1832." Despite the remodeling and the discreetly lettered sign announcing "Confederate Artefacts, Walter Highsmith, Prop.," you could see it had once been a bank. Of course, the words "DuBois Deposit Trust Company" engraved in the marble slab that topped four columns sort of gave it away. Even without the engraving, something about the double glass doors and the severity of the façade said "bank" to me. A granite hitching post out front testified to the days when plantation owners or carpet-baggers arrived on horseback to make their deposits.

I kept going, remembering that Walter had wanted to take Mom to dinner; maybe that's where she was. Mrs. Jones rocked on her porch as I came up the walk, a man seated in the chair beside her. He was probably one of her great-nephews. I waved and picked up my pace, hoping to make it to my apartment before she forced an introduction.

"Grace," she called. "This young man is here to talk to you."

Great. I retraced my steps. The man had risen at my approach, unfolding a gangly frame that probably topped six feet by at least five inches. He was about my age, thirty-ish, with sandy hair brushing his collar and an engaging smile. He wore tan slacks and a white shirt with a polka-dotted bow tie. He looked like he'd stepped out of a Norman Rockwell painting, except his gaze was a bit too sharp and his hair too long to fit in with Rockwell's characters.

"Martin Shears," he introduced himself, coming down two steps from the veranda to grip my hand. *"Atlanta Journal-Constitution.* Call me Marty."

"You're a reporter? From Atlanta?"

He nodded. "Yep. The political beat."

That confused me even more. "And you want to talk to me?"

"He's been waiting for forty-five minutes," Mrs. Jones confirmed. "He's a most charming young man." She winked at me behind Shears's back. "And he does like his lemonade." She nodded at the almost empty pitcher on the table between the rocking chairs.

"But I could use a beer now," Shears said. "Can I buy you one?"

"Uh, I guess so," I said, at a complete loss. Still, he didn't act like an ax murderer, and I didn't have any other plans for the evening.

He thanked Genevieve Jones for the lemonade and the pleasure of her company, making her blush and say, "Oh, go on with you!" Then he escorted me down the walkway to a yellow and white MINI Cooper. I didn't think he'd fit in such a small car, but he held the door for me and then slid easily into the driver's seat.

"It's your turf," he said. "Where shall we go?"

I resisted the urge to name The Crab Trap, foregoing the opportunity to spy on my mother's date, and gave him directions to The Pirate.

"Let's sit outside," Marty suggested when we had our beers. We claimed a table on the patio. Only one other couple sat at the far end of it. I began to relax under the influence of the beer, the gentle evening air, and the lappings of the ocean.

"So," I asked after a quiet interval, "what brings a big-city reporter to sleepy little St. Elizabeth?"

"What takes a reporter anywhere? The story." He sipped his beer and looked at me over the rim of his mug. His eyes were a light brown, fringed with sandy lashes under darker brows. The right brow had a thin white line of scar bisecting it near his nose.

I could think of only one big story in St. Elizabeth, but I couldn't imagine why it would interest an Atlanta reporter. "Constance DuBois's murder?"

"Close. I think her murder may tie in."

"To what?"

"To a story I'm working on about the governor."

"She was his cousin-in-law — hardly exciting news for your readers. I lived in Atlanta for going on four years and I know a murder doesn't make the paper unless it's a celebrity or a child or someone killed in a particularly inventive and gruesome way."

He gave me a half smile. "Touché. However, political corruption is news, especially when it may go as high as the governor. Isn't there a plan to build a Morestuf in St. Elizabeth? My investigation suggests that Gov-

ernor Lansky is taking kickbacks to smooth
the way for certain developers and that he's
been doing it for years. Ever heard of Sea
Mist Plantation?"

A chill that had nothing to do with the
cooling air wiggled up my spine. "Of course.
I've lived here all my life."

"Let's go take a look at it," he said, tossing money on the table to pay for the beers.
"And I'll tell you my story."

I chugged half of my beer and stood. As
we walked back to the MINI Cooper, I
asked, "Does your story start with 'once
upon a time'?"

"Sure," he agreed, holding the car door
for me. "Once upon a time there was a big,
bad wolf. And he wangled a position on the
city council and the zoning commission of a
small kingdom . . ."

By the time we reached Sea Mist Plantation, about ten minutes south of St. Elizabeth proper, Marty Shears had filled me in
on his investigation, in which Beau Lansky
played a key role in enabling developers to
build on wetlands and trample ecologically
sensitive areas, all for hefty bribes, sometimes disguised as donations to his campaigns or as scholarships for his children.
"Sea Mist Plantation was one of his early
forays into corruption, I think, and one of

the most controversial because it destroyed thousands of acres of wetlands."

We were walking around Sea Mist's town center, a collection of very high-end boutiques and pricy eateries that ringed a large, man-made lake populated by geese and other water fowl. A gator or two probably lurked below the surface, but maybe the homeowners' association dues funded gator removal. I found it hard to be too offended at the fate of Sea Mist's wetlands. The whole town of St. Elizabeth was soggy, with expanses of marsh in almost every view and fingers of water — streams, bayous, cricks — poking into housing divisions and flooding roads every time it rained. I kept my views to myself, though, knowing "wetlands" was a sacred word to the eco-conscious.

"Would he have been in a position to *stop* a particular group of developers from using the property?" I asked instead, thinking of Althea's story.

"Definitely," Marty said, steering me out of the way of three bicyclers. "Why?"

I debated sharing Althea's story with him as we turned down a side street where McMansions dominated lushly landscaped yards. I caught glimpses of the golf course between the houses, its fairways dotted with serene ponds and overhung with cypress trees, magnolias, and live oaks. Even this late in the evening, a foursome putted on a green in the distance.

Given Althea's sensitivity, I decided to tell her about Marty's investigation and let her choose if she wanted to clue him in about her husband William and Carl Rowan. "Why did you want to talk to me?" I asked instead, watching a Canada goose nibble at the grass in a nearby yard.

"I've been in town a couple of days, asking questions about the Morestuf development plan, and your name came up. People tell me you've been asking questions about Constance DuBois's death and Del Richardson from Morestuf."

"Word gets around," I said, kicking a pinecone off the sidewalk.

We stopped walking, and Marty propped his shoulders against a brick-encased mailbox at the end of a winding driveway. I faced him, appreciating the breeze that kicked up the scents of cypress and chlorinated water from a backyard pool.

"So what have you discovered?" Marty asked.

I stayed silent, wondering whether to trust him. On the one hand, he might know something that would help the police arrest

171

Constance's murderer and clear my mom. On the other hand, I didn't know him from Adam; in fact, how did I even know he was a reporter?

As if he guessed my suspicions from my silence, Marty said easily, "I'm legit, you know." He handed me a business card.

I waved it dismissively. "I could have one of these printed at any office supply store."

A flapping sound heralded the arrival of three more geese, and they landed on the lawn with a flurry of honking and jostling for territory.

Marty grinned, not at all put out by my lack of trust. "True. Look, this story's not going to come together overnight. Go home, look me up on Google or call the city desk, and then decide if you want to talk some more. We might be able to help each other. You know the area, but I know Lansky's history and the way he operates. Don't let the glad-handing and the Pepsodent smile fool you — he's a ruthless bastard."

"Do you think he could have killed Constance?" The thought popped out before I could stop it.

Marty shook his head, but he didn't look at me like I'd lost my mind for suggesting it. "He couldn't have pulled the trigger himself, he —"

"She was stabbed."

"Regardless. He was at a fund-raiser Wednesday night, in full view of dozens of the state's richest Democrats."

"Oh." I was disappointed, but a moment's thought told me it was beyond ludicrous to hope to clear my mom by pinning the murder on the governor. "And I guess there's really no reason for him to want her dead." I eyed the geese that had wandered closer to us in their search for grubs, or whatever geese eat. One lowered its head on its snaky neck and hissed. I scooted back a step.

"I don't know that I'd say that," Marty said deliberately. "The DuBoises have supported Lansky from the start. I think he even dated Constance before she married Philip and he got together with Anne, Constance's cousin. They've poured a fortune into his campaigns over the years, and I'm sure they've gotten a good return on their money. It's possible Constance knew where the bodies were buried, so to speak, and threatened Lansky in some way."

"You mean blackmail?" That didn't sound like Constance.

"Or an attack of conscience? Maybe she was going to spill the beans about their dealings? Who knows?" Marty shrugged.

173

That didn't sound much like Constance, either. But how well did I know the woman, after all? It was getting dark. I turned back toward the Sea Mist town center, and Marty fell into step beside me, taking one loping stride to my two. A golf cart puttered across the road in front of us, and the passenger lifted an iron in greeting.

"Friendly town," Marty observed.

"It's home."

"But you said you used to live in Atlanta."

"For almost four years." I found myself giving him an abridged version of my life in Atlanta, focusing more on my work at Vidal Sassoon than on my disintegrating marriage.

"So after the divorce, you flew back to the nest," he said. "Do you think you'll stay?"

"Not quite." I bristled at his comment. "I've got my own apartment. As to staying . . ." I hadn't really given it any thought. I'd assumed that I would stick around and I told him as much.

We had reached the MINI Cooper, and he opened my door. I slid onto the seat. "There are worse places to live, I guess," he said, looking down into my face with a curiously intent gaze. "But don't you miss the excitement of the city?"

I smiled ruefully. "Nope. I guess I'm just

not an exciting kind of girl." Or so I'd been told by a college boyfriend.

A smile crept across Marty's face. "Oh, I wouldn't say that." And he closed the door on my surprised look.

CHAPTER ELEVEN

[Tuesday]

Mom and Althea were already at the salon when I arrived Tuesday morning, holding mugs of coffee and stopping their conversation so abruptly when I walked in that I knew they were discussing me. Just like they had during my growing up years. I think Althea knew when I started getting my period before I did, and she always had remedies to suggest for Alice Rose's acne and my ingrown toenail. Telling Mom something was tantamount to telling Althea, something I'd sort of forgotten.

Althea had dark circles under her eyes, and her skin seemed to sag floorward, as if gravity had increased its pull on her tenfold overnight. Her hair was flat against her skull. My mom, on the other hand, looked sprightly in an aqua blouse I'd never seen before and a new shade of lipstick.

"Have fun at dinner last night?" I asked,

brewing my tea.

She actually blushed. "Walter and I had a nice conversation," she said. "He told me all about how he wants to remodel his store space, if his new landlady will let him." She gave Althea a sidelong glance. "It's going to look real nice, much more open."

Althea looked at me from under her brows. "I understand you think I fire-bombed the salon," she said.

"Mom!" I looked from one to the other, seriously annoyed. My mother busied herself straightening the cupboard where we keep the dyes. "I do not think you did anything of the sort, Althea," I said. "I only wondered, when I heard you had inherited the building —"

"If I murdered Constance to get myself a prime piece of St. Elizabeth real estate?"

"No! I just . . . I didn't . . . Did you even know she was leaving it to you?"

"Oh, simmer down, baby girl," she said, using a comb to fluff her hair. "I was pulling your chain. You're trying to find out what happened so you can clear your mama's name. I can respect that. Especially since we've already had three cancellations for today."

I looked at my mom. "Really?"

Mom nodded sadly. "Yes. But we don't

know it's because people think I had any-thing to do with Constance's death."

I could see she didn't really believe that.

"And, no," Althea added, "I had no idea Constance DuBois had put me in her will. I don't know what in tarnation made her do such a thing. I wouldn't take her blood money twenty-five years ago and I don't want it now."

"Maybe it's her way of saying sorry," I suggested. The first sip of tea felt and tasted wonderful. Ah, caffeine.

Althea snorted.

Just then, Stella walked in with Beauty in her arms. "Good morning, y'all," she said, letting Beauty jump down. The cat ambled to Mom and wove between her legs making little *prrp* noises. Mom bent to stroke her as Stella picked white hairs off her chocolate-colored blouse. "The doctor says Jessie's al-lergic to cats," she said mournfully. "I don't know what I'm going to do."

"Find her a new home," Althea suggested.

"But I've had her for five years," Stella said.

Althea cocked her head. "I thought the girl was twelve."

We all laughed when we realized she meant Jessie, and I poured Stella some cof-fee before filling them in on what I'd learned.

"So, Philip had a motive for getting his mom out of the way," Althea said, "and so did Lucy Mortimer and Walter Highsmith."

"Walter didn't do it," Mom put in. "He's such a gentle man."

A vision of the gentle man waving a sword around in this salon not quite a week ago made me raise my eyebrows.

"Let's not rule anyone out at this point," Stella put in sensibly, "except us, of course."

"And there's Del Richardson, the More-stuf guy," I reminded them. "He might have some kind of underhanded deal going with Beau Lansky that either or both of them might take drastic measures to protect." I told them about Marty Shears. I had looked him up online last night and even read a few of his articles. He wrote well and had won several awards for political reporting. I'd called him and agreed to meet him the next day. He was in Atlanta today, he said, working on deadline for a different story. I got the feeling he was aiming for a national-level reporting job, and wouldn't be in Atlanta forever.

"I don't know about working with a reporter," Mom said, aligning her combs and scissors to prepare for the day's first customer. "It's really more the police's job.

179

Do you think we should pass some of this along to Special Agent Dillon?"

"I think Grace has a flair for this investigating stuff," Stella said. "I mean, there's no reason we can't tell the police and keep looking into things ourselves, too. Right?"

Mom bit her lower lip. "I'm worried that —"

Althea interrupted her. "Grace's tougher than she looks, Vi, and more stubborn, too. You might as well just tell her to keep on with her detecting, because she's going to do it anyway. And she's already dug up my old secret, so I say what the hell. But don't you go worrying your mother any more, you hear?" She gave me the "don't mess with your mom" look I'd seen many times over the years. When I nodded, she checked the clock on the wall. "Since my first appointment's cancelled, I'm going to run to the Piggly Wiggly. You need anything, Vi?"

"Half a pound of okra, thank you, Althea. If it looks good. I'm going to make gumbo tonight."

Before Althea could leave, I suggested she tell her story to Martin Shears. "He might be able to track down some leads the police overlooked," I said.

She wagged her head from side to side. "It's been too long. My William's gone. I

180

accepted that years ago. But if you think my story would help this reporter track down Constance's murderer, you tell him. I don't want to talk to him." Slipping her handbag over her arm, she left.

"Did Rachel find out anything?" Stella asked me as the door shut behind Althea.

Mom zinged a flinty look between me and Stella. "You got that child involved?"

I grimaced at Stella, who shrugged her shoulders, abashed. "We didn't ask her to," I said. "In fact, we tried to stop her. But she wanted to help you," I said, shamelessly transferring part of the guilt to my mom, "and she's only planning to talk to a kid at the high school." I didn't mention that the kid was Philip DuBois the Third, otherwise know as Trey.

"Mmpf," Mom muttered. "I still don't like it. What would I say to her mother if something happened?"

As Stella set out her nail polishes and Mom dusted her station, I checked the appointment calendar to find that my first client had cancelled, too. Debating whether that gave me time to meet Vonda for a cup of tea at Doralynn's, I looked up when the door jangled open. An attractive blonde stood on the threshold, staring around curiously. Wearing skinny jeans and a snug blue tee shirt over a chest even my former mother-in-law would consider ample, she seemed familiar, but I didn't recognize her until she spoke.

"Ruthie told me you do the best cuts in town," she said, the New York accent reminding me of breakfast Sunday. Angie the waitress. No, Amber.

"That was kind of her," Mom said, coming forward. "Do you need a cut?"

"A trim, really," the girl said, fluffing out her blonde hair. It fell to her shoulder blades. "Can you fit me in?"

"Sure," I said, coming forward. "Let's get you shampooed." I gave her a smock from the closet and led her to the sink. I noticed a bandage wrapped her left hand, and a metal splint protruded from it. "What happened?"

"I broke a finger playing softball," she said ruefully, lifting the bandaged hand. "For Doralynn's team. We won, though. Beat those Roving Pirate swabbies by six runs."

I laughed and turned on the water.

"This is such a beautiful house, with all the gingerbread and everything," Amber said when she settled into my chair with her hair wrapped in a towel. "I love the old homes down here on the square. And the gardens. Where I come from, the houses look like little boxes. No personality. It must be wonderful to work in a historic house like this."

"The best part is the commute: walk downstairs and you're at work," Mom laughed, overhearing. "The worst part is the upkeep. Hundred-and-fifty-year-old plumbing has its drawbacks."

"How much do you want off?" I asked Amber, combing her hair.

She slid a lock of damp hair between two fingers and stopped an inch from the ends. "Like that?" She watched as I secured most of her hair onto the crown of her head with colorful plastic clips. "Do you have any ghosts?" She looked around wide-eyed, as if expecting an apparition to float through one of the walls.

I laughed, and Amber crinkled her nose and giggled. "Maybe like a Southern belle in one of those hoop gowns waiting for her fiancé to come home from the wars?"

"I've never heard of any ghosts," I said, cutting a thin layer of hair. "Mom?"

"Not in this house," Mom said. "And I've always been grateful for it. I don't need footsteps in the attic or cold spots on the stairs. But some of the other houses in town have ghosts, or so people say," she added, seeing disappointment in Amber's face.

"There's a Ghost Walk every Friday night from Memorial Day to Labor Day. A guide takes you around to the haunted houses on the square and tells ghost stories."

"Oooh," Amber's blue eyes sparkled. "That sounds like fun. I hope we're still here so I can do that."

"I thought you were staying for the summer," I said.

"I'd like to," she said, "but I might have to move on before then." Her full lips set in a straight line.

I didn't pursue the subject, asking instead, "Have you ever considered bangs?"

The day moved slowly with the usual flood of clients slowed to a trickle. I had trouble controlling my anger each time the phone rang with another cancellation. And the women didn't even have the guts to tell the truth. I heard more stories about sick children and unexpected visits from out-of-town guests than you could shake a stick at. By the time Rachel bounced in after school at three o'clock, Mom was working on her gumbo in the kitchen and I was ready to hurl the phone at the wall.

"Wow, it's, like, dead in here," Rachel said, surveying the empty salon. "The high school's not this empty on a Monday in July."

"That's not very helpful, Rachel," Stella said. She'd been on her cell phone most of the afternoon, calling allergists to see about getting her Jessie treatment for cat allergies.

"Sorry," Rachel said. She tossed her backpack under the counter and ran her fingers through her hair. The black strands looked shorter to me, and the bangs looked more ragged, as if she'd gone after them with nail scissors. "Like it?" she asked, pirouetting. "I got the urge this morning to do, you know, something different."

"It's different," I conceded. "Do you want me to even it up?"

"Oh, no! Trey likes it this way," she said slyly. "He's asked me to the prom."

"Trey DuBois?" Stella asked. "Way to go, Rach!" She high-fived the girl. "What are you going to wear? You would look so beautiful in pink."

"I was thinking black," Rachel said. Surprise.

"With maybe a net skirt," she went on, using her hands to sketch the skirt's fullness in the air, "and a black denim vest and fingerless gloves." She wiggled her fingers.

"Prom is so special," Stella said, obviously dismayed by the picture Rachel painted. "Don't you think —"

"Stella!" I put my hands on my hips, glad

185

Mom was in the kitchen.

"Oh, right," Stella said with a guilty glance toward the door. She lowered her voice. "Did you find out anything from Trey? About his dad's job?"

The three of us huddled into the Nail Nook. I noticed Rachel had a small tattoo of a lizard at the nape of her neck and hoped it was temporary. "Well," she breathed, "they're not moving to New York. Trey's really psyched 'cause he just got invited to work out with the Bulldogs for a couple of weeks at the start of the summer."

I didn't care if Trey was going to the Olympics. "Did he say anything about Philip's reaction to Constance's death, or anything about the bank?"

"Well, I could tell that he wasn't real broken up about his nana's death," Rachel said, twisting her mouth. "That's sad. He seemed more interested in the money."

"What money?" Stella asked.

"I couldn't really ask him that, like, right out," Rachel said, batting at the cauldron earring so it swung against her cheek. "But he seemed to think things were going better at the bank and that they'd have more money because his mom and dad are going on an expensive cruise next month. They'd cancelled the trip a month or so ago, but now it's back on. Trey said he's having a party while they're gone and I'm invited." Her eyes shone with anticipation.

"Don't go," Stella and I chorused.

Rachel pursed her mouth into a sulky moue. "It's not like you're my parents."

I'd never managed to sneak off to a classmate's party when I was in high school, maybe because I was never popular enough to get invited, but Vonda had gone to a couple, and I winced at the memory of some of her stories — all the drinking and necking . . . and worse. "No, we're not," I said gently. "But we're your friends. And you can get yourself in big trouble at some of those parties if there are no adults around. You don't want to put yourself in a position where it's easy for someone to take advantage of you." Ye gods, I sounded more like my mother every day. I wasn't surprised when Rachel shrugged off my warning, the way I was sure I'd ignored my mom's cautions.

"I'm not stupid," she said, "and I don't drink alcohol. Anyway," she changed the subject, "do you think Trey's dad killed Mrs. DuBois to get her money?"

I looked at Stella. "We don't know," Stella said. "There are other people who benefited from Constance's death, too." And she gave

Rachel an edited version of Lucy Mortimer's and Walter Highsmith's complaints with Constance, carefully not mentioning Althea's inheritance.

The salon door jingled open, and the three of us swung around guiltily. Special Agent Dillon stood on the threshold, quirking an eyebrow at us. "Let me guess," he said, pointing at me, Stella, and Rachel in turn. "Nancy, Bess, and George."

He surprised a smile from me and a laugh from Stella. Rachel blushed in that confusing way teens have of being perfectly at home socially one moment and insecure the next. "I've got homework," she muttered, ducking under the counter to get her backpack.

"It'll be busier tomorrow, Rachel," I called after her as she sidled past Special Agent Dillon. "Come in at the usual time."

"Sure thing," she said over her shoulder.

"Do you have a moment?" Special Agent Dillon asked me, motioning toward the door.

"Sure." I followed him out onto the veranda. The heat mugged me, giving me a foretaste of the summer to come. I plucked my blouse away from my body to allow the air to circulate. Dillon seemed oblivious to the heat in his blazer and khaki slacks. He headed to the far corner of the veranda from the damaged end, leaning back against the railing in a spot shaded by the centuries-old magnolia tree whose roots rumpled the yard so it looked like an unmade bed.

"We haven't come up with anything useful on this," he said, nodding toward the repaired section of the veranda. "We recovered shards of glass and determined the perp used a Heineken bottle."

"So you're looking for a snobby beer drinker?"

He gave me a half smile. "Over seventy cases of Heineken were sold in St. Elizabeth last week, and that doesn't take into account beer sold in the county or empty bottles left sitting in a garage or a recycling bin. There's no way we'll be able to trace the perp through the bottle. We didn't get any fingerprints."

I wasn't too surprised. "So you're not going to catch who did this."

"Probably not," he admitted. "Not unless it turns out to be kids and one of 'em brags to a buddy." His gaze followed a fat bee traveling from blossom to blossom on the magnolia tree, its legs furred with yellow pollen.

"But you don't think it was kids."

"No." His eyes came back to my face.

"And the note was a dead end as well. Common bond paper sold by the truckload in office supply stores, drugstores, and convenience stores nationwide. No fingerprints there, either. If we had a suspect, we could compare the handwriting, but as it is . . ." He shrugged.

I took a deep breath, pretty sure he was going to be annoyed with my continued sleuthing, to use Nancy Drew's favorite word. "Well, let me tell you what I've found out."

When I'd finished, he said, "We already talked to Walter Highsmith, of course."

I noticed he didn't reveal what the police had learned, if anything, from their conversation with Walter.

"But this Lucy Mortimer isn't on our radar screen. And a victim's nearest and dearest — in this case, her children — are always under suspicion."

I was surprised by his openness. "So you're not mad at me?"

"For what? Trying to help your mother?" The magnolia's shadow veiled his eyes, and I couldn't read his expression. "Would it make any difference if I were?"

I bit back the yes that sprang to my lips. His opinion mattered to me, but I didn't know why and I didn't want it to. "Our business is falling off," I said instead.

He frowned. "I'm sorry to hear that."

"So it would be nice if you would arrest someone," I added, "and clear everything up." I put my hands on my hips and tried to look annoyed.

"I'll get right on that," he said, straightening. His eyes narrowed slightly as they studied my face. "Mrs. Terhune employs Althea Jenkins, right?"

I stood straighter, not liking where this was going. "Yes. She's Mom's best friend."

"We reviewed the victim's will yesterday, and it seems Ms. Jenkins comes in for a substantial inheritance."

"Mm," I said noncommittally, spoiling it by adding, "She didn't know about it."

"And no one saw her at the town hall meeting."

"She was sick."

He raised his dark brows. "How do you know?"

"She told us."

It was his turn to say, "Mm."

His obstinacy was making me mad, even though I'd had the same suspicions for a nanosecond. "She didn't kill Constance," I said, glaring at him. "And she certainly didn't do the Molotov cocktail." I jerked my head toward the far end of the veranda.

"No way would she risk hurting Mom."

"She's one of several inheritors we need to talk to," he said, pushing away from the rail. "Just routine."

I blew a raspberry.

His mouth quirked at the corner, but he didn't comment. "If you could manage to stay out of trouble for ten minutes so I don't have to investigate arson attempts and threatening letters, maybe I could make more progress on the murder case."

I couldn't tell if he was joking or serious. "So it's my fault you haven't caught the killer?"

He flicked my cheek with his finger as he passed me on his way down the steps. "Just keep a low profile," he said.

I watched him walk toward his car, liking the breadth of his shoulders and his long, easy stride more than I wanted to admit. "You won't hear a peep out of us," I promised.

CHAPTER TWELVE

I returned to the salon to find Mom chatting with Stella, so I didn't mention Dillon's suspicions about Althea. The faint scent of cooked sausage from the gumbo clung to her. She picked up a message slip when I came in. "Oh, Grace, Mrs. Jones called. She wants you to call her back."

I dialed the phone, curious as to what my landlady wanted. She'd never called me at work before. I hoped nothing had happened to her. It wasn't that bad, but it was bad enough. A utilities work crew had severed the water main while doing construction on the street behind her property. We would have no water for at least twenty-four hours.

"I'm going to my niece Marjorie's to stay," Mrs. Jones said, cheerful despite the inconvenience. "She's the one whose boy is an architect, remember? I've already got my suitcase packed. He's going to pick me up on his way home from work." After collisions with a mailbox, a parked car, and a couch left on the curb for Goodwill collectors, Mrs. Jones didn't drive anymore. For which her insurance company and the citizens of St. Elizabeth were grateful.

"I'll stop by and get some overnight stuff," I told her. "Thanks for letting me know."

Mom immediately offered me my old room. As I walked back to the apartment, I heard myself telling Marty Shears that I had my own place, that I hadn't run home to the nest after my divorce. Recently, it felt like I'd spent more nights at Mom's than in my apartment. Ye gods. I threw clothes and toiletries into a duffel bag almost at random, then remembered I was meeting Marty Shears the next morning and packed a tan cotton sundress with a design of stylized leaves in green, cream, and rust. The dress's halter top bared my shoulders, and I hadn't worn it since before the divorce. I wasn't quite sure why I packed it, but I tossed in matching sandals before I could overthink it and locked the apartment as I left.

Mom, Althea, and I ate gumbo in the kitchen, carefully avoiding talk of the salon's declining business. Althea mentioned that the police had questioned her just before she came over. I poked my fork at a shrimp in my gumbo, wondering if I should have

194

warned her. Mom looked startled. "Why ever for?"

Althea sent her an ironic look. "It's no secret that there was no love lost between me and Connie DuBois," she said. "And then she ups and leaves me the old bank building." She blew on her gumbo to cool it. "I wonder if that's why she did it?" she said, a crease appearing between her brows. "Did what?" I asked.

"Left me the building. To make me look guilty." Almost before she finished the sentence, she was shaking her head. "Nah. That would presuppose she knew she was going to be murdered, and that's just plain ridiculous."

"No more ridiculous than the idea that you might have killed her," Mom said.

The rest of the evening passed companionably, and I tucked myself into bed before ten. I was sound asleep when a knock on my door and an urgent "Pssst!" woke me.

I pushed myself up on my elbow. I could just make out Mom's figure, clad in a striped nightie, in the doorway. Her hair was flat on one side from being slept on, and she had her glasses on. She was looking over her shoulder toward the stairs.

"What's up?" I said, something in her

195

posture bringing me to full alert.

She tiptoed closer. "Someone's in the house," she whispered. "Listen."

I stilled myself and tried not to breathe, straining to hear. The bedside table clock read 2:15. After a moment, I heard a scraping noise, no louder than an emery board rasping across a nail, and then faint footsteps. Were they coming up the stairs or going down? I flung the sheet away and swung my knees off the bed, bumping my mom. "Sorry. Call the police," I said, already moving quickly and quietly toward the door.

"Grace," my mom hissed. "Grace Ann! Don't you even think —"

Pausing only long enough to grab Alice Rose's old baton from the closet, I dashed into the hall. My bare feet made barely audible squeaks on the wood floor. At the top of the stairs leading to the kitchen I hesitated, peering down into the darkness. Sweat from my palm made the baton slippery. A bumping sound, like someone colliding with a piece of furniture, spurred me on. Heedless of the noise I made, I took the stairs two at a time and fumbled for the light switch when I reached the kitchen. The screen door was thudding shut as the lights sprang to life. Clutching the baton tighter, I raced toward the door, stubbing my toe on a chair that was out of place. The pain brought tears to my eyes and words my mother wouldn't tolerate to my lips. Hopping on one foot, I banged through the screen door and glimpsed a dark figure streaking down the alley that ran behind the houses and shops. I started after him, but my bare feet and braless state slowed me too much. I gave up after a block. In a last-ditch effort, I hurled the baton as far as I could. It glinted silver as it spun end over end, falling short of the fleeing figure that disappeared into the shadows behind the old bank building, Walter's shop. "Damn!"

Limping, I retrieved the baton and was headed back to the house when a swirl of red and blue lights lit up the alley. "This is the police," a harsh voice called. "Drop your weapon!"

The blinding glare of headlights made me scrunch my eyes closed. I wanted to point out that a baton wasn't much of a weapon, but the voice didn't sound like it would welcome discussion. Opening my eyes a crack, I raised my hands overhead and let the baton fall to the ground. It bounced off the rubber knob and ricocheted onto my already hurt toe. "Ow."

"Grace, is that you?" Hank's voice came out of the darkness.

Great. Just great. "Yes," I called back. I lowered my arms, feeling like an idiot.

"We got a call about an intruder." His tall form suddenly loomed in front of me, solid and comforting. It was just the uniform, I told myself, feeling shaky as the adrenaline leaked out of my system.

"He — or she — is gone now," I said, pointing to where the intruder had disappeared. I squatted to retrieve the baton, holding my tee shirt hem down with one hand.

Hank signaled to his partner, who started shining his flashlight between the trashcans and around the sheds that lined the alley. "Damn, Grace, why don't you ever wear one of those sexy nighties I bought you?"

Hank's whispered question reminded me that I was once again wearing my red Bulldogs tee shirt. I'd thrown out the tarty wisps of cheap red lace and teal satin he called lingerie the day I served him with divorce papers, dumping coffee grounds and egg shells on them for good measure.

"What I wear or don't wear to bed and who I do or don't wear it with is none of your business, Hank Parker," I said. "Shouldn't you be trying to catch the burglar?"

An expression of mingled astonishment

and anger clouded his face. "You're not cheating on me?"

I rolled my eyes. "Hank. We're divorced. Kaput. Splitsville. I can date whoever I want." Not that I was dating anyone. But I could. I stalked toward the house.

His relieved laugh followed me. "There's no one new. You're sleeping at your mom's."

With analytical skills like that, he'd make detective in no time. Scary thought. Mom appeared in the doorway, backlit by the kitchen light, and I marched toward her. I was still a few feet from the kitchen when another figure strolled around the house, coming from the front.

I stopped. Special Agent Dillon, in jeans with holes in the knees and a black tee shirt, swept his eyes over me from my bare feet with their Tahitian Coral nails to the hem of my tee shirt at midthigh to my sleep-snarled hair. His stern expression relaxed until I was convinced he was biting back a grin. "Practicing your twirling?" he asked with a nod at the baton.

"We had a break-in. I chased the burglar." I hefted the baton, wishing I were wearing something more dignified. With my hair tumbling around my shoulders and no makeup, I probably looked like a "before" picture in one of those women's magazines.

"Shouldn't that outfit have fringe if you're going to do a majorette routine? And little white boots?" This time the smile leaked through and his shoulders shook.

"Ha-ha. Very funny, Marsh. I don't know why a big-shot detective like you showed up for a simple B and E, but since you're here, how about doing some detecting?" I glared at him. It occurred to me that I didn't even know what town he lived in, but it couldn't be too far away because he always managed to show up when something happened at our house. Mom's house.

"I came because I recognized the address," he said, shepherding me toward the house. He waved off another patrolman who would have approached. "I'm glad you're okay, although I could spank you for chasing after an intruder with no better weapon than a baton. Don't you at least have a nice, solid Louisville slugger?"

Before I could tell him Alice Rose and I never went out for softball, preferring tap (both of us), volleyball (me), and cheerleading (Alice Rose), we had reached my mom. Wearing a robe over her nightgown, she held the screen door open. "I think I found where he got in," she said. Her expression was calm, but I saw the pulse fluttering at her throat. I hugged her and then followed her into the mudroom, which opened off the kitchen and led to the carport. Shards of glass glinted from the utility sink's basin. Above it, a hole gaped in the window.

"Have you checked to see what's missing?" Special Agent Dillon asked, the humor gone from his voice as he studied the scene.

"Nothing that I can see," Mom said. "Grace probably scared him off before he could take anything."

She gave me a look that told me I'd be hearing about my rashness before the night ended. I thanked my lucky stars that the water main breakage had resulted in my sleeping here tonight. The thought of my mom confronting an intruder on her own made me shiver. I put my arm around her shoulders and faced Dillon. "We'll check more thoroughly in the morning, okay?" I said. "My mom needs to get back to bed."

"I'm not an invalid, Grace," she said. She slipped out from under my arm and walked back into the kitchen, dignified even in her old robe and scuffed slippers. "In fact, I think I'll make some tea for these nice officers." She looked out the kitchen window at the flashlights bobbing in the alley. "Unless you'd prefer coffee?"

"Sure," Special Agent Dillon said absently. "I don't like this," he muttered, almost under his breath.

"Me, either," I agreed, sure he was referring to the Molotov cocktail, the threatening note, and now the break-in. "Do you think it all ties back to Constance's death?"

He frowned as we joined Mom in the kitchen. "I don't see how it could," he said. "But . . . you didn't see anything that night, or pick up anything from near the body, that you didn't tell me about, did you?"

"You mean like the murderer?" I asked, miffed with his tone. "Or the murder weapon? No." I thought about what his question implied. "You think the murderer thinks we know something?" The idea chilled me.

A knock heralded Hank's arrival. "No sign of the intruder, sir," he said to Dillon. His eyes slid to me. "Grace here must have scared him off. She has that effect on men."

Special Agent Dillon didn't return his grin. "Thank you, Officer Parker."

"Have some coffee," Mom said, pouring some into a disposable cup.

"Thanks, Violetta." Hank reached for it, but somehow Mom fumbled as she was handing it over, and it splashed onto his hand. "Damn!" He sprang back.

"I'm so sorry, Hank," Mom said in a not-sorry voice as he danced around, waggling his scalded fingers in the air. "I don't know how that happened. Let me get you another cup."

"No, thanks," he gritted. "I'll go to a drive-through." He stalked out of the kitchen, banging the screen door behind him. "I'm coming by for my NASCAR things tomorrow, Grace," he yelled over his shoulder.

"I'll see you in the morning," Dillon said. "Make sure you lock up after me. And put a board over that window for tonight. Call a window company in the morning, first thing."

"Jawohl, herr kommandant," I said with my best German accent, clicking my bare heels together. The man definitely had a bossy gene.

"Grace," my mother sighed. She turned to Dillon and offered her hand. "Thank you for coming over," she said.

"You're welcome," he said, patting her hand. "I think you should consider staying somewhere else for a couple of days. Just until we can get a handle on what's going on. I can't think this break-in was a co-incidence."

Mom shook her head and pulled her hand away. "I've lived through my husband's death, more hurricanes than I can count, and a fire in this house," she said serenely. "I'm not going to be chased away by any two-bit burglar or vandal."

"How about by a murderer?" I asked.

"If he'd wanted to murder us, he wouldn't have run off like that," she said sensibly.

"She's got a point," I told Dillon.

He threw up his hands. "I'll make sure a patrol car keeps an eye out around here. Get a dog. The barking would at least give you a heads-up if your burglar comes back."

"I'll sleep with the baton under my pillow," I said, twirling it through my fingers. "And I'll go down to the sporting goods store in the morning and pick up a baseball bat."

Special Agent Dillon shook his head as if I were a lost cause and let himself out the screen door without even a "good night."

"Sweet dreams," I called after him, closing and locking the door.

I sent Mom up to bed and found an old piece of plywood to nail over the mudroom window. By the time that was done and I'd checked all the doors and windows three times, it was almost four. I trudged up the stairs to bed, determined to visit Belk's in the morning, not a sporting goods store, and buy a pair of pajamas with more complete coverage than my tee shirt.

CHAPTER THIRTEEN

[Wednesday]

I had decided to spend Wednesday doing my interviews for the Morestuf committee, and Mom had no problem with me taking the morning off, since so many clients had cancelled that she and Althea could handle the remainder on their own. The forlorn look on her face convinced me to redouble my efforts to find Constance's killer. Wearing the sundress and sandals, and carrying a notebook, I kissed Mom's cheek and headed to Doralynn's for my meeting — it was not a date — with Marty Shears.

"You look very pretty this morning," Ruthie greeted me, her German accent still strong, even after half a century in America. She was only a shade over five feet tall but had a sturdy body and an attitude that made her seem taller. Her hair was a wiry mass of gray and white that she let Mom trim exactly four times a year. "It is for your date with that handsome man, *ja?*" She nodded toward Marty, who was reading a newspaper in a booth by a window. "He told me he was waiting for you."

"It's not a date," I said, blushing. "It's a business meeting."

She gave me a knowing wink. "Whatever you say. But what *I* say is that when a young woman dresses up to meet a young man, it's a date." With an emphatic nod of her head, she tucked a menu under her arm and led me to the table.

Marty folded his paper and rose to greet me, earning a smile of approval from Ruthie. She laid the menu on the table, promised to bring tea, and disappeared.

"You look pretty refreshed for someone who was chasing intruders down the street in the middle of the night," he remarked, sliding back into the booth. He wore a yellow shirt today with a paisley bow tie. A lock of sandy hair hung down on his forehead, and his grin warmed the room.

Holding my skirt against my thighs, I slid in opposite him as Ruthie reappeared with my tea. I took a careful sip. "Where did you hear that?"

His grin grew broader. "I'm a reporter. People tell me things."

Amber came over with a cheery greeting

and took our orders. When she had gone, I told Marty Althea's story, warning him that she refused to be interviewed. He listened intently, eyes focused on my face, taking a sip of coffee now and then. When I finished, he leaned forward. "This is potentially huge," he said, his words coming faster than usual. "If I could tie Lansky to a murder, or even to a swindle . . ." His eyes got a faraway look. Was he composing his Pulitzer acceptance speech? He brought his attention back to me as the food arrived. "Where is Carl Rowan's widow now?" he asked. "Maybe she knows something. Maybe she left St. Elizabeth so quickly because she was paid off."

I hadn't given Rowan's widow two seconds of thought. "I suppose that's possible," I said, buttering a piece of toast. "Constance did try to buy off Althea, sort of."

Marty pulled out his BlackBerry and began tapping on it. "I'll get my researcher on it. Do you know her first name?"

"No. I can ask Althea." I pushed my plate away. "Your turn. Have you discovered anything about the murder?"

Marty spread his arms along the back of the booth. "As a matter of fact —"

"Miss Terhune," a voice interrupted. "Your mother said I would find you here."

I looked up to see Special Agent Dillon standing beside the booth, his navy blue eyes dark, his face set in stern lines. "I had a few more questions about last night's incident," he said, studying Marty.

I introduced the two men. Marty rose to shake hands. He topped Dillon by about five inches, but his slim, graceful build looked somehow insubstantial next to Dillon's solidity and flagpole-straight posture.

"You're the investigator in charge of the DuBois case," Marty said with an easy smile. "I've been trying to get an interview with you, but your public information officer keeps stonewalling me. Have you got —"

"You're a reporter?" Dillon's eyes narrowed. He looked from me to Marty, and a trace of contempt crossed his face.

The Atlanta Journal-Constitution," he said, pulling out a business card. "Can you tell me —"

"No comment," Dillon said.

"We're on the same side, here," Marty said, obviously used to being no-commented. "We both want to find out —"

"I don't think so," Dillon cut in. "I want to bring Mrs. DuBois's killer to justice. You want a byline and a sensational story — even if what you reveal taints a jury pool or helps the murderer get off."

Marty measured him with a glance and stood a bit stiffer. "Well, perhaps you can confirm what I heard. Apparently, the murder weapon was a sword. What do —"

"Where did you hear that?" Dillon asked, anger threading his voice. "Don't tell me — you have 'sources' at the coroner's office." He sounded disgusted, whether at Marty or the leaks from the autopsy team, I didn't know.

"The state crime lab, actually," Marty said, unfazed by Dillon's hostility.

"Why didn't you tell me that?" I asked, puzzled by the change in Dillon's attitude. Last night he'd been . . . concerned. This morning, he seemed pissed off. "About the sword, I mean."

"The St. Elizabeth Police Department doesn't share information on open investigations with private citizens," Dillon said stiffly. "And we just got the report this morning."

"Apparently it's a Civil War–era blade," Marty put in, unhampered by restrictions against sharing. "Trace amounts of metals left in the wound confirm it's not a modern blade, at any rate."

"Know anyone with a Civil War sword?" Dillon asked.

Amber came over with our bill. "Here you go, Special Agent," she said with a smile, handing him a cup of coffee before sliding the bill onto the table.

Dillon accepted the cup of coffee that Amber brought over, unasked. He returned her smile. "Thanks, Amber."

Her newly trimmed blonde hair bounced in a ponytail against her shoulders as she headed toward the kitchen.

An irritation I reluctantly recognized as jealousy nipped at me. Ye gods, I berated myself. He's a cop who wants to put Mom in jail. Get a grip. My reasonable side stepped in: well, he doesn't really *want* to arrest her. But he would if he had the evidence, my grumpy side argued. I made myself answer his question.

"Every third person in the state, probably," I said. "Lots of folks still have great-great-great-granddad's sword over the mantle or in a box in the attic. And then there are plenty of collectors." My mind zipped to Walter Highsmith. He had swords galore. Were any of them missing?

"Do you or Mrs. Terhune have a sword?" he asked.

"No," I said. "And it's ridiculous to think that either of us could have been lugging one around at the town hall meeting without someone noticing."

"That holds true for everyone at the meeting," Dillon said. "Although I suppose you could hide one in — what? A bassoon case?" He seemed to relax a bit — maybe it was caffeine deprivation that made him snappy.

"Yeah, that wouldn't stand out," I said skeptically. "It was a town hall meeting, not a high school band concert."

"A duffel bag?" Marty suggested.

"A golf bag?" Dillon said.

"A tote bag." Marty held his hands a yard apart. "Some of the bags women carry these days would conceal a bazooka."

"One of those tubes you put rolled-up posters or architectural drawings in."

I rolled my eyes at their game of hide-the-sword one-upmanship. "I've got to go," I said, dropping a ten on the table to cover my breakfast and sliding out of the booth. "How about if someone left the sword in their car and retrieved it on their way to meet Constance?"

Both men stared at me silently, identical chagrined expressions on their faces. Enjoying my small triumph at having left them speechless, I headed for the exit, winding around the clumps of tourists waiting for a table. Since I needed to interview business owners, I might as well start with Walter

Highsmith and kill two birds with one stone.

Walter Highsmith was setting up a mannequin when I arrived at Confederate Artefacts. He didn't hear me push through the door, and I watched him for a moment, unobserved. With the loving care of a mother getting her son ready for picture day at school, he buttoned the soldier's tunic over the mannequin's plastic chest and smoothed the fabric with his palm. He fussed with an epaulette to make it sit straight and filched a speck of lint from braiding on the jacket's cuff with tiny tweezers. Finally, he placed a brimmed hat pinned up on one side, with a feather curling down, on the mannequin's luxurious brown locks. When he stood back to admire the effect, I said, "He looks very handsome, Walter."

Walter spun around, his sword clanking against the mannequin's legs and rocking it. He grabbed for the mannequin and steadied it before turning to me, the ends of his mustache quivering. "Miss Grace! You shouldn't sneak up on a soldier like that. I could have pulled steel on you." He patted the scabbard hanging from his belt.

To appease him, I asked, "How come that uniform coat is straighter than yours and a different color?"

He puffed up his cheeks, and his eyes shone at the opportunity to lecture someone on his passion. "Confederate officers, Miss Grace, provided their own uniforms, most of which were tailor-made to the owner's taste. After the first year of the war, most of the jackets were some shade of gray. The jackets could be tunic-style, like this captain here" — he patted the mannequin's shoulder gently — "a shell jacket, or a frock coat like mine. Most of them, though, had standing collars" — he stretched his neck up so I could see his collar, somewhat obscured by his jowls — "and two rows of seven brass buttons." He darted to one of a half-dozen display cases and extracted a button. "Generals had eagles on their buttons, like this." He held the shiny button on his palm, and I dutifully examined it.

"So, I guess you're not a general," I said, studying the buttons marching down the front of his coat.

"No, ma'am. I'm a colonel from Georgia's Twenty-first Infantry Regiment. Our numbers were decimated at Second Manassas — we lost three-quarters of the men engaged there." He sighed like he'd ordered the troops to their deaths. "I was one of only seven surviving officers to surrender at Appomattox. Oh, the ignominy." He bowed his head.

"I'm sure it must have been very difficult," I said, entertained by his playacting. At least, I hoped he was acting and not clinically delusional. "But if you can rejoin me here in the twenty-first century, we need to talk about Morestuf."

Walter straightened. "Morestuf, fah! Carpetbaggers." He stroked his goatee with three fingers. "Actually, Miss Grace, I don't anticipate they will bother me too much. It's not as if they deal in the same merchandise as I do." He looked around his shop proudly, his eyes going from the unit flags and pennants hung from the ceiling to a troop of mannequins arrayed in different uniforms to the display cases crowded with canteens, knives, bullet molds, and soldiers' personal effects, and finally landed on a wall crisscrossed with swords and pistols. "And if I don't look to the right when I drive out of St. Elizabeth, I won't ever have to know it's there." He nodded several times, clearly pleased with his head-in-the-sand approach.

Maybe, though, he had the right idea. I made some notes, determined to have something concrete to show Simone and Lucy when we reconvened. Wandering over to the weapons wall, I studied the swords.

"What do these go for?" I asked.

"It varies." Walter bustled to my side. "These are reproductions. I sell them for ninety-nine dollars."

I felt slightly disappointed, having imagined myself to be standing in the presence of history.

"But the real thing . . . that's a different story. A sword someone finds in the woods or digs up in their field — it still happens — probably won't be worth much because it will be pitted and damaged and won't have a provenance. I won't say they're a dime a dozen, but they'd only fetch a few hundred dollars. Swords in better condition might go for fifteen hundred or so, and swords with the original gold gilt on the hilt largely intact, etching on the blade, documentation about the original owner, especially if he was famous or fought in important battles, and with a scabbard in excellent condition, might sell for eight, nine thousand."

"Wow." I ran a finger down the blade of the sword nearest me, admiring its cold sleekness until I remembered Constance had died with one of these thrust through her heart. I stepped back. "How often do you sell a real Confederate sword?"

He shrugged, more in shopkeeper mode

than soldier mode now. "During the tourist season, maybe one a month, although I do a significant business in reproductions. Less often during the off-season. Then, most of my sales are to collectors off my website. I did sell one last week, though, to a walk-in customer." He tightened his lips until they disappeared beneath the mustache.

"Really?" I tried to sound casual. "Do you remember the buyer's name?"

He snorted. "Of course. It was Constance Lucinda Wells DuBois." He enunciated each syllable of her name. "She came in Monday afternoon. Before I got the eviction notice, I need hardly tell you."

I dropped my notebook. "Really? What did Constance want with a sword?" I bent to retrieve my notebook.

"She said it was a gift. For Philip. His fortieth birthday was last Tuesday." His face crumpled into a suspicious frown. "What is it about swords today, anyway? That detective was in here asking me almost the same questions not two hours ago."

"What a coincidence," I said, fanning myself with the notebook. It seemed warm in the shop. "I just got interested in the swords when I saw your display. My questions are really supposed to be about More-stuf, for the committee, you know." I was pretty sure Special Agent Dillon would lock me up if I told anyone the police had identified a sword as the murder weapon. I sought for a way to distract Walter. "Uh, if you get to remodel the shop, what are you going to do?"

His face brightened. "Set up a mock battle scene between our forces and the Union invaders. See, if I can knock out this closet" — he patted the wall beside him — "I can open up the office space that's on the other side and use it all for a battle, complete with life-sized mannequins for troops. I have an artillery piece in a storage unit that I've always wanted to display here."

Having started him on his favorite topic, it was hard to stop him, and it was fifteen minutes before I could escape. As I strolled the short distance to the next store, my reflections were disquieting. Walter sold Constance a genuine Civil War–era sword Monday, and she gave it to her son on Tuesday. The same son who was desperate to forestall an audit, to keep his job, to avoid prison. But was he desperate enough to run his own mother through with a sword?

Entering the next shop, I put aside my gruesome thoughts and concentrated on the interview. By one o'clock, I had conducted six interviews, and the results were predictable. Shop owners who dealt in goods that Morestuf didn't carry, like Walter with his historical artifacts, and Ben Falstaff with his microbrew store, had no objection to the Morestuf going up. The sporting goods store owner, however, and the clothing retailers were vehemently against granting permission for the Morestuf's construction. I sighed as I entered Animal Kingdom, the pet supply store and grooming salon that sent all its furry clients home with cardboard crowns, because "Your pet deserves to be a king."

The odor of wet fur and sawdust smacked me in the face as I entered. The right side of the store had aisles stacked with aquarium filters, dog collars, and kitty litter. The back of the store held terrariums full of creepy-crawlies — tarantulas, snakes, and lizards — along with wire cages with kittens, bunnies, and a couple of rescue puppies. Parakeets twittered from a round cage in the middle. To my left, the grooming operation was behind a floor-to-ceiling glass wall through which I could see five tables and two deep tubs. Three of the tables were occupied. On one, a cocker spaniel lay patiently as a groomer teased burrs out of its coat. On the second, a Great Dane towered over the petite woman clipping his toenails. And on the third, a Yorkshire terrier quivered, looking like a drowned rat with its fur plastered to its thin body. The store's owner, Amy Chiem, toweled it dry. She beckoned me in when I knocked on the glass.

"Hi, Grace," she said. "Are you here to talk about the Morestuf moving in?" The Georgia accent coming from a woman who looked Vietnamese threw a lot of people. Truth was, Amy was born and bred in Georgia, although her folks had emigrated from Saigon in the '70s.

"How did you know?" I pulled out my notebook.

She smiled. "Ben gave me a call after you stopped by Just Brew It. I don't know if I can help you much. I'm not thrilled about a Morestuf — they'll probably undersell me on pet food — but I think, in some ways, it'll be good for the town." She tossed her long black ponytail over her shoulder and picked up the terrier to dry its tummy. "Competition, capitalism . . . it can't be all bad, right? I mean, I could use a cheaper pharmacy, and being able to buy a bathing suit that doesn't cost as much as an AKC-registered pup can't be all bad. I mean, Filomena's has some cute stuff, but four hundred dollars for a bikini? Please."

"I know what you mean. Of course, there's always the Internet."

She grimaced, crinkling the skin around her almond-shaped eyes. "I like to try stuff on before I buy it. Especially bathing suits." She turned on a blow-dryer and began to fluff the Yorkie.

I moved closer to talk over the noise of the dryer, and the dog bared its teeth at me. "That wouldn't be Peaches DuBois, would it?" I asked.

"Yep." She used a wide-toothed comb to detangle the dog's topknot and clipped a pink barrette in place. "She's a nice dog, aren't you, Peaches?" Amy cooed. The dog licked her chin with its tiny pink tongue.

"Hm. Well, thanks for this." I waggled my notebook at her. "I appreciate your time."

"No problem," Amy said. "Let's do happy hour one of these days after work."

"Sounds good to me." I turned and bumped into a man who had come through the door. "Sorry!" I said, as the man steadied me with his hands on my shoulders.

"Grace, isn't it?" Greg Hutchinson, Simone's fiancé, smiled down at me. In jeans and a white golf shirt, he looked much more approachable than he had at the funeral. His golden hair was damp at the ends, as if he had recently showered.

"Good memory."

"I work on remembering names," he said with an easy smile. "In my job, it's essential."

"Peaches will be ready in just a moment," Amy put in.

"What do you do?" I asked.

"I'm a Realtor."

"Oh." I was surprised. For some reason, I'd thought he was a lawyer like Simone. "How did you meet Simone, then?"

"She hates it when I tell people, but we met at one of those speed-dating events." He grinned, creasing his cheeks. "You know . . . where the women sit at tables and the men rotate every five minutes so you meet lots of potential dates in an hour. We hit it off from the start. In fact, we left before the event was over and had dinner near Central Park. The rest, as they say, is history."

"But you're not from New York, originally, are you?" I asked, hearing something in his voice. "You sound like you've got Southern roots."

He laughed. "You've got a good ear. No, I grew up in New York, but my mom was a Southern gal, so I guess I picked up a bit of her accent."

"So, will you and Simone go back to New

221

York after you get married," I asked, "or will you settle down here?"

Amy tried to hand him Peaches before he could answer. The dog growled at him. "Doesn't she have a leash?" Greg asked Amy, eyeing the dog with disfavor. "She hates me," he admitted. "I think she's jealous."

"Don't feel bad," I said, "she growls at me, too."

Amy snapped a sparkly blue leash to Peaches's collar and put the dog on the linoleum. She immediately tugged toward the door, her toenails skittering on the slick floor.

"Anyway," Greg said, jerking her back with a pop of the leash, "we haven't decided. We both really like New York City, and my job is there, but Simone has a lot of business interests here now that her mom's passed on. The Misty Sea Plantation, or something."

"Sea Mist," I said.

"Right. At any rate, we'll be here until after the wedding."

"When will that be?"

"As soon as possible," he said, letting Peaches drag him toward the door. "I'm anxious for her to make an honest man out of me." And with a smile and a wave, he followed Peaches out the door.

"Simone's a lucky woman," Amy observed from behind me. "That is one good-looking man. And he seems nice. Some girls have all the luck."

Then, as we both remembered that Simone's mother had been murdered a week ago, she reddened and said, "What was I thinking? I take it back."

I didn't have to reply because a woman walked in holding a large black-and-white cat at arm's length so his back legs dangled. I understood almost immediately why she was carrying him that way, as the pungent stink of skunk permeated the air. Ew. "Catch you later, Amy," I called, holding my breath and sidling around the woman to the door.

I returned to Mom's for lunch and fixed myself a sandwich in the kitchen without disturbing my mom and Althea, who seemed to each have a client, judging by the voices I could dimly hear drifting from the salon. That was good, at least. I sat at the kitchen table with my turkey, Swiss, and avocado sandwich, wondering if I could fake the rest of the interviews with downtown business owners, since I could predict who would say what based on the morning's conversations. As I was reluctantly admitting I should at least go through the motions — maybe ask fewer questions? — a knock sounded on the door. I looked up to see Hank's tall figure through the screen door. He was here for his NASCAR stuff, I knew. I hesitated before letting him in, tempted to call my mom. No, I was a big girl. I'd been married to the man for three years, for heaven's sake; I could put up with his innuendos and off-color remarks without my mommy there to protect me.

I rose and held the door open. "Hi, Hank."

He bent to kiss my cheek, but I stepped back. "Aw, Grace, don't be so standoffish," he complained.

"Let's get your stuff so you can be on your way," I said. "It's up here." I started up the stairs leading from the kitchen to the upstairs hall. Hank followed close behind. Too close. If he goosed me, I was going to kick him down the stairs and file an assault suit. But he kept his hands to himself. I stopped in front of the hall closet we used for out-of-season clothes, the vacuum cleaner, and other miscellany.

"It's up there." I pointed to the shelf stacked with light bulbs, vacuum bags, and nine-volt batteries for the smoke alarms. A large box with a winery logo on it took up much of the space. I'd had to use a step ladder to get it up there, and I stepped aside so Hank could wrestle it down.

He leaned into the closet and grabbed the box, grunting as he shifted it forward. "My autographed Jeff Gordon jacket better not be wrinkled," he said. He lifted the box off the shelf and staggered, knocking some coats from their hangers.

"Careful," I said, as he steadied himself. His knee bumped the upright vacuum, and it fell backward out of the closet, bringing more clothes with it. As I righted the vacuum, exasperated by Hank's clumsiness, one final thing clanked down. Hank, holding the big box against his chest, couldn't see over it. But I could see the item plain as day. At first, the shape made me think it was an umbrella, but then I recognized it. It was a sword. An evil length of steel that glinted in the light from the overhead bulb. Except where brownish stains streaked the patina from the tip to a point fourteen inches up its length. I felt dizzy.

Hank set the box on the rug and followed my gaze. It took him a couple of seconds. "That's the sword that killed Constance DuBois," he breathed.

I nodded mechanically, my brain spinning, not making sense out of the weapon lying in the hall.

"I found the murder weapon." I could tell from his expression he was already thinking about promotions and congratulations. His excitement turned to consternation. I could see doubt forming on his face like cumulus clouds spoiling a calm day. "What's it doing here, Grace?" Doubt gave way to suspicion. "I would never have believed it if I hadn't seen it with my own eyes." He shook his head and pulled out his cell phone.

"Believed what?" I said impatiently.

"Violetta did it, after all. Your mama killed Constance DuBois."

CHAPTER FOURTEEN

Full of self-importance, Hank Parker arrested my mother in the salon. All my efforts to stop him were in vain.

"How do you know I didn't do it?" I asked in desperation after he'd called in his find.

He looked down at me. "You're not stupid, Grace. Aggravating and too nosy for your own good, but not stupid."

I guess finding credit card receipts from cheap motels in the laundry hamper and discovering his infidelity made me "nosy."

"You wouldn't hide the murder weapon in a closet and then invite a police officer to go through it."

"I didn't invite you — you insisted," I said. "Maybe I forgot it was there."

He shook his head and clomped down the main stairs that led to the original foyer where a door opened into the salon. Pulling handcuffs out of his jacket pocket, he marched in and announced, "Violetta Terhune, you're under arrest for the murder of Constance DuBois."

"Mom, a sword fell out of the closet upstairs. I think it's the one that was used to stab Constance."

My mother looked up from sweeping hair clippings near her station. The only client, Mrs. Toller, dropped her copy of *Soap Opera Digest* and looked from Hank to my mom, mouth agape. I was glad the salon wasn't full of customers to witness my mom's humiliation, but why, oh why, did Euphemia Toller have to be here? She spread gossip faster than a wildfire ate up dry hay fields.

Althea rolled her eyes and said, "Hank Parker, you always were one to put your mouth in gear before your brain was engaged. What the hell do you think you're doing?"

"Apprehending a murderer," he said doggedly.

"You wouldn't recognize a murderer if you tripped over him," Althea said. "John Wayne Gacy could walk in the room right now and you'd probably invite him for a game of pool."

"He's dead," I said.

"Doesn't matter. The point is that Hank here is better suited to selling vacuums door-to-door than policing St. Elizabeth. He should've stayed in Atlanta where most of the folk are criminals anyway, so he couldn't go far wrong arresting one of them."

"Althea," my mom broke in, laying a hand on her friend's arm. "It's okay. If Hank wants to arrest me, he can."

"Thank you, Violetta," Hank said. "If you'll stick out your wrists please." The handcuffs clinked as he held them up. "You have the right —"

"I don't think you need those," Mom said with a slight smile. "I promise to behave myself. Just let me wash up first." She went to the sink and began to wash her hands. The scent of the lavender soap perfumed the air.

Hank looked torn. Clearly, department policy dictated that officers cuff their suspects. However, I suspected he couldn't see himself wrestling my mother to the ground to get the cuffs on her.

"I'll just be going now, Vi," Mrs. Toller said breathlessly, struggling out of the smock. "My hair's dry enough."

In point of fact, it was dripping on her gingham blouse, outlining the bony shoulders beneath.

"I'll finish you off," Althea offered.

Her tone was rough enough to make me wonder if she intended the double meaning.

"No, no," Mrs. Toller said, scuttling to the door. "I've got to be going."

Sure she did. The sooner she left, the sooner she could spread the word of Mom's arrest around St. Elizabeth.

"I want to see this sword," Althea announced and strode toward the door. "Coming, Vi?"

"But you can't —" Hank objected.

Mom followed Althea, and I followed Mom, leaving Hank to trudge up the stairs in our wake.

"At least don't touch it," he said when we reached the landing. His voice had gone from authoritative to resigned.

Mom and Althea stared at the blade lying in the hall. "I've never seen it before," Althea announced, "and neither has Vi."

"Actually," Mom surprised us by saying, "I think I have. Walter showed me one just like it anyway, about ten days ago. I remember it because of the engraving there by the hilt." She slid her glasses a little down her nose. "Doesn't that say 'Captain Louis Abercrombie'?"

Hank, Althea, and I squatted to read the tiny script. "I think so," Althea said.

Heavy knocks thudded on the front door. Hank's compadres. I hoped Special Agent Dillon was with them and that he'd listen to reason.

"Okay, Violetta, time to go," Hank said. He escorted her down the stairs to the door, his hand encircling her upper arm. He pulled open the front door to allow a trio of uniformed officers, two forensics types, and Special Agent Dillon into the foyer. He was wearing a dark gray suit today, complete with red-striped tie. He scanned the foyer, and his gaze drifted up the stairs.

"If I'd known there was going to be a party, I'd have worn my party dress," Althea said, giving the cops the evil eye as they crowded into the house.

"I had to speak at a Rotary Club luncheon," Special Agent Dillon said, apparently taking her remark as a comment on his suit.

"The murder weapon is upstairs," Hank said, pointing. At a nod from Special Agent Dillon, the woman holding a camera and a short man with a kit disappeared up the stairs. "And I've detained the suspect." He nudged Mom forward.

"Good afternoon, Special Agent Dillon," she said with a wry smile.

"Hello, Mrs. Terhune. Miss Terhune," he

nodded at me. "Let me go inspect this sword, and then we'll talk."

"Should I take her down to the station?" Hank asked.

"I was thinking the kitchen," Dillon said. "I could use a cup of coffee. Thanks for your quick notification, Officer Parker, but since you're off duty, we'll let you go now. You can write up your report when you come in this evening. Good work."

The emotions flitting across Hank's face told me he was torn between gratification at the praise and resentment of his dismissal. After a long moment, he released Mom's arm and started back up the stairs, muttering something about getting his box. Special Agent Dillon followed him. Mom, Althea, and I drifted into the kitchen.

"Well, it doesn't look like that detective is going to haul you off to the poky," Althea said. "Thank God he's got a bit of common sense. Unlike that Hank Parker." She shot a look at me.

I held up my hands. "Hey, don't blame me. I divorced him, remember?"

"But only after you married him," she said. "Why you were so set on tying yourself to that —"

"Althea, that's ancient history," Mom broke in, setting mugs on the counter.

The words "ancient history" reminded me: "Althea, do you remember Carl Rowan's wife's name?"

"Martha. No, Martina," she said. "I only met her a handful of times. She seemed like a timid little thing, without the gumption God gave a mealy bug. Why?"

"That reporter I told you about wants to try and track her down, see if she knows anything from back when Carl and William disappeared."

"Were murdered, you mean," Althea said.

At that moment, Dillon stepped from the stairs into the kitchen, followed by the technician with the kit. "I'm going to have to ask you all to get fingerprinted," he said, accepting a cup of coffee from Mom, "strictly for elimination purposes."

"Are there prints on the sword?" I asked.

After a moment's hesitation, he nodded. "Allen can get your prints right now."

The technician, a slight, fortyish man with a pug nose and reddish hair said, "Who's first?"

I raised my hand and crossed to where he was laying out an ink pad and cards on the kitchen table. I let him press my fingers into the pad and tried to let my hand go limp, as directed, while he rolled each finger on the card and then pressed all four fingers down together. He filled out some information at the top of the card, and then it was Althea's turn. Finally, Mom stepped forward.

"So, tell me what happened," Special Agent Dillon instructed me.

I summed it up as concisely as I could. "When Hank bumped the vacuum cleaner over, the sword fell out," I finished. "I'd never seen it before and had no idea it was there."

"What made you think it was the murder weapon?"

I gave him a look. "Bloodstained sword? You do the math."

He accepted my sarcasm without comment. "Did you touch it?"

I shook my head.

"Did anyone else touch it? Think."

"Not that I saw. We all went up to look at it, but no one touched it."

"Any idea how it got in your closet?"

I'd been giving that a lot of thought and I did have an idea. "I think the intruder put it there. He or she didn't break in to steal something. He broke in to plant the sword."

I could tell by the way he received the idea that he'd already thought of it, but he didn't say anything. Allen called him over, and they looked at the fingerprint cards together under a small microscope, comparing them with another card Allen pulled from his kit.

"You're sure?" Special Agent Dillon asked softly.

"Yes, sir," Allen replied. "Twenty-one points sure."

Special Agent Dillon looked up, and his gaze went from me to my mom. He sighed heavily. "Mrs. Terhune," he said, "your fingerprints are on the murder weapon. I'm going to have to ask you to come down to the station. You might want to call a lawyer."

Mom paled but nodded her head.

Althea shook her head, disgusted. "And just when I was thinking you had some sense. You're as dumb as that box-of-rocks Hank Parker."

"I've got no choice," he said.

I gave my mom a hug. "I'll call a lawyer and meet you down there," I said. "We'll get this straightened out in no time."

"Of course we will," she said. Her voice was calm, but she clung to me for a moment. "Let Stella and Rachel know we'll be closed this afternoon, won't you?"

"Sure," I assured her, trying to will back tears of anger and fear. "Don't worry about anything."

I dashed over to Confederate Artefacts, hoping Walter Highsmith could give the police an innocent explanation for Mom's prints on the sword. When he heard my story, he closed up shop immediately and accompanied me to the GBI regional headquarters in Kingsland. Walter identified the sword Dillon showed him as the one he'd sold to Constance DuBois and even produced his copy of the receipt. He also corroborated Mom's story that he'd shown it to her soon after he acquired it, and told the police he'd handed it to her.

"I always wear gloves when handling my stock," he said, "but I didn't give Violetta a pair when I suggested she check the balance. You can always identify a fine weapon by how well it's balanced," he added, slipping into pontificating mode. When the investigators — Special Agent Dillon was called out for a phone call — wearied of his Civil War Swords 101 lecture in which the words "presentation blade," "etching pattern," and "Ames Foot" jumbled together unintelligibly, they escorted us to the door with the clichéd admonition not to leave town. It was awful that Mom was the number one suspect, but at least she'd been allowed to leave GBI headquarters.

"I'm so sorry, Violetta," Walter said, stroking his goatee. "I got you into this when I shared that sword with you. It's all my fault."

"I'd say it's the killer's fault," I said.

My mom hushed me and thanked Walter for coming to the station. The three of us drove home in silence after that. I was shaken by Mom's arrest and I knew she must have been more scared, even though Walter's evidence had gotten her released quickly.

"Do you want me to stay?" I asked after we dropped Walter off and walked back into her house.

"All's well that ends well," she said, making shooing motions. "I'm fine, Grace," she added when I looked skeptical.

I still had time for a couple more interviews before meeting Lucy Mortimer for my private tour at the Rothmere mansion. I reminded Mom of the committee meeting.

"Good," she said. "Althea and I were going to catch the new Hugh Jackman movie. Don't wait up if I'm not home when you get back."

I collected my notes, called Mrs. Jones to check on the water situation (still no running H_2O), and conducted a couple more hurried interviews before hitting the road for Rothmere mansion.

The former plantation occupied a prime bit of real estate perched on a slight rise overlooking the Satilla River, three miles west of St. Elizabeth. Fields of alfalfa and cotton and a grove of pecan trees eddied out from the home like ripples on a lake. When Phineas Rothmere willed the property to St. Elizabeth in the 1950s, the city sold the arable land, putting the money in a trust to fund the mansion's upkeep, and kept only fifty acres, the house, and a few out-buildings, including the original slave quarters, a chapel, and a threshing barn. The house itself stood in parklike surroundings of emerald lawn and English gardens. From grade-school field trips, I remembered the architecture was called Greek revival, which apparently means simple lines, columns, and gallons of white paint.

I parked in the lot to the left of the house and approached the front door. Visitor hours had ended at four thirty, half an hour ago, so the round foyer echoed with quiet as I pushed open the front door. The hush had an almost physical quality. The heart-of-pine-floored foyer, with its aqua-painted walls and woven-to-order rug, was bigger than my entire apartment. Being a slave-owning landholder in the nineteenth century had its advantages. As I was wondering who the woman was simpering from a portrait across the room, Lucy Mortimer slipped in.

"There you are," she said. Today's outfit consisted of a white blouse tucked into a brown and white skirt with a pattern so teensy I couldn't make out what it was. Her low-heeled shoes rated higher on the comfort scale than the stylish scale. She had corralled her mousy hair into a bun, but wisps had escaped and hung limply against her cheeks. Her eyes shone with anticipation behind the tortoiseshell glasses. "I wasn't sure that you would make it, what with your mother being in jail and all. Not that I blame her one bit. That Constance DuBois was asking for it."

"My mother was not jailed and she did not kill Constance," I bit out. "Where did you hear that?"

Lucy took a step back at my tone. "Euphemia Toller is a docent here." She fluttered her hands as if waving away unpleasantness. "Well, I'm glad to hear that she was mistaken. I've been looking forward to this all day."

I felt churlish that my excitement level was so much lower than hers, so I tried to fake enthusiasm for the next hour as she dragged me through every room of the mansion, filling my head with facts about generations of

Rothmeres.

"I saved the best for last," she said, pushing open double doors that led to the ballroom. "It's already decorated for the fund-raising ball Friday night." Yards of yellow silk draped from the ceiling, creating a tentlike effect. Masses of flowers — forsythia, roses, lilies, and many I couldn't identify — climbed temporary trellises and bloomed in pots and urns and stands along the walls. The scent was overpowering, and I sneezed. "Too bad they didn't have Zyrtec in Reginald and Amelia's day," I said, making a mental note to take a double dose before the ball.

Lucy's tight-lipped smile didn't approve of my humor. "All of the flowers came from the estate's gardens," she said as proudly as if she'd nurtured each bloom herself. Maybe she had. She crossed the expanse of polished-wood floor and threw open a set of French doors. "Isn't the view lovely?"

I dutifully followed her and admired the view: topiary gardens, a glint of the river in the distance, and a peaceful cemetery shaded by live oaks and contained by a wrought iron fence. A small yellow backhoe dug its tines into the earth on the eastern edge of the cemetery and gouged out a bucketful of dirt. "What's going on there?" I asked.

Lucy tapped a fingernail against the earpiece of her glasses. "They're digging a grave for the burial tomorrow."

"Is this a public cemetery, then?" I asked, confused.

She shook her head. "No. But when old Phineas Rothmere deeded the property to the city, he put in a clause saying Rothmere descendants could be buried here for free."

"Really? I figured the family had died out. Are there many of them left?"

Lucy nodded, looking a tad smug about her superior knowledge. "Dozens. Amelia and Reginald had fourteen children, you know, of which nine survived to adulthood. And even though all but two of the male Rothmeres were killed off during World War I — they were such a patriotic family — the line survives through the distaff side."

At my blank look she added, "Through the women."

"I'll bet there were some hard feelings when Phineas gave the plantation to the city, then," I mused. "Surely someone was counting on inheriting the property." The *beep-beep-beep* of the grave-digging machine backing up drifted up from the cemetery.

241

"Oh, yes. Some of the descendants, egged on by one of Phineas's nephews, filed a lawsuit, but Phineas was a crafty old coot and a lawyer, and his will was unbreakable. And, really, it takes a fortune to maintain a place like this," she added, "which is why we're having the fund-raiser. You'd need to be a multimillionaire to have a prayer of keeping it up." She cast a proud and proprietary look around. "And it would be criminal to let someone who didn't properly appreciate and understand the family's history take over." She shuddered.

Horrors. They might paint the kitchen an unhistorically accurate shade of white or plant a variety of rose that didn't exist in the 1800s.

"So, are there a lot of burials here, then?" I asked, watching the backhoe reverse and stutter forward again.

She closed the French doors and turned away. "Not so many," she said. "Not surprisingly, people want to bury their loved ones near where they live so they can visit them, and many of the descendants live in California and the Midwest. This is the first burial we've had since the early 1980s, actually."

We returned to the hall, and a change in the air currents told me a door had opened. "Anybody here?" Simone's voice called. The

242

pock-pock of stilettos crossing the foyer ricocheted like bullets. "I haven't got all day."

Lucy led the way back to the foyer, and we greeted Simone, who wore a pair of tobacco-colored linen slacks and a peach-colored shrug over a matching camisole. The color brightened her skin and made a nice contrast with her dark hair. "You look nice, Simone," I said.

She gave me a half smile. "Thanks. Greg and I are going out to dinner after this, to talk about the wedding. We're having such trouble getting the church and reception sites we wanted that he thinks we should elope." She twiddled the engagement ring around her finger, making the diamond flash.

"I think it's sweet that he's so eager to get married," Lucy said. "It reminds me a bit of Reginald's courtship of Amelia. They were married a month to the day after they met. So romantic!"

Simone and I exchanged a speaking look, and Simone suggested we get down to committee business. Lucy led us to her small office, which had a table — it looked like someone's recycled dinette set — for us to work at. Apparently Simone hadn't heard about Mom's arrest because she didn't mention it. I presented my data from the interviews, and Simone passed out complicated charts showing how a Morestuf greatly increased a community's carbon footprint. "We want to have a green community, right?" she said, taking it for granted that Lucy and I agreed. "So, we should recommend that the city vote against letting Morestuf build a store."

I wondered how much of her vehemence was due to her ecological conscience and how much came from knowing her mother had opposed the store. "I think we should present all our findings and let the townspeople decide," I said mildly. "I don't know that we're supposed to make a recommendation."

Simone glared at me and tossed her bangs out of her eyes with a flick of her head. "Look, it's not going to make any difference to you one way or the other, since your mom's salon will be long gone before Morestuf can lay its first brick. Just today I —" She stopped, apparently realizing that antagonizing me by detailing her plans for getting Violetta's shut down wasn't going to persuade me to vote with her. Her cell phone rang, playing "My Way." She glanced at the display and shut it off as I thought how appropriate her ring tone was.

"If that's the case," I said, feeling argumentative, "then I'm in favor of a Morestuf because I'll be unemployed and I'll need to shop as cheaply as possible." I crossed my arms over my chest.

Unexpectedly, Lucy sided with me. "Having a Morestuf in the area might give people more disposable income," she said. "That might help us see an increase in donations to arts and cultural causes."

Read: people might give more money to the Rothmere mansion and museum. Lucy didn't care diddly-squat about the town's theater group or the women's chorale society or the marine aquarium.

As storm clouds gathered on Simone's face, I held up my hands placatingly, deciding to be an adult. "Look, I'm not saying I really want a Morestuf. Heaven knows, I don't want Del Richardson to have a reason to hang around St. Elizabeth. I'm just saying it's not up to us: we present our data impartially and let the town vote."

"Fine," Simone said in a not-fine voice. She slammed her leather folder shut, huffing papers off the table.

As she bent to pick them up, Lucy asked, "Are you coming to the gala, Simone? What kind of costume are you wearing?"

Simone straightened, her face slightly reddened. "I'm going to be a Southern belle, of course, and Greg's going to be a dashing Confederate officer. I got my gown in Atlanta. What about you?"

"You'll see," Lucy said with a sly smile.

They looked at me expectantly. "I'm going as a maidservant." Renting a crinolined gown and hoop skirt was well outside my budget.

"A maid?"

From Simone's tone you'd have thought I said I was going as a camp follower . . . and planning to conduct business on the premises. Truth was, I was going to be a lot more comfortable than they were. A maid's simple cotton dress and apron were a lot cooler than the elaborate silk gown and layers of petticoats and underthings most of the women would be wearing. And the price was right: Stella, an accomplished dressmaker, had made matching costumes for all of us — me, Mom, Althea, and herself.

We agreed that Simone would put together a PowerPoint briefing of all our findings and email it to the mayor. What happened after that was up to him.

Chapter Fifteen

When I left Rothmere, I was looking forward to a quiet glass of wine with Vonda, but when I arrived at Magnolia House to pick her up, she hustled me inside. Her brown eyes were wide with agitation and her platinum hair looked liked she'd been pulling at it.

"I just got a call from a family reunion group that's arriving tonight. Apparently, the hotel they thought they were booked into messed up the reservations, so they're coming here. Five families! And of course Ricky's taken RJ on a camping trip, and they're out of cell phone range." She sounded like she thought he'd done it on purpose. "Please, please, please help me make up beds and put out towels."

"Then do I get wine?"

"Absolutely," she said with a grin. "A whole bottle."

Too bad I wasn't wearing my maid's

uniform. I shuttled the fluffy sea green towels Vonda used to all the bathrooms and made sure supplies of soap and toilet paper were adequate. Then, I helped her make the beds. As I flapped a top sheet and watched it drift down to the bed, I told her about my day, starting with breakfast.

"Well, I can tell you why your detective was so cranky," she said with a sideways look.

"Why?"

"He's jealous." She plumped up a quilted bolster and placed it precisely on the finished bed.

"No way." I found the thought surprisingly pleasing and hid my smile by shaking a pillow down into its case.

"Of course he is. He finds you having breakfast with an attractive man — a big-city reporter — and he goes all snotty on you. He's got the hots for you."

We moved to the next room, a suite with an 1820s four-poster bed and anachronistic Jacuzzi tub. "Well, be that as it may," I said, "it didn't stop him from dragging Mom down to the police station today when her prints turned up on the murder weapon."

Polishing an antique wall mirror, Vonda looked at me over her shoulder. "Well, when you put it that way, you really can't blame him. I'm glad Walter Highsmith was able to explain how your mom's fingerprints got on the sword."

"Yeah," I agreed. "After he'd told his story, Dillon admitted that they found the prints on the blade, not on the hilt where you'd think someone would hold it to stab someone. The hilt was wiped clean — no prints at all."

"And what's up with this Martin Shears person? What's his stake in all this?"

I eyed her with mild surprise. "The story. He's a reporter."

"Hm. Seems to me there's not much of a tie between Constance's death and Beau Lansky."

"Probably not. Marty's thing is proving Governor Lansky is taking kickbacks. He's going to track down Rowan's wife and see if the DuBoises or Lansky offered her money when her husband disappeared. Maybe she knew something and that's why she took off so quickly."

"Maybe." Vonda didn't sound convinced. "I think his showing up here right now is strange. He pops into town, and someone tosses a Molotov cocktail at your mom's house and then breaks in. The timing's a bit too coincidental for my taste."

"You could say the same thing about Del

Richardson," I countered. "And probably about a dozen tourists we've never heard of. Just because a stranger shows up and then bad things happen doesn't mean there's a causal relationship."

Vonda sniffed, still doubtful but willing to leave the subject. "Have the police talked to Philip?" she asked. "Didn't you say Constance gave the sword to him?"

"She bought it for his birthday, at any rate." I smoothed wrinkles from the quilted coverlet in the small back bedroom that looked out on the garden. "I don't know if the police have talked to him or not, but I'm going to."

"Do you think you should?" A worried look creased Vonda's face. "I mean, if he killed his mother . . . Maybe you should let the police handle it."

"This was bad enough when people thought Mom might be involved just because we found the body. But now, someone's deliberately trying to implicate her in the murder. I'm going to find out who."

Spritzing the room with an aerosol container of a cinnamony scent, Vonda asked, "Do you think the murderer planned to frame Vi from the get-go?"

"How could he make the timing work? No, I think he or she only thought of framing Mom after we found the body and the police questioned us."

"Maybe your asking so many questions gave him the idea," Vonda said.

I stopped in the process of opening the linen closet to put back the unused bedding. "Are you saying it's my fault?"

"No! Of course not. Not really."

"Not *really?*" Despite myself, there was an edge in my voice, honed by doubt. Could I have precipitated this with my insistence on trying to clear my mom's name?

"No." She sounded definite. "I'm sure he only got the idea when people started talking about Vi being arrested, even though she wasn't. It was bad luck that Constance threatened to close down Violetta's and then went and got herself killed that same night."

"I'm sorry I jumped on you."

"Maybe now would be a good time for that wine." Vonda accepted my apology with a smile.

But before we had made it down the wide central staircase to Vonda's living quarters, we heard cars pulling up out front.

I peeked out the heavy crimson drapes at the front window. "It appears your guests are here."

"Dang." Vonda stripped off the ruffled apron she'd worn to clean and raked her fingers through her hair. "Rain check on the wine?"

"Sure," I agreed. I gave her a hug as the doorbell pealed. "I'll slip out the back."

[Thursday]

Midway through the morning Thursday, we were fairly busy at the salon. Although we'd had a few cancellations, we also had some walk-in customers. Most of them, I noticed, were special friends of my mom or Althea, but it was nice that they were making an effort to show their support. The usual hubbub of conversation and blow-dryers made the salon feel more normal than it had all week. And tomorrow would be busier, as even the women who thought my mom killed Constance DuBois would show up to get coiffed before the Rothmere Ball. The prospect of not having ringlets or an updo to complete their antebellum look would make them put aside their principles and patronize the salon again. I winced at my own cynicism as I trimmed the bangs of a middle-aged tourist from Nevada who gushed about the alligators she and her family had seen on an Okeefenokee boat tour the day before.

"So big and so . . . so prehistoric looking," she said. She studied her reflection

252

critically, her head cocked. "Maybe a bit shorter?"

I accepted her credit card at the register and wished her a good time on the rest of her vacation. As she went out the door, another woman entered. Another tourist, I thought, not recognizing her. She was petite and looked to be in her late fifties, with her hair expertly dyed a soft strawberry blonde and razor cut to feather around her face. She had a fair complexion with a fish-shaped port wine birthmark at the corner of her jaw. A royal blue jacket over a white A-line skirt gave her a vaguely nautical air. "May I help you?" I asked.

She glided forward with a slight smile. "Yes, thank you. My name is Barbara Mayhew. I'm here to see Mrs. Violetta Terhune, if she's available." Her voice was soft but assured, and testified to her Georgia roots.

The name rang a bell, but I couldn't place it. "She's with a client," I said, indicating my mother with a nod. "But if you don't mind waiting, I'll let her know you're here."

"Thank you." She drifted to the waiting area and looked around, flipping through the magazine pile before rubbing a fern frond between two fingers, maybe to see if it was real.

I went to tell Mom she had another

customer waiting. She looked over her shoulder at the woman and nodded. "Tell her I'll be another five minutes."

"I see you offer facials," Ms. Mayhew said when I returned to the counter. "May I ask what products you use?"

I smiled. "Our aesthetician, Althea Jenkins, uses only all-natural ingredients. No chemicals or preservatives to irritate your skin."

She raised her thin brows. "You mean she doesn't use a commercial product? She mixes something up in her kitchen sink?"

"I don't think it works quite like that," I said, not comfortable with her tone. "If you're interested in a facial, I can ask Althea to tell you about the products. We've never had a complaint; in fact, many women have told me it's the best facial they've ever had."

At that moment, Beauty emerged from the Nail Nook and sashayed to the front window where she sometimes liked to sit in the sun. "Lots of people are allergic to cats," Ms. Mayhew said, staring at Beauty.

"If you're allergic, I can put her in the back," I said, beginning to get a bad feeling about the pleasant-looking woman in front of me. "C'mere, Beauty." I scooped the cat up and carried her to the kitchen. Her plumed tail tickled my chin. "Behave yourself," I admonished her, shutting the door.

When I returned to the front, Mom was inviting Ms. Mayhew back to her station.

"I'm afraid I'm not here for a haircut," the woman said. "I'm from the Georgia Board of Cosmetology licensing. My sorority sister, Constance DuBois, sent me an email the day she died to urge me to investigate this salon's practices, and yesterday I heard from her daughter, Simone. And I must tell you that what I've heard and seen so far proves that they were right to have concerns. My staff tried to look up your cosmetology license, Mrs. Terhune, but couldn't find one."

"That's because I don't have one," Mom said calmly, her fingers clenching on the comb she held.

"And you use untested products for facials and allow animals to roam about the salon," she added. She shook her head. "Violetta's is clearly in violation of numerous regulations. Until such time as you can address these problems, I'm afraid I have no choice. I have to close the salon." She clapped her hands until she had everyone's attention. "Ladies, Violetta's is closed until further notice."

I felt like things were happening in slow motion. Customers' heads turning, their

255

slow migration to the door, my mother's face crumpling, Stella dropping a bottle of red polish that spurted little drops onto the floor. I heard nothing but a heavy buzzing in my ears and the refrain "closed . . . closed . . . closed" echoing in my head.

Just after noon, Mom, Althea, Stella, Rachel, and I sat around the kitchen table staring glumly into our mugs of tea, coffee, or cocoa.

"This sucks eggs," Rachel summed up our feelings.

"I'll have to tell Jessie she can't take flute lessons anymore," Stella said. "We can't afford them, what with Darryl only working part-time." Stella's husband Darryl was a mechanic whose hours had been cut back a couple of months earlier.

"I can't believe she objected to my facial products," Althea grumbled. "Why, I've been using them for nigh on forty years. Oatmeal and honey and avocado and sugar are much better for the skin than red dye number whatever and polyethylene something. My great-granny Stone gave me my recipes."

"My skin looks ten years younger since you started giving me facials, Althea," Mom affirmed.

It was true. Her skin and Althea's looked years younger than their peers' skin; I'd noticed it before. I eyed her closely. She sounded normal, but a stricken look in her eyes told me she was taking the closing hard.

"And no one's ever complained about Beauty," Stella said, stroking the cat that lay on her lap. "Never."

"It's like Constance is reaching out from the grave to get back at us," Althea said darkly. "She never could stand not getting her way. I don't suppose she's changed just because she's dead."

"Oh, hush," Mom said. "There's nothing more we can do for today. Let's pretend we're on vacation and do something fun."

I looked at all the morose faces; no one looked like fun was on the agenda.

Mom continued in a determinedly cheery voice, "Tomorrow, we can get together and figure out a plan for reopening Violetta's. There must be a way. We'll look at those documents Mrs. Mayhew left and see what we need to do." Her foot tapped restlessly, a sure sign of her agitation.

Rachel drained her cocoa and pushed to her feet. "I've got to get back to school. Lunch is, like, almost over, and I can't be tardy again. Maybe we could find something on the web that would help us. I'll look when I get home."

"Thanks, Rachel," Mom said, squeezing the girl's hand.

Rachel banged out the back door in her black Crocs, and I stood up. "I'm going to see if there's water in my apartment yet," I said. I arched my back, trying to dump the load of gloom that slumped my shoulders. "I'll call you later, Mom." I'd have stayed if she'd said something, or even looked at me, but the set of her mouth told me she'd rather be alone.

I was going to the bank. The silver lining to being temporarily (I hoped) unemployed was the opportunity to track down Constance's killer. And I was going to start with the man who owned the sword that killed her.

CHAPTER SIXTEEN

I settled on my approach and called for an appointment before driving to the bank. I told Philip's secretary that I was interested in a loan, that I was thinking about setting up my own beauty shop now that Violetta's was defunct. She sympathized and told me Philip could see me in half an hour. I thanked her and hung up, refining my strategy. I'd ask his advice and play up to him. Somehow, I'd ask about the sword and see how he reacted.

The bank was only five minutes down Confederate Avenue, and I parked in the small lot east of the drive-through banking lanes. Inside, a short line of people waited for one of the two tellers to assist them while a handful of suited men and women did busy things at desks. A large poster on an easel advertised "Free iPod with New Account!" A carpeted hall led to what I presumed were offices in the back.

I was a few minutes early, so I wandered around the lobby examining the abstract art on the walls. Susan DuBois, Philip's wife, owned an art gallery on Bedford Square, and I'd bet her shop supplied these turquoise, black, and red squiggles with sprays of tiny white dots that looked like what ended up on my bathroom mirror. Sure enough, cards tucked into each frame credited Susan's gallery, Artrageous, with loaning the paintings and discreetly listed prices. Seeing the number of zeroes on one of the price tags told me that displaying them in a bank was appropriate because you'd have to take out a loan to purchase one.

I was still wondering why someone would pay as much as the average mortgage for a painting that looked like my two-year-old nephew had done it when I heard a familiar voice. I turned to see Del Richardson and Philip DuBois emerge from an office down the hall.

"I'm looking forward to doing business with you," Richardson said. He wore a black suit and black cowboy boots and the ubiquitous Stetson. Sling a guitar over his shoulder and he'd look like Johnny Cash. His smile didn't have any of Cash's warmth, though; he looked more like a crocodile who'd

260

struck a deal with a hapless zebra foal. Not that Philip was a babe in the woods — judging by his expression, he was sure whatever deal he'd struck with Richardson would pay off nicely.

As if Richardson felt my gaze, he turned his head and saw me. For a moment, his face hardened and his eyes narrowed. Then, he smiled, said something in a low voice to Philip, and sauntered my way. My muscles stiffened as he got close, but I held my ground, putting a mildly enquiring look on my face.

"If it isn't Miss Snip-snip," he said. "What brings you here? Looking for a loan to tide you over now that your place of employment is shut down?" He laughed.

"We're temporarily closed for renovation," I lied.

He laughed again, an unpleasant sound that grated on my ears. If a wolverine could laugh, that's what it would sound like. "Yeah, right. And I'm the Easter bunny."

"What brings you here?" I turned the tables on him. "Looks like you get along better with Philip than you did with his mother. How convenient for you that he's in charge now."

His smile froze. "You missed your chance to profit from this store being built, missy.

261

Others know enough to open the door when opportunity knocks."

"Yes, well, opening your door to a stranger can get you killed. Excuse me." I skirted around him and headed down the hall. My hands were shaking, but I tried to keep my steps steady so he wouldn't see how he'd upset me.

Offices opened off the gray carpeted hall, and I glanced in each one as I passed, wondering if I'd see Janelle, the head teller who was Stella's friend. A cardigan sweater was draped over the chair in her office — I identified it by the nameplate in a slot by the door — but she wasn't there. Probably just as well. Philip's secretary was away from her desk, but Philip's door stood open. Through the crack I saw the corner of a desk and credenza, a slice of window, and most of a huge saltwater aquarium. I knocked.

"Come," Philip called.

I pushed the door wider and walked in, suddenly wishing I'd changed my casual work clothes of khaki slacks and red blouse for something more businesslike. Philip, bug-eyed and thin-limbed, looked formal and unapproachable in a gray pinstriped suit and white shirt. A yellow tie with a faint red pattern and well-shined shoes completed his attire. His thin hair was combed strategically over the bald spot on his domed head. As I stood there, feeling suddenly as awkward as if I really wanted a business loan, he shrugged out of his jacket and hung it on a coat tree behind his desk. "I've got to feed the fish," he said, nodding toward the aquarium, which probably held at least two hundred gallons. "You don't mind, do you?"

"Of course not," I said. I dimly remembered a large fish tank at the DuBois house from the one time I'd been invited there. It had been for one of Simone's grade-school birthday parties, back when you had to invite the whole class so no one's feelings got hurt. When Simone's real friends made it clear they didn't want me in the way while they played pin the tail on the donkey, I sat in front of the aquarium, watching the fish dart back and forth, telling myself it was a stupid game, anyway, and I didn't really want to play. Philip and a friend, who must have been thirteen or fourteen, ambushed us with water balloons while we were eating cake on the patio. Some of the girls, dressed in taffeta and velvet, burst into tears. I thought getting wet was fun. I didn't have many other memories of Philip except for seeing him pick up Simone after school a few times once he got his driver's license. He was off to college before we made it to junior high, and I didn't remember hearing anything else about him until he got engaged to Susan and they staged the wedding of the year.

Now, blue tang and oscars and sergeant major fish swarmed toward the top-left corner of the aquarium, obviously knowing the routine. A foot-long shark circled at the bottom of the tank, stirring up puffs of sand and debris, its gunmetal gray hide making it look sleek and deadly as a torpedo. Sharks gave me the shivers. I knew they almost never attacked humans, but statistics didn't comfort me when I braved the surf.

While Philip busied himself with containers of fish food and took something briny smelling out of a small refrigerator, I studied the office. Behind his desk hung the usual diplomas and photos of himself with Georgia dignitaries, including Beau Lansky and the Democratic senator. One featured a brunette beauty I recognized as a former Miss Georgia who had gone on to make her fortune in Hollywood playing a succession of butt-kicking action heroines.

"Wasn't that Del Richardson I saw on my way in?" I asked, watching Philip plop tiny shrimp into the tank.

"Probably," he said, his back to me so I couldn't read his face.

"Is the bank involved with financing the Morestuf?"

He turned and gave me a disapproving look. "We don't discuss our customers, Miss Terhune. We're very discreet."

"Oh, of course. That's good." Strike one, I thought, as he rolled up a sleeve and plunged his hand into the tank to fiddle with the filter. I drifted to the other side of the office. On the wall that adjoined Janelle's office hung a display of swords similar to what I'd seen in Walter's shop. I stepped closer to examine them.

Mounted at eye level, each of the four swords had a framed document next to it giving details of its owner's life and the battles he had fought in. The names — Great Cacapon, Bulltown Swamp, Forty Mile Creek — reverberated from the wall. I skimmed the documents, not wanting to get sucked into the history. A fifth mount showed where another sword was missing, and I stood before it, gazing at the empty space. My heartbeat quickened. Constance *had* given him the sword.

"Looks like you lost a sword," I said, trying to keep my tone casual.

Philip wiped his fish-foody hands on a

handkerchief and joined me at the wall. "Missing only in the sense that I don't have it yet," he said. A tightness in his voice caught my attention.

"Oh?"

"My mother's mother's family was named Abercrombie. For my fourteenth birthday, Great-grandpap Abercrombie gave me this sword." He pointed to the second sword from the right. "He told me the story of one of our ancestors, Daniel Abercrombie, who fought with that sword in the Revolutionary War. He died at Yorktown."

I studied the card next to it more closely, feeling a bit stupid for not having noticed the battles cited were not from the Civil War.

"He got me started collecting Abercrombie family swords. At least one Abercrombie from each generation became a career soldier, and besides Daniel's sword, I've got swords from the French-Indian War, the War of 1812, and World War I." He pointed at each of the swords in turn. "I have an agent looking for swords in England so I can expand my collection to the pre-Colonial Abercrombies, and every Civil War collector with an Internet connection knew I was looking for Louis Abercrombie's sword." His protuberant eyes gleamed behind the lenses of his glasses.

Past tense? Hm. "Wow. It must have been hard to trace your family back that far."

"Great-grandpap Abercrombie did the genealogy," he said. "He was a historian."

"So there's no sign of the Civil War sword?"

He went still and studied my face, his eyes narrowed. I affected innocence, pretending to study the sword from the French-Indian War, which was considerably more beat up than the others.

"I didn't say that," he said slowly. "In fact, Walter Highsmith came across it not long ago and sold it to my mother. She was going to give it to me for my birthday. Or so the police tell me. I understand from them that it turned up in your mother's closet." His voice took on a distinctly nasty edge.

"Oh, my goodness, was that the same sword?" I gasped, simulating amazement and sorrow. "How horrid. I'm so sorry. I suppose the police also told you that they think an intruder broke in and left the sword there, hoping to frame my mother for Constance's murder."

"The detective mentioned that as one possibility," Philip said. His tone made it clear he wasn't convinced. He moved away from the sword wall to his desk.

I could sense he was about to turn the

conversation, and asked as if thinking aloud, "I guess you won't want the sword now? I mean, after all . . ."

He looked at me as if I just didn't get it. "Don't be ridiculous. It's a piece of my family history. The police need it as evidence in the investigation, but I'm holding them accountable. Just as soon as they wrap this up, I'll insist on having the sword back."

I hoped my expression didn't reveal the distaste I felt. Displaying the weapon that murdered your mother on your office wall seemed colder than cold to me.

He must have read something of my thoughts because he said, "To paraphrase: Weapons don't kill people, Miss Terhune. People do."

Ye gods. I wondered if he'd at least clean the blood off the blade.

Philip slicked a hand across his balding pate, maybe checking to make sure his comb-over was still in place, and sat behind his desk. Folding his hands on the leather blotter, he fixed a businesslike expression on his face and said, "So, tell me about this plan of yours. You want to establish your own salon and you need a loan, right?"

I endured a trying half hour of grilling about my professional qualifications, my business experience, and my intentions. I left with a stack of loan application forms, feeling pretty certain that DuBois Bank and Trust had no intention of loaning me enough to buy a cup of coffee. I didn't know if that was because Philip really thought I was too big a risk, or if he was getting payback for what he saw as Mom's role in Constance's death, or if he blamed me for getting his precious sword confiscated by the police. And I still wasn't convinced Constance hadn't given him the sword. His birthday was the day before she died — why wouldn't she have given it to him as planned? I'd tried to work my way back to that question, but he didn't give me an opening. I had to admit that his obsession about the sword made it seem unlikely he would murder his mother with it, much less hide it in Mom's hall closet.

I arrived back at Mom's house to find her sitting on the veranda alone, a glass of iced tea in one hand, a closed-in expression on her face. It took her a moment to notice me and when she did, the smile I got was a ghost of her usual smile. I hurried up the stairs.

"Oh, Mom, this'll get straightened out in no time," I said, sinking to my haunches beside her and reaching for her hand. It rested slackly in mine. "We'll find a way around the rules, and Violetta's will be open again in a couple of weeks."

"I'm not so worried about that, Grace Ann. If I have to, I can go to cosmetology school and get my license. It'd take the better part of a year, maybe, but I've got enough saved to get by. So does Althea. And Stella could get on at Chez Pierre in a heartbeat. No, with Violetta's closed and nothing I have to do, I'm looking back and asking myself if I haven't wasted my life."

I was aghast. I'd never heard Mom talk like this. Of course, I was too young to remember much about her reaction when Daddy died, but since then, I'd never heard her express doubts about the path her life had taken. "How can you say that?" I asked. "You've got a wonderful life."

"I do," she acknowledged. "I've got you, and Alice Rose and her boys, and lots of friends."

"Friends who love you."

She nodded. "But is that enough? Have I done what the Lord wanted me to do with my life or have I opted out? Is cutting hair a calling, Grace, or did I close my ears to the Lord's voice because I was too afraid to try something else, to move maybe, or get more education?"

"You've never been afraid of anything."

270

"Oh, baby girl." Mom looked at me rue-fully. "Little do you know."

I wasn't sure I wanted to know, but I kept quiet. Even at thirty, having long outgrown the conviction that Mom was perfect, it made me uncomfortable to come face-to-face with her fears.

"After your daddy died, I was paralyzed with fear for the better part of two years."

"Not paralyzed," I objected. "You came up with a plan to keep the house, and heaven knows Alice Rose and I never knew things were hard, except for all of us missing Daddy."

"I guess I did keep moving forward," she said, "but at the time it felt like I was sinking in quicksand. The life insurance policy was enough to keep food on the table, but I was so afraid we were going to lose the house. Then Althea and I came up with the idea of turning the haircuts and facials we'd been doing for friends into a business, and money began to trickle in. Before long, it seemed worthwhile to turn the whole front of the house into a salon and things snow-balled from there. But now . . ."

She seemed to drift away again, and I gave her hand a sharp squeeze. "You do more than cut hair," I told her when she looked at me. "You take care of people. Remember

271

when Jamie Southerland ran away and you stayed up for two nights with her mom? Or when Minna Jackson needed a job that time her husband walked out and you trained her to do shampoos? And you raised all that money for the Farleys when their house burned down. You've helped keep a community together. That *is* a calling."

"You really think that?" she asked, a note of hope in her voice.

"Absolutely. C'mon." I stood up and tugged on her hand.

"Where are we going?"

"To the harbor. We're going to rent a paddle boat for an hour and forget all this. I'll never forget that time when I was a junior and I stumbled over Hank making out with Sally Preston and we broke up. And I hid in my bedroom and cried and cried until you told me a little exercise and sunshine would help and dragged me down to the harbor."

"We must have paddled for three hours that afternoon," Mom said, a real smile lighting her face. "I could hardly walk the next day, my legs were so sore. It was all Hank Parker's fault. You should have dumped him then and there."

"I did. But then I took him back. I'm a slow learner."

"No, Grace Ann. You have a big heart," she said fondly.

She let me pull her up, and we hugged for a long moment. Both of us were a bit teary eyed when we broke apart.

"Get your hat and your sunblock," I said. "And let's get paddling."

Sticky with sunblock and sweat, but pleasantly tired and much less stressed, I dropped Mom at the house two hours later before heading to my apartment and some too-long-put-off gardening tasks. I figured I might as well deadhead the azaleas, since I was already a sweaty mess. Twenty minutes later, with browning blooms at my feet, I heard a voice call my name.

"Back here," I yelled from behind my apartment. I snipped another azalea from a bush as Marty Shears appeared around the corner. I swiped my forehead with my arm, feeling scruffy in my crumpled outfit in the face of his crisp Bermuda shorts and turquoise cotton shirt. Sunglasses dangled from a lanyard around his neck.

"I've got a line on Martina Rowan," he said, holding up his steno pad. "She initially moved to Richmond, where she had family, but then remarried and followed her new husband to Newark. I'm catching a flight up there this afternoon."

"Wow," I said, impressed. "That was quick. Why don't you call her?"

"It's too easy to duck a phone call," he said. He brushed away a fly buzzing around his neck.

"You must really think she knows something that will help you get Lansky."

"A gut feeling," he said. "I've learned not to ignore it over the years. Anyway, I'll be back tomorrow evening, in time for the Rothmere gala."

"Are you going?" I asked, surprised. Since he wasn't from St. Elizabeth, it never crossed my mind Marty would attend a fund-raising function for a local landmark.

"I bought a ticket yesterday." He grinned at my surprise. "Save me a dance?"

The warmth in his eyes as he looked down at me threw me into confusion. "Uh, sure," I stammered, clicking the pruning shears open and closed.

His smile broadened. "I'll look forward to it. By the way, have you discovered anything new?"

I told him about the sword turning up in Mom's closet, which he'd already heard about, and my interview with Philip. "Del Richardson was there when I arrived," I said, "and it looked like he and Philip were up to something."

"What kind of something?" Interest flickered in his eyes.

"Some sort of deal. Richardson implied it had to do with the Morestuf."

"I wonder . . ." A crease appeared between his brows.

"What?"

"Could Philip DuBois be Richardson's conduit to the governor now that Constance is gone? That would make sense," he answered his own question. "Lansky's too high-profile now to risk a face-to-face meeting. Now that everyone has a cell phone with a camera, you never know when you're on *Candid Camera.*"

"They talked at Constance's viewing," I reminded him.

He waved it away. "Too public. They can't risk that kind of encounter more than once. No, the more I think about it, the more I'm convinced there's a go-between." He glanced at his watch. "I've got to run or I'll miss my plane. Here." He wrote on a page of his notebook, tore it out, and handed it to me. "My cell phone number. Call me if you find out anything interesting."

I tucked it into my pocket. "You do the same."

He leaned down and kissed my damp

275

cheek. "See you tomorrow." Without waiting for a reaction, he trotted down the sidewalk and eased into the MINI Cooper.

I stood there for a moment, feeling the imprint of his lips on my cheek, wondering how I felt about it. Pretty good, I decided with a slight smile. I was looking forward to the ball.

CHAPTER SEVENTEEN

Finally finished with the gardening, I desperately needed a shower. Two days' worth of pent-up heat rolled over me when I unlocked my door. Ugh. I turned on the window air-conditioning unit and went straight to the sink. The tap sputtered for a moment when I turned the faucet, then spit out some rust-colored liquid, before running clear. Hallelujah. I showered, enjoying the ping of the water against my skin. As I shampooed my hair, a thought came to me. I had meant to follow up on Althea's story about William and Carl Rowan's disappearance, but I'd never made it to the newspaper archives. With half the afternoon in front of me, and no job to occupy my time, I decided to see if I could find the old newspaper stories.

Wrapped in a towel, I dried my hair, shaping the light brown strands into a bell around my face. I would get highlights, I decided, studying my reflection in the mirror. I'd have my mom do them tomorrow before the ball. Throwing on a pink tee shirt and a pair of madras shorts, I turned off the air conditioner, opened a window to let the fresh air flow through the apartment, and hopped back in my car.

The *St. Elizabeth Gazette* had its offices in a squat, two-story building in a light industrial area that dated to the 1960s. The sand-colored bricks of the façade were pitted from the fury of various hurricanes. Glass doors opened into a small lobby with linoleum floors and fluorescent lighting. The air inside was dry and cool. I glimpsed a labyrinth of cubicles through the open door on my right and heard the sounds of CNN overlaid by the clickity-click of several keyboards. A young woman with frizzy hair and cat's eyeglasses directed me to the morgue in the basement and a Mrs. McGowan.

Expecting dimness and dust, I was pleasantly surprised by the well-lit staircase and clean basement. Mrs. McGowan turned out to be a lanky woman in her sixties clad in jeans and a Western shirt with pearl snaps. She sat at a large metal desk positioned under a window well that let in natural light. Her hair was an unlikely shade of red cut in

278

a shag that had last been popular in the '60s, and the aroma of cigarettes hung around her. A butt smoldered in the ash tray she quickly shoved in a drawer when she caught sight of me. A half-guilty, half-defiant expression gave way to a smile when I introduced myself and told her what I was looking for.

"Piece of cake, hon," she said in a raspy voice, pushing back her chair and leading me to a small room with two microfiche readers in study carrels. "You wait right here and I'll get the films you need." She returned within minutes to hand me a stack of open-topped envelopes with the translucent brown of microfiche flats peeping out. "I brought you all of 1983 and 1984." She gave me a brief tutorial on operating the microfiche viewer and walked out, saying, "Holler if you need anything else, hon."

After a few minutes, I got the hang of zipping across the card. Althea had said William and his buddy disappeared in February of 1983 so I started at the beginning of the month. A headline about the paper mill laying off workers . . . a paragraph about a Rothmere relation being buried in the family plot . . . half a page about potential development of beach property . . . The headline "Local Men Disappear" caught my eye. It was published on an inside page two days after the men's disappearance, since the *Gazette* came out weekly on Thursdays, and the article was relatively short.

"Two local men, William B. Jenkins (32) and Carl G. Rowan (37) were reported missing by their wives Tuesday morning after neither one returned home Monday night. Witnesses say the men left a poker game together at eleven o'clock. Police are investigating but say there is no reason to suspect foul play at this point. They urge anyone who may have seen either of the men to call their stop crime number, 847-5463 (TIP-LINE)."

Uninformative, I thought, scooting the microfiche to the next week's issue. Birth announcements . . . results from a local fishing tournament . . . a local boy drowned . . . This time, the men's disappearance rated several paragraphs on page one, beneath the drowned boy. The article repeated the information from the previous week, detailed the police's efforts to locate the two men (interviews with locals and disseminating the men's descriptions to other law enforcement agencies), and provided photos that were too grainy for me to tell anything other than one man was white and the other black. By the third week after their disappearance, the reporter had to fall back on interviews with the wives and friends of the men, since the police had "no further leads." In Althea's interview, she announced her conviction that the men had been killed and urged the police to continue investigating. There was no mention of the DuBois family or of Carl Rowan's land development deal gone sour, either because Althea hadn't brought it up (unlikely) or because the paper hadn't cared to annoy a major advertiser.

The interview with Martina Rowan yielded nothing but a photo of her — a plump blonde with Farrah Fawcett hair winging away from her face — and the news that she was leaving St. Elizabeth. "This town has too many memories," the article quoted her as saying. "I don't feel I can raise my children here where people will forever be saying that their father deserted us."

I skimmed through several more issues, but the articles got shorter and shorter until they petered out altogether under the weight of no new developments and waning public interest. Sifting through the slick microfiche flats, I located the one for February 1984 and found a brief follow-up article on the anniversary of the men's disappearance. It noted that their disappearance remained a mystery, that Martina Rowan and family had left the area, and that Althea Jenkins still maintained the men were murdered. The reporter wrapped up with the results of an informal poll she took on the streets of St. Elizabeth: three out of four people didn't even recognize the names William Jenkins and Carl Rowan. "If 'no man is an island' as the poet maintains," the reporter concluded, "what does it say about our community that two men can vanish without a trace and be so quickly forgotten by the police and the citizenry?"

What, indeed? I slid back up the article to find the byline: Adrienne McGowan. Hm. Sorting the microfiche envelopes back into chronological order, I sought out Mrs. McGowan at her desk. She looked up from her computer screen as I approached. "Find what you need, hon?"

"Maybe," I said, handing over the microfiche. "One of the articles I read was by an Adrienne McGowan. Is that you?"

She nodded, her fringe bobbing. "Yep. Call me Addie."

"So you used to be a reporter?"

"Still am, when I feel like it," she said. She dug the ashtray out of her drawer and lit a cigarette. "You don't mind?"

I shook my head.

Blowing a stream of smoke out her nostrils, Addie said, "But I got tired of covering the brangling at city council meetings and the good deeds at Elk Club meetings. Meetings, meetings, meetings. And when something exciting did happen, like the youth minister at Sunrise Methodist getting caught with that fifteen-year-old, or those men vanishing, the publisher was too inclined to kowtow to the powerful men around here, rather than let me tell it how it was. So, I still do some reporting when the mood strikes me or the story's right, but mostly I'm happier down here in the morgue." She leaned back in her chair, crossed her arms over her thin chest, and exhaled smoke at the ceiling.

I wondered why she hadn't moved to a bigger city for more opportunities as a reporter but knew it would be rude to ask. "So, did you find anything while you were reporting on the disappearance that didn't make it into the articles?"

She gave me a considering look. "Why are you so interested?"

I explained about Althea's relationship to our family and my interest in Constance DuBois's death.

"You think there's a link between the men's disappearance twenty-six years ago

283

and Constance's death?" She sounded intrigued rather than disbelieving.

"I don't know," I admitted, hitching my hip onto the edge of her desk. "But this reporter I've been talking to from Atlanta, he thinks it might be related, that there might be a tie between the DuBois family and the governor and some shady land deals."

"I always thought Lansky was on the take," she said, stubbing out the cigarette. "When Althea Jenkins told me her suspicions about what happened with Carl Rowan's land and Philip DuBois Senior, I knew Lansky was involved somewhere. But I never found proof, and my editor wouldn't even let me put Philip's name in an article unless I preceded it with 'the revered' or 'the upstanding citizen' or some such pig slop. No way was he going to let me hint that DuBois had ruined Rowan on purpose to steal his land. I nosed around for a couple of years, but after DuBois had his heart attack, I let it drop. By then, Lansky was in Atlanta as a state representative and well on his way to the governor's mansion. I didn't vote for him."

"Was there anything else you discovered that you couldn't print?" I asked. I surreptitiously slid the overflowing ashtray away from me.

She hesitated, twisting her mouth to one side. Finally, she said, "I always thought the boy knew something."

"What boy?" I straightened in my excitement and slipped off the edge of the desk, bruising my hip. "Ow."

"Careful," Addie said with a slight smile. "Rowan's boy. He must have been eleven or twelve when Rowan disappeared. The girls were younger — ten, I think, and eight. The mother wouldn't let me talk to the kids, and I'm pretty sure the police didn't interview them, either. Well, why would they? But I'd catch him looking at me while I was in the house, talking with his mom, and it was just a feeling I got, that's all."

"What was his name?"

"I don't remember. Maybe he'd talk now," she said, sitting up straighter. Her pale hazel eyes sparkled, and I knew she must've been a pistol in her younger years. Probably still was. "If we could track him down. Wouldn't that make a doozy of a story if he could shed some light on the disappearances all these years later?"

I caught some of her enthusiasm, although it seemed unlikely that the kid would remember anything from a quarter century ago, even assuming he knew something at the time. "I could look up his birth certificate to get his name," I suggested. "And you could research it."

"Done!" Addie crowed. "I'll let you share the byline."

I raised my hands to shoulder height. "Oh, no. I don't want my name in the paper. I'm just curious to see what he has to say."

"Give me a call after you've been to the town hall," Addie said, handing me a business card.

My enthusiasm dimmed somewhat as I returned to my car and headed toward Bedford Square. I felt like I was getting sucked into Althea's tragic mystery without getting any closer to finding out who killed Constance so I could clear my mom's name. The two cases seemed to overlap on several levels, with the DuBois family firmly embroiled in each case and iffy development speculation — with Rowan's seafront property twenty-six years ago and now with the Morestuf deal — playing a role both times, too. Was it a coincidence that Althea Jenkins's name was front and center in each case? I winced at the thought and gripped the steering wheel more tightly. Revenge is a dish best served cold. The line — was it Shakespeare? — ran through my mind and

I couldn't dislodge it. Althea wasn't the vengeful type, I told myself, and really, would anyone wait a quarter century before settling a score?

As I was telling myself the idea was ludicrous, I parked in front of the town hall. Greeting a couple of people I met on the stairs, I stopped in front of a third-floor door with frosted glass on the top half stenciled with the word "Records." Inside, a counter topped with Plexiglas barred access to the room. Row upon row of sliding files stood behind the counter. No one was in sight. I dinged the bell and waited, reading the notices posted under the Plexiglas, including the charges for copies of records.

"Yeah?" A ponytailed young woman appeared on the other side of the counter. Maybe twenty or twenty-one, she had serious freckles across her cheeks and forearms, and chewed gum with a loud smacking sound.

"I'm looking for a birth certificate. The last name is Rowan and the boy was born between 1972 and 1974." I thought a three-year span would cover whatever margin of error there might be in Addie's estimation of the boy's age. "Can you look that up?"

"Nope." *Smack, smack* went the gum.

Her response took me aback. "Can't or won't?"

"Can't." She looked bored.

"Why not?" Her unhelpfulness was irritating.

"Because we don't have those records." A trace of triumph erased her boredom, and I figured she was pleased to have a good excuse not to do her job.

"Where are they?" This was like pulling teeth.

"Burned up." She pronounced the words with relish.

"Oh." That stopped me for a moment. "What happened?"

"They put the records from the seventies in storage when they renovated this place — put air-conditioning in, I think," she said. *Smack, smack.* "The warehouse burned down. So, if you got born, got hitched, or kicked the bucket in St. Elizabeth in the 1970s, there ain't no record of it." The thought seemed to bring her pleasure. "I guess it's almost like you don't exist," she added.

Creepy thought. Accepting the dead end, I said, "Thanks for your help," and turned to go.

"You know," the girl called as I turned the doorknob, "you're the second person this month that's come in looking for the Rowan boy's certificate. Isn't that weird?"

Beyond weird. I turned back to her. "Who else wanted it?"

"I don't know his name," the girl shrugged. "Just like I don't know yours."

"Grace Terhune," I volunteered.

"I'm Kayla," the girl said. Still no smile. *Smack, smack* with the gum. "Anyways, I told him what I told you, about the records being burned and all. He had an exact date, though."

"For what?"

"The birth. August 20, 1973. I remember because my mom's birthday is August 21."

I tried to think of something else to ask Kayla and fell back on, "What did he look like?"

She puckered her brow. "Tall, blondish, kinda old." The muscles of her jaw knotted and released, knotted and released in a hypnotizing rhythm as she chomped the gum.

I wasn't sure what that meant to a twenty-year-old. " 'Kinda old' like in his thirties or like in his sixties?"

"I dunno. Somewhere in between?"

Maybe it was Marty. The description fit. That made sense. The researcher who located Mrs. Rowan must have turned up information on the kids, too. But why hadn't he mentioned it to me, if it was Marty? I experienced a sudden pang of anxiety that made me uncomfortable.

"Thanks," I told Kayla again.

"Happy to help," she said as I stepped through the door.

CHAPTER EIGHTEEN

The day was diving toward evening as I returned to my car. It was hard to believe I'd been laid off that morning, thanks to the DuBois women and Barbara Mayhew. What with the tension of talking to Philip DuBois, the paddle boating, and running all over St. Elizabeth investigating a twenty-six-year-old mystery, not working was exhausting. I returned to my apartment, called Addie to tell her I'd hit a dead end, and decided another shower was in order. I let cool water spray over me for an unconscionably long time and emerged feeling refreshed. A spritz of cucumber-melon body splash and I felt like a new woman. Maybe Vonda would want to make good on the wine rain check. I called her up, and she offered to meet me at The Pirate.

"I've got to get out of here," she said. "This reunion family are a bunch of polka fanatics, complete with their own instruments, and if I hear one more accordion solo I'm going to shoot someone. Ricky can man the fort tonight."

We arrived at the bar simultaneously. "Let's get our wine to go and walk on the beach," I suggested. Despite the day's activities, I felt antsy and didn't want to be cooped up in the bar.

"Sure," Vonda agreed. "I don't think I could stand to watch that, anyway." She nodded discreetly toward a couple kissing at a corner table. When they broke apart, I recognized Simone DuBois and her fiancé. A bottle of champagne nestled in a bucket on a stand beside the table.

The bartender handed Vonda and me plastic cups of wine, and we passed the cuddling couple on our way out. Simone glanced up, and a dazzling smile broke over her face. "Grace, Vonda!" she exclaimed, as if we were best friends and she hadn't just shut down my mom's business. "You can be the first to hear our big news. Greg and I got married today!" She waggled her ring finger to display the diamond-encircled wedding band that had joined the engagement ring.

"I'm a lucky man," Greg announced, snagging the hand and kissing it. Simone giggled, more than a little tipsy.

We stared at them in astonishment. Vonda was the first to recover. "Well, congratulations," she said. She raised her wine cup. "A toast to the bride and groom: may you have many years of happiness together." We all raised our glasses and drank.

"We eloped," Simone explained unnecessarily. "We'll have a huge reception later this summer."

"But I couldn't wait any longer to call her my own," Greg added, a goofy grin spreading across his face.

"The whole white wedding celebration thing didn't feel right without my mom," Simone said, a hint of sadness intruding on her face.

"Of course not," I said gently. "You did the right thing."

"I certainly did," she said, shedding the sadness as she leaned over and kissed her new husband. When the kiss showed no signs of ending, Vonda and I crept away.

Ninety minutes later, when Vonda reluctantly said she had to get back to the B&B, I called my mom. She said she was fine alone for the night, so I drove back to my apartment, ready for some time on my own. Closing the bedroom window, I turned the air-conditioning back on to cool things off.

I couldn't sleep if I was too warm. Fixing some mint tea, I slipped on my UGA tee shirt and curled up in the recliner to read Georgette Heyer's *False Colours.* The light-hearted story was one of my faves and I could probably quote parts of it from memory; still, it never failed to comfort me or lighten my mood. When I got to the part where Kit agrees to impersonate his twin brother, I yawned and headed to my room. It might be only nine o'clock, but I was exhausted. And I'd be up late the next night at the Rothmere ball. I wondered suddenly if Special Agent Dillon would be there. Feeling a little tingle of anticipation, I brushed my teeth and climbed into bed, pulling up the crazy quilt my Nana Terhune made me.

I was just dropping off to sleep when a whisper of sound jolted my eyes open. I lay as still as a rabbit in a hawk's shadow, straining to hear. I breathed in and out through my mouth, trying to slow my breaths, afraid I wouldn't hear whatever it was over the thrum of blood pounding in my ears. It came again, a raspy shush. Maybe the forsythia bush scraping against the side of the apartment? No, it was closer than that. In the room. I couldn't lie here like a sitting duck, waiting for whoever it was to make their move.

"Stop right there or I'll shoot," I said. My voice trembled. I leaned to my right to turn on the bedside lamp, wishing I really had a gun in the drawer.

The soft white of sixty watts illuminated the room. My eyes darted to the doorway. No one blocked the opening. I scanned the room. The bathroom door was wide open and no one crouched in the shower stall behind its glass door. The closet door was still closed. I hadn't heard its distinctive squeak, so no one had jumped in there. An unsettling thought popped into my head. Maybe someone had hidden there earlier and was waiting for me to fall asleep before attacking. The sound I heard could've been the intruder brushing against some clothes. I felt light-headed.

With my eyes glued to the closet door, I ran through my options. One, open the door and confront whoever was hiding there. If I'd had a gun, that might have been doable; without one it was sheer stupidity. Two, quietly reach for the phone and call 911. But the intruder would hear the beeps as I dialed and might leap out of the closet. I could be raped or kidnapped or dead before the police arrived. Three, sneak out of the room and run like mad for the front door, then call 911 from Mrs. Jones's house. I liked option three.

Still watching the closet — had I seen a shadow move across the half-inch space between the door and the floor? — I silently lifted the covers and slid my legs over the side of the bed closest to the door. I could do this. The skritching noise came again and I tore my gaze from the closet. He wasn't in the closet — he was under the bed! Just as I was wondering if Mrs. Jones would hear me scream, my eyes caught a flicker of movement. Ye gods! A fat, evil-looking water moccasin was coiled on the floor not three feet from my bare foot. I froze.

Its heavy, triangle-shaped head tracked slightly back and forth, mouth open to show the white lining that gave it the name cottonmouth. The snake's muddy gray body, thick as a man's wrist, was coiled, ready to strike. I couldn't reach the phone from where I sat, not without moving my foot. And I was afraid if I so much as twitched a toe, the snake would strike. I could clearly see its fangs and imagined them piercing my flesh, injecting toxin. After only five minutes of holding my position, I realized I wasn't going to be able to win this reptilian game of freeze tag. The snake would outlast me. Already my tense muscles cried out for movement and I felt a cramp developing in my calf. I had to do something.

My eyes scanned the bed for anything within reaching distance. My pillow. Maybe I could drop my pillow on the snake and at least distract it long enough to get my foot back on the bed. It would still be between me and the door, but once I was out of striking range I could call for help. Moving slower than I ever had in my life, I inched my right arm behind my back to get a grip on my pillow. I tugged it a centimeter at a time until it was beside me and I could lift it onto my lap. I was sweating by the time I had it in both hands. Stuffed with goose down, the pillow made an unwieldy weapon. Yet, if I could drop it on the moccasin, its softness might smother the snake for a critical moment or two. With any luck, it would be a bit sluggish from staying immobile on the cool wood floor.

The snake had not relaxed its posture since I put my foot on the floor. My calf twitched as the cramp took hold and the snake tensed. It was now or never. Slowly easing the pillow to my left, I held it just off the edge of the bed. Should I heave it toward the snake or drop it between my foot and the snake? Thrusting the pillow toward the cottonmouth, I jerked my foot onto the bed and rolled to the middle as the snake struck. It banged against the box springs and I cried out involuntarily. I gave myself a couple of seconds to catch my breath, then scrambled to my feet in the middle of the bed and lunged toward the window. I wasn't going to play hide and seek with a poisonous reptile all night. I knew moccasins could climb; I'd frequently seen them sunning on tree limbs stretched out over the Satilla River. I knew it was seeking warmth as the air-conditioning continued to do its job. And the warmest spot in the apartment was my bed.

I wasn't up to seeing if I could out-race it to the door, and the bathroom wasn't an option because the gap beneath the door and the floor was large enough for the snake to squeeze through. I climbed onto my bedside table, knocking a book and the lamp to the floor. With a crash of ceramic, the light went out. Damn! Not knowing where the snake was, I balanced precariously on the narrow table and jerked at the window sash. It flew open and I thrust a leg out, completely forgetting about the screen. It gave with a ripping sound and I swung my other leg onto the sill. Thanking the good Lord that I lived in a one-story apartment, I pushed off and crashed through an oleander bush on my way to the ground. I

298

landed with a thud on my right side. The bitter scent of crushed oleander and the piney smell of the mulch engulfed me. Breathing heavily, I took stock of my situation. My flesh stung where the oleander's branches had scraped it open, I felt bruised and I thought my ankle was twisted, but no bolts of pain shot through me so I figured I hadn't broken anything. Gingerly pushing myself upward into a sitting position, I brushed mulch and dirt off my nightshirt and out of my hair.

Standing took a fair amount of effort, since I discovered I was trembling, my legs shaking so badly they hardly supported me. Forcing myself to move, I hobbled toward Mrs. Jones's house and a telephone. No way was I reentering my apartment to make the call. As I rang the doorbell and waited for Mrs. Jones to answer, I wondered for the first time how the snake had gotten into my apartment. The answer that came to me made me shake so hard I was sitting cross-legged on the veranda when Mrs. Jones opened the door.

It was midnight by the time the police awakened a snake wrangler — a man who made his living trapping nuisance gators and snakes that had taken up residence

299

inside people's homes, boathouses, or sheds — and he corralled the moccasin. By then, I was feeling calmer, partly because Mrs. Jones had put a slug of brandy in the cup of chamomile tea she brewed me and partly because Special Agent Dillon and a couple of patrol officers — not Hank, thank goodness — were inspecting the outside of the apartment with flashlights.

"He's a feisty one," the man said when he emerged from the apartment. Clad in thigh-high boots and gloves, he carried a heavy canvas bag that bucked and wiggled in an alarming way. Tucked under his other arm was a long metal tool.

"What are you going to do with it?" I asked, hugging the rose-printed robe Mrs. Jones had loaned me tightly around my body.

"Turn 'im loose in the Okeefenokee where he won't bother nobody," he said. "Ain't no point to killing him. You can't blame him for doing what he did. He was just being a snake."

That was all fine and dandy, but if he wanted to go on being a snake, he'd better stay out of people's houses. "How did he get in, do you suppose?" I asked.

"Dunno." The man shrugged. "Did you have the door open, or a window?"

"The window," I admitted. "But it has a screen."

"Maybe came up through a hole in the crawl space," the man said, depositing the bag in a special container in the back of his truck. He clanked the snake-catching tool in beside it.

Dillon came around the side of the apartment as the man climbed into his truck. "Thanks, Tyrone," he said, shaking the man's hand. "I appreciate your coming out at this hour."

"Anytime." The man grinned and put his truck in gear.

"Hey, Special Agent," one of the officers called from the side of the house. "Look at this."

I trotted beside Dillon as he headed around the corner.

The cop shone his flashlight at the window. "Here's where your snake got in, miss." Using the heavy end of the flashlight, he slipped it under a flap in the screen and lifted it. "Unless that moccasin was real handy with a Super Leatherman," he said, "I'd say someone slit your screen and dumped it inside. You got any enemies?" He looked at me with concern and a hint of suspicion on his young face.

"No," I said as Dillon replied, "Dozens.

301

And making more every day." His voice and expression were deadpan.

I glared at him as the patrol officer looked from me to Dillon and back, trying to decide if Dillon was kidding.

"It's all right, Officer Hernandez. I'll take it from here."

Hernandez rounded up his partner, and the two of them returned to their patrol car.

"You know," Dillon said, as the car bumped down the driveway, "I don't think I've had a whole night's sleep since I met you."

The tag stuck up from his green shirt, and I reached out to tuck it in, snatching my hand back when I realized what I was doing. "That's not my fault," I said. I turned on my heel and headed barefoot back to Mrs. Jones's veranda. She'd offered me a guest room for the night, and I'd accepted, knowing I wouldn't get any sleep in the apartment and not wanting to alarm my mother by showing up on her doorstep at this hour.

Special Agent Dillon grabbed my arm to stop me. "This is getting serious, Grace. The attacks are escalating. That snake could have killed you, or at least put you in the hospital."

"You think I don't know that?" To my

fury, tears leaked from my eyes.

"And whoever it is," he went on inexorably, "has figured out where you live. The other incidents — the Molotov cocktail, the note, the intruder — all happened at your mother's house. "Don't the two of you have a relative you can visit some place like Oregon or Illinois until we close this case?"

"What if you never solve it?" I asked, scrubbing the tears away with the back of my hand. "Do we just start over again in Peoria? I don't think so."

"What happened today, Grace? Who did you talk to, what did you do to trigger this response?" His voice was grave.

I couldn't read his face in the darkness. The light over Mrs. Jones's door puddled on the veranda and didn't seep beyond it into the darkness where we were still standing. Becoming aware that Dillon's hand still held my arm, I shrugged it off. "Well, first thing this morning a lady from the State Board of Cosmetology closed down Mom's shop —"

"I'm sorry. I hadn't heard that."

"You must be the only one."

He must have heard the tears in my voice because he said more gently, "Let's sit."

In silence, we walked to the veranda stairs and sat on the steps. I tucked my feet up

303

under the hem of the robe. A cluster of moths beat frantically against the light over the front door. That's how I feel, I told them silently. Like I'm beating my head against this case to no effect. The light's yellow glow illuminated Dillon's profile with its crooked nose and strong chin as I continued with the account of my day.

"Okay," he said when I finished. "There's a lot of moving parts here. You antagonized Del Richardson again, and probably Philip DuBois, and if this case is connected to Carl Rowan's and William Jenkins's disappearance, you may have made someone nervous by visiting the newspaper."

"Who would know I went there?" I asked.

He shrugged. "In this town . . . potentially ninety percent of the population. This Adrienne McGowan might have talked to someone, or you could have been tailed —"

"You think someone's following me?" The idea was preposterous. An owl hooted nearby. I shivered and wrapped my arms around my knees.

"It's not likely, but you should be careful. Don't go off somewhere on your own. Stay in a crowd. Stay alert and observe the people around you."

"Oh," I said, remembering, "you should know that Marty Shears located Mrs.

304

Rowan and he's gone to talk to her."

I felt rather than saw Dillon stiffen beside me.

"What's wrong?"

"I'm not sure I trust Shears. He's putting a lot more time and effort into this than the 'story' would seem to warrant. What's his stake in this really?"

He sounded almost as if he were talking to himself, thinking things through out loud. "You sound like Vonda."

"Give me Mrs. Rowan's full name and I'll check her out."

"Her first name's Martina," I said, "but I don't know her last name. Marty said she remarried and lives in Newark." Saying the names together made something click. "Martin and Martina," I said slowly. "You don't suppose —"

"I'll check on Shears, too," Dillon said, not following up on my thought. Or maybe he was. "First thing tomorrow I'll call the *Journal-Constitution* and see what they have to say about him. And I can call Newark and get a detective there to talk to the Rowan woman."

He stood and reached down a hand to haul me to my feet. "I meant it when I said you and Mrs. Terhune should leave town for a while. You've poked a hornet's nest —

305

I wish I knew where, damn it — and I don't want to see you get stung."

I tried to read his face, but it was in shadow again. "You don't think my mom killed Constance anymore, do you?"

"No, I don't," he said. "Despite the evidence against her, my instinct says she didn't do it. Someone wants us to think she did, though, and that worries me."

The relief that rushed through me made me sag. "Thanks. And thanks for coming out here tonight. I know it's not really your job."

I caught a glimmer of white teeth as he smiled. "Rescuing damsels in distress makes a nice change from investigating robbers or tracking down gangbangers."

"I'm not a damsel in distress," I protested, "and I rescued myself."

"Well, maybe I wanted to assure myself you're really okay," he said.

Before I could think of an answer, he slid past me and strode toward his car.

The door behind me squeaked open, and I whirled. Mrs. Jones stood in the doorway, her hair frilling around her head and a turquoise silk robe belted at her waist. "Is he gone then, dear? My, he is a handsome one. Why don't you come in and have another cup of tea and tell me all about it."

CHAPTER NINETEEN

[Friday]

I didn't want to tell Mom about my close encounters of the reptile kind, but I figured she'd hear it from someone else if I didn't. The cops who'd shown up had probably told their wives and girlfriends, or Tyrone the snake wrangler might have mentioned it over morning coffee at his favorite diner, so I fessed up first thing to an audience that included Althea and Stella as well as my mother. We were all gathered in the empty salon, ostensibly to fill out the paperwork Barbara Mayhew had left and figure out how to reopen Violetta's. Despite my making light of the fear that had immobilized me, and referring to the moccasin as "Sammy the Snake" to make it seem less threatening, Mom paled and Stella gasped when I got to the part about dropping my pillow on him. Althea murmured, "I'd bet on you against a herd of snakes, baby girl."

I shot her a look, but she seemed to be serious. "Thanks," I said. Who knew Althea thought I was brave or resourceful or whatever you'd need to be to vanquish a herd of snakes? Although I didn't think a group of snakes was called a herd.

"Well, that's the last straw," Mom said.

We all turned to look at her. Dressed in a pale green tee shirt with strawberries on it and matching cotton pants with a drawstring waist, she looked springlike and implacable. She adjusted her glasses and eyed each of us in turn. "I am not putting any of you at risk any longer. It was prideful of me to insist on staying in this house no matter what. Well, I won't let whoever is doing these things hurt Grace or any of you. We'll go stay with my sister Flora in Decatur for a few days. We can be packed and on the road by noon."

When Mom spoke in that tone, there was no point in arguing with her. Althea opened her mouth but shut it again without saying anything. Stella said, "I think that's wise, Violetta."

"What about the Rothmere gala?" I asked. "We already bought the tickets and Stella worked so hard on the costumes. We could leave tomorrow morning, first thing."

We all looked at each other. "Okay," Mom

conceded. "I guess one more day won't hurt. But I want you to spend the night here, Grace Ann, where I can keep an eye on you."

"Yes, ma'am." I made a joke out of it, but truth to tell, I wasn't too comfortable with sleeping in my apartment tonight. I knew I'd lie awake listening for the rasp of scales on wood or the metallic ripping of a knife slicing through screen. That morning, I'd borrowed a hoe from Mrs. Jones's garden shed to take with me when I picked up clothes, holding it awkwardly in the crook of one elbow while I grabbed my navy and white striped seersucker slacks from the closet and a white shirt with a ruffled neckline from a drawer.

"Let's get back to business," Althea said, pulling a spiral notebook from her flowered tote. "I talked with a very helpful young man at the Consumer Products Safety Office and did some research on the Internet yesterday about marketing organic cosmetics. It looks to me that as long as I give the customers a list of the ingredients in my masks and lotions, and mix up a fresh batch for each customer, like I do anyways, then the State Board won't have anything to complain about."

"That's wonderful, Althea," Mom said.

"Can you give me some highlights while we talk?" I asked her.

She gave me a surprised look, since I'd been refusing her offers to highlight my hair for months, but didn't say anything. "Of course."

Althea shot me a knowing look. "Uh-huh. Guess someone's expecting to meet up with a special beau at the ball tonight."

"Oh, hush," Stella said.

My face warmed and I hid my reddened cheeks by sticking my head under the sink hose to dampen my hair. With the wet strands sticking to a smock, I sat at my mother's station and smoothed the foils while she mixed up two colors of highlights.

"And," Althea said, in the voice of one building to a climax, "I think we can package some of my recipes and sell them."

"That's a fine idea," Mom said. "Why ever didn't we think of that sooner?" She sectioned my hair with the pointy end of a comb.

"I was thinking little white pots or tubes with purple lids," Althea said. "I've phoned a couple of companies that do that sort of thing and I'm going to talk to them next week. They have labs to help with the formulations and stabilizing the products." She beamed and I could see her pride in her products and her excitement at the prospect of marketing them.

"And I talked to a lawyer about Beauty being at the shop," Stella said. She looked like she hadn't slept much the night before, with her skin duller than usual and a pimple forming on her chin. I wondered how badly she and Darryl needed the money she'd been making from Violetta's. "She said that as long as we post a sign saying 'Cat on Premises,' or something similar, that everything's okay. Of course," she added, "I could leave Beauty at home, and we wouldn't have to worry about it."

"Absolutely not," Mom said, tugging at my hair. "Beauty is the shop mascot."

Stella sent her a grateful smile.

"And I guess I'll enroll in beauty school," Mom said with a wry smile, "and work on my cosmetology license."

Althea snorted. "You could teach at a beauty school."

I had an idea for how we might get Mom a license without her having to go back to school, but I wanted to run it by Mrs. Mayhew before I got everyone all spun up about it. I smiled as I listened to the women discuss their plans. It was amazing how in only twenty-four hours the mood had gone from depressed to purposeful. If Mom and

Althea ran the country, I was pretty sure the government wouldn't be bailing out failing businesses. They'd never asked for handouts, wouldn't accept any if offered, and knew the power of hard work and a good attitude. I hoped I'd inherited half of Mom's gumption.

Some time later, she carefully slid the foils out and rinsed my hair with warm water. She began to blow-dry it, and I watched my reflection anxiously, eager to see how the highlights turned out.

"Wow," Stella breathed, "the golden highlights around your face make your skin glow."

"And your eyes look greener," Althea put in.

I'd effected transformations on my customers many times, but I hadn't expected simple highlights to make such a change in my appearance. Strands of gold and wheat framed my face and caught the light. Even the natural light brown looked brighter and glossier somehow. My brows and eyelashes appeared darker and more dramatic against the lighter hair. I shook my head, making my hair dance. "I love it," I told my mom. I turned to give her a hug. "I feel like a new woman."

"You're still my baby," she said, hugging

me back.

The day passed more quickly than I anticipated. Getting ready for the gala felt like a
slumber party as we did each other's hair
and nails. Stella and Althea went to their
homes to get dressed, and Mom and I went
upstairs. My black, Civil War–era maid's
costume with white lace at the wrists and
neckline was fitted through the bodice,
emphasizing the bosom my ex-mother-in-
law thought was inadequate and accentuat-
ing the curve of my waist before swelling
out into a full skirt. In the interest of
comfort, I skipped the pantaloons that were
historically accurate and stuck with my
Jockey hipsters. I tied a white apron around
my waist and put a cap that wasn't much
more than a frill of lace on my head. Althea
had pulled my newly highlighted hair back
into a bun, calling attention to my cheekbones and the smooth line of my jaw. I applied makeup minimally, a little mascara
and lip gloss, to stay almost historically accurate. Slipping on a pair of low-heeled
black pumps that were not remotely correct
for the period, but which my skirt hid, I
glided downstairs to wait for Mom.

She came down ten minutes later, looking
much as I did, except that her short, spiky

313

hairdo and rimless glasses were too clearly twenty-first century. "I'm not wearing a wig and I'm not going to wander around blind as a bat," she'd said when Stella did the costume fitting and mentioned the anachronism.

"Well, Scarlett O'Hara's got nothing to fear from us," I said, "but I think we make comely serving wenches."

"I hope no one asks us to pass hors d'oeuvres," Mom said, making a face at our reflections in the hall mirror. "I may be dressed like a servant, but I intend to have fun at this party."

That fear proved groundless when we arrived at the mansion to find the staff, both male and female, wearing modern dinner jackets and pleated-front shirts with slacks. The grounds twinkled with fairy lights strung in the trees and shrubs. Light spilled from the windows of the house and the open front doors. An old-fashioned carriage drawn by four glossy horses stood in the circular drive as if Governor Brown and his wife, Georgia's first family during the Civil War, had just alighted.

"That's a nice touch," I said to Mom as we passed the equipage with its smiling coachman holding the reins. A horse snorted and tossed his head as if agreeing with me.

"It is," she said. "Lucy Mortimer's always been a stickler for details."

Lucy herself greeted us in the foyer. I almost didn't recognize her. Gone were the dowdy shirtwaist and the boring skirt and blouse. Unlike my mom, she had ditched the tortoiseshell glasses. Maybe she was wearing contacts. A gorgeous maroon gown hugged her shoulders and showed a moderate amount of cleavage. Its full skirt belled over a hoop. Her brown hair was twisted up into a complicated mass of ringlets. A replica of a beautiful cameo hung on a black velvet choker at her neck. She looked like the portrait of Amelia Rothmere that hung behind her come to life.

"You look magnificent," I told her.

"How kind of you to say so," she said. "Thank you for coming this evening."

Even her elocution had changed. I exchanged a look with Mom. It was almost creepy.

"Hi, Lucy," Mom said. "It looks like you've done a great job with this party. I hope you've raised lots of money."

Lucy waved a languid hand. "Oh, the servants did all the hard work. I just drew up the menus."

By "servants" I assumed she meant maintenance personnel and gardeners. Personally, I thought she was getting a bit too much into character. I nudged Mom, and we joined the throng of people headed for the ballroom. The women had gone to town with elaborate gowns in jewel tones of sapphire, emerald, and ruby. Fringe and lace draped bosoms and flirted at hems and cuffs. One woman's wig looked more Marie Antoinette-ish than Scarlett O'Hara-ish, but it didn't spoil the overall effect. Many of the "belles" had trouble maneuvering their hoops, and we had to stop for more than one traffic jam in the wide hallway. The men, not to be outdone, looked dashing in their Confederate soldier uniforms, pirate costumes, and riverboat gambler attire. I saw one man who looked more like he belonged at the court of Charles the First than in Civil War Georgia, and another who wore a modern tux, but most of them had made an effort. I paused at the door to the ballroom when we reached it and looked around, but I didn't see either Marty Shears or Special Agent Dillon. Of course, the latter had never mentioned that he was coming, so maybe he wasn't here. I ignored the small jab of disappointment that thought gave me.

Music swelled from the ballroom, almost

316

drowned by the chatter of two hundred or so guests. I was relieved to recognize a Madonna track; at least the organizers had had enough sense not to inflict Civil War–era music and dances on us. My Virginia reel and quadrille were a little rusty. Servers moved around the room with trays of food, and a bartender mixed up martinis and margaritas at a station near the terrace doors. Mom and I drifted in that direction and ordered glasses of wine when our turn came.

"Do you see Stella or Althea?" Mom asked, craning her neck to try and see over the crowd.

My greater height gave me an advantage, but I didn't see them, either. Very few of the women were wearing black, so it would be easy to spot them when they arrived. I spied Vonda, beautiful in a yellow silk ball gown copied from one that had been in her family for generations. The original was on display at the Smithsonian. Vonda waved a mittened hand when she saw me and started working her way through the crowd.

"You look very . . . subservient," she said after hugging me. "*Love* your hair. Hi, Violetta."

She and Mom exchanged greetings and Mom wandered off, saying something about finding Althea.

"And you look very *Gone with the Wind*," I returned. "Where's your Rhett?"

"Ricky's back at the house with RJ," she said. "The reunion family is still there. But they leave tomorrow morning, and Ricky and I are having a date night tomorrow night." Her eyes sparkled.

"It's about time," I said, happy for her. She and Ricky belonged together, and I was pleased that they were patching things up.

A Confederate officer I didn't recognize, sword clanking in a scabbard at his side, strolled up and offered his hand to Vonda. "Dance with me, pretty lady? I'm off to war tomorrow and would like to take the memory of your pretty face with me."

"La, sir, you flatter me," she said, batting her lashes. Waggling her fingers to me, she headed toward the dance floor, where the women's hoopskirts looked incongruous swaying to the beat of "Play That Funky Music," like a mass of colorful jellyfish bells tossed by the surf.

Scanning the room, I saw many people I recognized, including salon clients, people from church, and Mayor Faricy with his wife. Simone DuBois — no, Simone Hutchinson — and her new husband stood in the doorway. She wore an elaborate green ball

318

gown and had her dark hair styled in ringlets that caressed her cheeks. Greg was a dashing carpetbagger complete with a Clark Gable mustache. Susan DuBois strolled over to greet them, but I didn't see Philip. I spotted Mom, Althea, and Stella in line at the bar on the far side of the room. As I watched, the fire chief — What was his name? Roger something? — joined their little group. My mom smiled at him, and I raised my brows. I wasn't sure I'd ever seen that particular smile. Hm, maybe Walter had some competition for my mother's favor. I looked around but didn't see Walter Highsmith. Vonda waved to me from the dance floor, and I waved back. Dancing beside her was Amber from the restaurant, laughing into the face of a bearded pirate. Marty Shears still wasn't here. I wondered if he'd been detained in New Jersey.

A hand on my shoulder made me turn. A lawman straight out of the 1800s, complete with gold star pinned to his vest, stood smiling at me. He looked dashing and a bit dangerous, and my breaths came a little faster as the surging crowd bumped him closer to me.

"Marshal Dillon, I presume?" I asked.

"You didn't really think you were the first one to come up with that, did you?" Special

319

Agent Dillon returned. "Would you care to stroll on the terrace? It's damned hot in here."

What I really wanted, I discovered, was to dance with him to the strains of the dreamy waltz just starting. I imagined his strong arm around my waist, my right hand clasped firmly in his. Startled by the direction of my thoughts, I mumbled, "Sure. I could use some air."

Holding my wineglass high, I followed him to the open doors and out onto the terrace. It ran the length of the house and had a stone balustrade. Shallow staircases led down into the garden from both ends and the middle. Beyond the twinkle of the fairy lights strung over the topiary, dark fields stretched into the distance. An almost full moon cast shadows in the garden and glanced whitely off the grave stones and statuary in the cemetery. A wisp of night breeze cooled my sweating forehead, and I drew in a deep breath. "I don't know how women put up with these clothes," I said, fluffing the skirt to encourage air flow around my legs. "They're stifling."

He studied me for a moment. "You look nice," he said. "There's something different."

His compliment pleased me, but I hid it,

saying prosaically, "Highlights."

"Um." His mouth crooked in a half smile. "The upstairs maid attire doesn't fit your personality, though."

"Oh?"

"Well, you're not exactly the meek, obedient type, are you? I'd think any plantation owner giving you an order would get nothing but back talk."

"I don't know why you say that, sir," I said demurely, eyes downcast.

Dillon laughed. "Maybe because you've ignored everything I've ever said to you."

"My mom and I are leaving tomorrow," I said, proving him wrong. "We're going to stay with my Aunt Flora in Alabama."

"Good. Maybe then I can concentrate on finding Mrs. DuBois's killer."

Was he saying I disturbed his concentration? I felt a little tingle at the thought. It's more likely, my sensible side said, that he's saying you get in the way. Another couple appeared on the terrace and strolled toward the far end. The music was upbeat again and I found myself tapping my foot to the beat.

Dillon caught my eye and stepped closer, hand outstretched. "Would you —" His cell phone rang. He pulled it from his pocket and looked at the screen. "I have to take this," he said. "Excuse me." He descended the middle stairs to the garden, his finger plugging one ear, saying "Dillon," as he went.

I leaned against the stone railing, feeling the hard edge of it against my stomach and the rough stone under my palms. Five minutes passed. I could no longer hear Dillon — had he been called away on a police emergency? — but voices behind me told me others were seeking the relief of the night air on the terrace. As I was debating whether to return to the ballroom or wait longer for Dillon, a man's voice floated up from beneath me and to my left.

"We can't talk here . . . meddling beautician . . . Meet . . . five minutes."

Del Richardson! Who was he talking to? And why did he mention me? I leaned as far over the balustrade as I could, but I couldn't see anyone in the darkness below. Without stopping to think, I lifted my skirts and ran down the stairs at the left end of the terrace. A dark figure slipped behind a topiary stag as I reached the grass. I didn't see whoever he'd been talking to. The man emerged from behind the stag and headed for the bottom of the garden and the cemetery beyond. His stride and height told me it was probably Del Richardson. I had to see who he was meeting. My black dress gave me an edge in remaining unseen, but my cap and apron had to go. Snatching the cap from my head and untying the apron, I balled them up and stuffed them into a huge ceramic urn planted with what smelled like mint and rosemary. As I walked, I folded the lace cuffs up inside my sleeves.

For a moment, I thought I'd lost Richardson, but a man's silhouette broke away from the shadow of a huge magnolia fifty yards in front of me, and I ran toward it. The thick grass underfoot was dense and muffled the sound of my footsteps. I was grateful not to be wearing a hoop skirt as I trailed the man. Within minutes it became clear he was headed for the cemetery. A good place for a secret meeting. None of the donors laughing and dancing at the ball would go farther than the terrace, or maybe the garden if they were looking for a private place to snatch a kiss. The squeak of an unoiled hinge told me Richardson had opened the cemetery gate.

An old live oak grew twenty feet from the cemetery entrance, and I paused in its shadow to get my bearings. Something tickled my neck, and I swatted at it, turning so fast I almost fell. Ghostly tendrils of Spanish moss trailed from the branch above and fingered my cheek. I let my breath go. Peering around the trunk, I saw nothing unusual, just a few rows of gravestones and the gentle sweep of a marble angel's wing. The smell of freshly turned loam was strong in my nostrils, and I remembered watching the backhoe dig a grave on Wednesday. Leaving the safety of the gnarled tree, I crept toward the gate, tripping and almost falling on an exposed root. Maybe I'd do better without the pumps. I kicked them off, and the cool grass tickled my feet. I scrunched my toes in it for a moment, getting used to the feel, and then tiptoed the remaining steps to the fence. Twigs and acorns pressed into my soles, but the grass provided enough cushion to keep them from being too painful. I felt along the cold iron until I came to the gate. Richardson had left it ajar, and I sucked in my stomach and plastered my skirts to my legs to avoid bumping it as I sidled through. I didn't need its rusty complaint alerting Richardson and his cohort.

A cloud shrouded the moon, and I paused, trying to get my bearings in the near total dark. The murmur of voices came from in front of me and to my right, so I crept that way, arms extended in front of me. Banging my knee against a granite headstone, I bit my lip hard to keep from crying out. I waited a second for the pain to ebb, then edged forward again. My dress rustled slightly, but I hoped the sound blended with the sighing of the breeze through the tree leaves. A break in the clouds allowed the moon to emerge again, and a gaping hole appeared at my feet. Ye gods. One more step and I would have tumbled into the grave I'd watched the backhoe dig. Some kind of hitch must have prevented the burial.

I stepped back carefully and drew in a deep breath. The voices were louder now. Inching around the empty rectangle, I started forward again until I saw the silhouettes of two men. Dropping to a crouch, I duckwalked as close as I dared, stepping on my long skirt and almost pitching onto my nose. I stopped when I reached an ornately carved tombstone about twenty feet from the men. Still in a crouch, I put one hand on the ground for balance, feeling the crisp grass against my palm, and the other on the smooth surface of the marble marker. I leaned forward until I could just see around the edge of the gravestone.

Del Richardson was facing me, easily recognizable in his riverboat gambler vest and hat. The other man was shorter and slighter and wore a Confederate uniform.

With his back to me, I couldn't tell who it was.

". . . Lansky's on board," the unidentified man said.

Was it Philip DuBois? I couldn't tell for sure because his voice was little more than a whisper.

". . . usual terms, I guess?" Del Richardson said. He said something else the wind snatched away and ended with ". . . take care of that reporter and the Terhune gal."

My eyes widened, and I put a hand to my mouth. He knew about Marty. And he had plans for "taking care" of us, whatever that meant. I was afraid it meant poisonous reptiles in my bedroom . . . or worse.

A twig snapped behind me, and both men froze, looking in my direction. I dropped down, flattening myself against the grave. My black dress merged with the shadows, but I knew the white glimmer of my face would give me away. The chemical smell of fertilizer assailed me as I plastered my face to the ground.

"What was that?" Richardson asked.

"A possum or a 'coon, maybe," the other man said. I was almost positive it was Philip. Except . . . had I caught a glimpse of a mustache when he turned to look my way?

I lay still for a long two minutes before

daring to peep around the tombstone again. Both men were gone. I backed away from my hiding place on my hands and knees, not sure which direction Richardson and Philip — if it was Philip — had gone. They were probably back in the ballroom by now, but I didn't want to take any chances. I had reached the brink of the empty grave when my knees started complaining. I couldn't hear anything, so I stood cautiously. My dress was probably a muddy mess. I could only hope my apron would cover the worst of it. I didn't need Mom asking suspicious questions about what I'd been up to.

Another twig cracked, this one closer, and I started to turn. Something hard and metallic thwacked the back of my head and knocked me off balance. Pain sang through my head and reverberated down my spine as my toes scrunched, trying to grip the grass. I windmilled my arms to keep from falling, but a second blow across my shoulders knocked me forward. I plunged into the grave.

CHAPTER TWENTY

My head throbbed like a woodpecker was trying to drill through my skull. An unpleasant coppery taste filled my mouth. I brought a hand to my face to brush away dirt. Dirt? I lay still for a moment, trying to think where I could be. I opened my eyes to darkness broken only by a thin glimmer of starlight overhead, beyond the walls of the tunnel. I frowned. I couldn't be in a tunnel. After another second of confusion, memory returned. The grave! I was in the grave at the Rothmere cemetery. Someone had hit me. I sat up and dirt cascaded from my chest and shoulders. An inch or so covered my legs. Ye gods, my attacker had tried to bury me! Maybe he was still up there.

I peered fearfully up at the rim of the grave, but no sinister silhouette blocked the view. I had to get out of here. He might be coming back. Trying to ignore the pounding in my head, I struggled to my feet. Nausea overwhelmed me, and I braced myself with outstretched hands against the solid-packed walls of the grave. When the dizziness passed, I stood against the right wall and reached both arms up. My fingers just gripped the lip. I scrabbled for purchase with my bare feet.

A hand grabbed my wrist.

"Help!" I screamed, throwing my weight backward.

"Grace! Grace, it's me." Special Agent Dillon's head appeared above me. "Give me your other hand."

Almost sobbing with relief, I grasped his hands. With a grunt of effort, he hoisted me up until my elbows reached the top. I used them to brace myself as I scrambled the rest of the way out of the grave and fell onto my back. Dillon knelt beside me and smoothed a lock of hair off my face. "Are you okay?" he asked, his voice gruffer than usual.

I rolled my head back and forth a scant half inch. "No. My head hurts."

"Where?"

"All over."

His hands gently worked through my hair, fingers examining my scalp.

"Ow," I said, wincing away as his fingers pressed against a tender spot behind my left ear.

"You've got a big lump," he said. "And probably a concussion. Anything else hurt?"

I thought about it for a moment. "Just bruised," I said.

"Can you tell me what happened?"

I explained about overhearing Richardson and the mystery man talking. "I was headed back to the house when someone hit me. I don't know how long I was in there."

"Not long, I don't think," Dillon said grimly. "I scared away your assailant. I heard running footsteps after I came through the gate. Whoever it was dropped that." He pointed to a shovel lying at the foot of the grave.

"He was trying to bury me, wasn't he?" I asked. "I was covered with dirt —" I broke off on a sob. Dillon put his arm around my shoulders and coaxed me to my feet.

"I imagine your attacker was hoping they'd plant a coffin on top of you and fill in the hole with no one the wiser," Dillon said in a carefully controlled voice. "When I couldn't find you in the ballroom, I came looking for you. One of the guests on the veranda said she thought she saw you in the garden. When I didn't find you there, I wandered down here. Did you see who hit you?"

I started to shake my head, then thought

better of it. "No. Not even a glimpse."

"Could it have been Richardson or DuBois?"

"I guess so. I thought they'd gone back to the ball, but if they spotted me, one of them could have doubled back."

"Can you walk?"

I took a tentative step. It jarred my head, but I could do it.

"We'll take it slowly," Dillon said, sliding a hand around my waist.

His arm was strong and warm, and I leaned against him gratefully as we climbed up the slight rise to the mansion. We skirted the garden, staying outside the pool of light from the mansion's windows, and worked our way to the parking lot. Dillon looked down at me. "You need a doctor," he proclaimed. "I'll drive you."

"I don't need —"

"It wasn't a question," Dillon said.

"My mom —"

"I'll give her a call so she won't worry about you. And I'll call and get someone out here to pick up that shovel and dust it for prints. There might be useful footprints, too, although we probably trampled them."

My head hurt too much to argue further, so I let him lead me to his car. At the ER in Brunswick, they x-rayed my head and

331

proclaimed that it was intact, although I had a slight concussion. "You'll have a doozy of a headache," the doctor warned, scribbling on a prescription pad.

Like I didn't know that. I took the pain pills the doctor handed me and swallowed them with water from a paper cup.

"You shouldn't be alone tonight," the doctor said, looking from me to Special Agent Dillon.

"I'll sleep at my mom's," I said hastily.

"Fine. She'll need to wake you a couple of times to make sure you're lucid. Make sure she talks to the nurse before you leave."

"Your mom should be here soon," Dillon said as the doctor strode out of the examining room. "She said she'd meet us here. Why don't you lie down and rest until she comes?"

I glimpsed my pale face, mussed hair, and muddied black dress in the mirror over the sink and didn't feel inclined to argue. I slumped back on the examining table, feeling pleasantly woozy as the pills took the edge off my headache. Special Agent Dillon looked down at me, the fluorescent lights bouncing off his marshal's star. A faint stubble hazed his jaw line, and the crow's feet around his navy eyes seemed more prominent than usual. I blinked, sleep pulling at my eyelids. "What's your first name, anyway, Marshal Dillon?" I asked.

A half smile crooked his mouth. "John," he said. "My name is John."

[Saturday]
Wild dreams plagued my sleep. Amelia Rothmere — or was it Lucy? — announced her determination to save Tara, come what may, and my mother, dressed as a Civil War nurse, asked me silly questions like who the president was. I told her that guy from Illinois . . . Lincoln. Del Richardson asked me to dance and turned into an alligator as we spun around to a Bee Gees song. Then I was falling into a deep pit . . . falling, falling. I jerked awake before I hit bottom. Breathing heavily, I lay still for a moment, trying to orient myself.

Yellow gingham curtains; 1950s-era print of Jesus with the little children, one boy holding a model airplane, little girl seated on Jesus' knee; white rocking chair in the corner. My old bedroom. Tension drained from my muscles. My headache was substantially better. Thank goodness.

Mom came in before I could muster the energy to get out of bed. Steam wisped up from a mug of tea, which she put on the bedside table. "How many fingers am I holding up?" she asked.

"Twelve," I said. At her frown, I amended, "Three."

"Good. And what day of the week is it?"

I thought a moment. "Saturday."

A smile plumped her cheeks. "No permanent brain damage, I guess. The doctor said you've got a hard head. He wasn't telling me anything I didn't already know. I'll go scramble you an egg." She left.

Pushing to a sitting position, I groped for the mug and took a swallow of hot tea. Ah, much better. Caffeine can fix all sorts of problems medical science doesn't have a clue about. I took another pain pill with my second swallow. My mind played back images from the ball and my dreams, and I knew I had to see Lucy Mortimer before we left today. Mom wouldn't be happy, but I was going back to Rothmere before we hit the road to Decatur. I finished my tea and dressed slowly, examining bruises on my knee, thighs, and arms. I was glad I couldn't see my shoulder blades where the shovel had whacked me the second time. I brushed my hair and left it loose, enjoying the play of light on the highlights.

I stepped into the kitchen, clutching my tea, to find Special Agent Dillon forking up eggs at the table. "That better not be my egg," I said by way of greeting.

"Good morning to you, too," he said. He took a sip of coffee.

"I'm making you another egg," Mom said, scrambling the contents of a cast-iron skillet with a spatula.

"That was a fine breakfast, Mrs. Terhune. Thank you," Dillon said.

"Thank *you* for pulling my daughter out of that grave," Mom said.

Dillon relaxed back into his chair and pulled out his notebook. "Speaking of which, we talked with the Rothmere staff last night, including Miss Mortimer, and she said the grave was dug for a Nathan Philpott, a distant Rothmere relation, but his casket ended up in Dallas due to an airline snafu. The burial that was supposed to be Friday is now scheduled for later today."

I was incredibly grateful not to be spending eternity underneath Nathan Philpott. I took the plate of eggs and toast from Mom with a murmur of thanks and joined Dillon at the table.

"The shovel," Dillon went on, "was already at the grave site, so the minister or Mrs. Philpott could tip in a ceremonial shovelful of dirt. So, that makes the attack on you seem like a crime of opportunity, not premeditated," he finished, leveling his gaze at me.

"Then it was probably Richardson or Philip — if it was Philip," I said, peppering my eggs.

"Or someone who saw you leave and followed you, like you followed Richardson."

"But that could be anyone," I said in dismay, my vision of Special Agent Dillon arresting and interrogating Del Richardson evaporating.

"I can rule out a few people," Mom said. "Althea and Stella were talking to me, and Vonda was on the dance floor the whole time. I also chatted with the Kitchenses and Roger MacDonald for quite a while. I let folks know we'd be out of town so they can keep an eye on the house."

"What about Philip DuBois? Did you see him?" I asked.

She thought a moment, pursing her lips. "No, but Susan was with Simone and her fiancé."

"Husband," I said. "I forgot to tell you that they eloped. Vonda and I ran into them at The Pirate Thursday night."

"Well!" My mom took in the news. "I'm glad Simone had enough respect for her mother not to have a big wedding celebration before Constance is cold in her grave."

"What about Lucy?" I asked. "Or Walter?"

"As far as I know, Lucy was still in the foyer, greeting people," Mom said. "And Walter didn't come. He refused to buy a ticket because he was so mad at Constance for terminating his lease. Then, after Constance died, they were all sold out."

I bit my lip. That didn't make sense. Marty Shears had told me he'd secured a ticket only a couple of days ago. Which reminded me I hadn't seen him last night.

Special Agent Dillon interrupted us by standing. "This won't get us very far," he said. "The time period is too tight. Would you be able to swear, Mrs. Terhune, about anyone's whereabouts between, say, eight forty-five and nine o'clock precisely? Did you check your watch?"

Mom shook her head.

"People were coming and going all night long, dancing, standing at the bar, walking on the terrace, using the restroom," he continued. "Establishing a rock-solid alibi for most of them would be impossible. Not to mention, the attacker doesn't have to be someone who was at the party at all."

"So, what do you suggest?" I asked, dabbing at my mouth with a napkin.

"Go to Aunt Flora's like you planned," he said promptly. "We got some prints off the shovel handle. Maybe we'll get lucky and get a hit in AFIS."

"I need to go out to the Rothmere mansion and talk to Lucy before we go," I told them. I stood and collected all our plates, putting them in the sink.

"I'll come with you," Mom and Dillon said simultaneously. They exchanged glances and chuckled.

I was touched by their concern, but I thought my errand would go better if I was on my own. "That's not necessary. I need to have a conversation with Lucy. I'll make sure she knows you all know that I've gone to see her. I'll be perfectly fine. No strolling in the cemetery or exploring dark basements," I said, crossing my heart with my index finger.

"We should plan to leave no later than noon if we want to get to Flora's by dinner time," Mom said, tacitly accepting my plan.

"I'll be back," I promised. I hugged Mom. "Thanks for the breakfast."

Special Agent Dillon walked out with me. "Check in with me before you leave," he said. "And make sure I've got a way to reach you at your aunt's."

"Will do, Marshal," I said. "I'll call you after I talk to Lucy. I may need your help with something."

He looked curious but didn't press me. "As long as it's not snake removal," he said, getting into his car.

Arriving at Rothmere, I was struck by how different it looked this morning. Gone was the magical antebellum atmosphere. Only a pile of horse apples in the circular carriage way marked where the coach had stood. Maybe it had turned back into a pumpkin. A caterer's van was parked, back doors open, near a side entrance. Maintenance workers with telescoping poles removed lights from the trees. Groundskeepers stabbed trash with a pointy tool and put it in garbage bags. The grass beyond the parking lot was flattened and muddy where cars that wouldn't fit in the lot had parked. The great doors stood open, and I walked in, seeing similar signs of postparty cleanup. A bucket and mop stood abandoned in a corner. Jeans-clad workers from the caterer lugged cartons of dirty glasses to their van. A vacuum whirred in a distant room. Ignoring it all, I went directly to Lucy's office and tapped on her door.

"She's in the museum," a voice said from behind me.

I turned, thanked the helpful caterer's assistant, and headed toward the museum, the former carriage house. A covered path connected the main house to the museum, and a small card announced the museum's hours. A larger poster advertised the new exhibit that would open Monday. I opened the door on the cavernous space large enough to hold at least four carriages without crowding. Windows and skylights had been added not that long ago — I remembered the fund-raising campaign — to brighten the exhibit space. On my left, mannequins wore Rothmere family clothing from the eighteenth and nineteenth centuries. Displays of jewelry and personal artifacts were neatly labeled in glass cases around the walls. Professionally done placards discussed plantation farming techniques, slavery, and the effects of the Civil War on the plantation lifestyle.

I spotted Lucy squirting glass cleaner on a case and wiping it with old newspaper. "Lucy," I called from the doorway, not wanting to startle her.

She turned, dropping the crumpled newspaper. With her tortoiseshell glasses back in place and a beige cardigan over her shoulders, Lucy looked nothing like the plantation housewife she'd impersonated last night. "Oh, Grace. I was going to call you later today. I was so sorry to hear about your accident. I wouldn't have had such a thing happen at Rothmere for the world."

I'm not sure I called getting thumped with a shovel and dumped in a grave an "accident," but I let it go. "I'm feeling much better," I said. "Just a little leftover headache."

I crossed to the display case where she was standing. "What's the theme of the new exhibit?" I asked, studying the documents in the glass case.

"Civil War love letters," she said proudly. "And not just from the Rothmeres. This one" — she pointed to a brief note on yellowing paper — "is from Jefferson Davis to his second wife, Varina. And Robert E. Lee wrote this one to his wife, Mary Custis Lee, moments before the Battle of Antietam. It's taken me years to persuade museums and private collectors to lend their documents."

"I'm sure it's fascinating," I said, "and I'll come view the exhibit when it opens. But I want to talk about last night." For a town not much larger than an amusement park, St. Elizabeth hid a lot of secrets. And Constance had been privy to too many of them. One of them, I suspected, had gotten her killed. I needed to be sure it wasn't Lucy's secret. "That cameo you wore — it was Amelia Rothmere's, wasn't it?"

Lucy blinked behind her glasses. "It was just like it," she said. "And my dress was a copy of —"

"The cameo wasn't a copy, Lucy," I said gently. "Constance DuBois was holding you responsible for the disappearance of some Rothmere artifacts, wasn't she? And she was going to have you dismissed as curator. Did she know you took them?"

Lucy looked to the left and right, as if searching for an escape route. "I couldn't . . . I wouldn't . . . I didn't steal —"

I chose my words carefully, not wanting to scare her into silence. "I'm sure it didn't seem like stealing to you, because you . . . identify so closely with the Rothmeres." I stopped short of saying she thought she *was* Amelia Rothmere.

"They're my — they're like my family," she said. Pulling a lace hanky from her pocket, she dabbed at her eyes under the glasses. "I knew Amelia would want me to have that brooch," she said, sniffing defiantly. "It's not as if anyone else around here cares that the brooch was Reginald's betrothal present to Amelia, or that she gave the Wedgwood tea cup to their daughter Caroline after she almost died of typhus. These are family memories, not just baubles

342

for people to gawk at." She glared at me. "You have no proof that I took anything," she said belatedly. She took a step toward me. Fluid sloshed in the spray bottle she still held in her right hand.

I stepped back, keeping a wary eye on the container of glass cleaner. I didn't think she'd attack me, not with the workers outside to hear me if I screamed, but I wanted to stay out of spraying range. "You should know that I told the police I was coming here."

Her face turned an ashy gray. "You turned me in? Not even Constance —"

"I didn't tell him why I was coming to see you," I said, feeling sorry for her.

She paused for a beat, then gasped and said, "You thought I might hurt you? How could you? I've never hurt anyone, ever. Did you think I — ?" She faltered. "Constance?"

"No," I said. "No one thinks that." Not anymore. She was too genuinely confused and horrified. "And I don't think anyone else has figured out about the jewelry and mementoes. But someone will, Lucy. That's why I came today. You need to return the stuff you took. 'Find' it all in a box in storage if you want, but you've got to replace it."

Her lips thinned to a mulish line. "What

343

gives you the right?"

I hesitated, not sure how to phrase it. "It's not about right, I don't think. Well, it is, in a way, but not completely. I think the people who visit Rothmere, who come to pay their respects to the Rothmere family, would appreciate seeing the mementoes that meant so much to Amelia and Jeremy and Caroline and —" I broke off, not remembering any of the other names.

"Reginald and Elizabeth and the others." Lucy looked thoughtful. "I guess it was a bit selfish of me."

Not to mention criminal. I stayed silent, letting her find her own way.

"If the items that have gone missing turn up, can we keep this just between us?" she asked, her expression hovering between supplication and defiance.

I found myself troubled by what I was doing. I'd written her impersonation of Amelia Rothmere off as a harmless delusion. What if it was more than that? And who was I to decide that because she'd "borrowed" the mementoes for her personal enjoyment, rather than to make money off them, that her thievery was any more acceptable? "I don't know, Lucy," I said honestly. "I hope so."

She turned away from me, her shoulders

slumped. "Fine."

"There's one other thing," I said. "I need a favor."

CHAPTER
TWENTY-ONE

I returned to Mom's half an hour later to find her and Althea heading out. "We're off to Walter's," Mom said as I parked. "He wants to show Althea his plans for the renovations."

I got out of the car and joined the women on the sidewalk.

"I told him he can do whatever he wants," Althea said grumpily, "but he insists I approve his plan as his new landlady. He says if he does some of the work himself, it won't cost much at all. I can't imagine why Constance left the building to me. I can see it's going to be a big, fat pain in the patootie. Maybe Walter would like to buy it." Her face brightened.

"Want to come with us?" Mom asked. "Then we can pick up some sandwiches at Doralynn's and hit the road."

There was no easy way to say what I'd come to say. "I think I know where Carl

Rowan and William are," I said baldly.

Althea staggered and dropped her purse. Coins and a lipstick rolled across the sidewalk. Mom steadied her while I bent to retrieve the purse's contents.

"Grace Ann, you can't throw ideas like that around without preparing a body for them," Mom said. Althea stayed uncharacteristically silent.

"I'm sorry. I didn't mean to break it to you that way. But after I got knocked into that grave last night, it came to me. The last time a Rothmere was buried at that cemetery was in 1983, about the time Carl and William went missing. I saw it in an old issue of the newspaper. I think whoever killed them put their bodies in the grave and let them get buried under the casket."

The other women were silent for a moment. Althea pinched at her lips with her thumb and fingers and then said, "I guess it could have happened like that. How do we find out for sure?"

"I've already talked to Lucy Mortimer, and she's going to get an okay from the Rothmere Board of Directors to dig up the casket and look beneath it. Since we're not actually opening the casket, she doesn't think we need to notify anyone else, like the health authorities or anything. And since

347

the grave diggers are already there today because of Nathan Philpott's interment, she figures they can do the work this afternoon."

"I need to sit down," Althea announced.

Mom led her to the veranda and disappeared inside to get some water.

"I'm sorry, Althea," I said, worried by the dazed look in her eyes. "Would it have been better if I hadn't said anything, if I'd just let it be?"

"No. If there's a chance that I could finally know . . ."

Mom returned and handed her friend a glass of water. Althea's hands were shaking so hard the glass clinked against her teeth as she drained it. A young mom went by on the other side of the street, pulling two toddlers in a red wagon. We waved.

"Better?" Mom asked.

Althea nodded. "I think Walter's going to have to wait a bit. Let's go out to Rothmere."

Mom sighed, resigned. "I guess this means we're not getting to Flora's today."

The Rothmere cemetery basked peacefully in the early afternoon sun. The sun, directly overhead, warmed my arms bared by a sleeveless yellow blouse and banished shadows, leaving the terrain, so seemingly uneven and dark the night before, a swathe of emerald. The marble angel gleamed. Dozens of small white butterflies flitted from dandelion to dandelion in the spaces between the graves. A blanket of carnations, lilies, and honeysuckle draped the newly turned mound of earth where Nathan Philpott had been laid to rest, sending out a sweet scent. With the grave filled in, my adventures of last night seemed unreal, something I'd seen in a movie or read about in a book.

Mom and Althea stood beside me outside the wrought iron fence, watching the backhoe maneuver into position. Lucy Mortimer, wearing a broad-brimmed sun hat, stood an arm's length away. A cluster of crime scene technicians armed with baggies, brushes, and small spades, like an archeological team ready to dig up one of King Tut's relatives or a T. rex, stood in a knot under the big oak tree. Special Agent Dillon, jacket off, squinted his eyes against the sun's glare and tracked the backhoe's movements. I'd expected skepticism when I told him what I thought about Carl's and William's final resting place, but after I'd explained my reasoning and he'd called the paper to have them fax over the article about the 1983 burial, he'd said, "Interesting possibility. I'll get the appropriate permissions. We'll have to treat it like a crime scene."

I'd called Marty Shears, too, but his cell phone went directly to voicemail. I was getting worried about him. I'd try calling his paper to see if they'd heard from him when we finished at Rothmere.

A canvas screen around the gravesite provided some privacy for the exhumation. The grassy sod had been removed from the grave earlier and stacked to one side. A simple granite tombstone, engraved "Gemma Rothmere Lackland, January 16, 1903–February 3, 1983, Beloved Wife and Mother," stood sentinel over the barren rectangle of earth. Now, the backhoe bit into the soil. I winced, then steadied myself, hoping no one had noticed. The bucket swung around and tipped the dirt into a trailer positioned nearby. Pebbles rattled against the metal sides. The machine's engine growled and *beep-beep-beeps* sounded every time the backhoe reversed. A puff of diesel exhaust drifted my way. Another piece of equipment, like a small crane, was poised nearby, to lift the casket out, I presumed.

After five minutes of watching the backhoe work, Lucy approached Althea and Mom. "This is going to take quite a while," she said gently. "Don't you think we'd be more comfortable waiting inside? They can let us know when the casket's been removed."

After a brief hesitation, Althea nodded, and we crossed the broad lawn to the mansion. Dillon remained behind and shook his head at me when I gave him an enquiring glance. Two cups of tea later, he appeared in the doorway of the small sitting room where we sat, mostly quiet. The sun had burnished the tip of his nose and his cheekbones, and sweat damped his temples. His expression fit the task. "The casket's out," he said. We filed back to the cemetery after him, Mom and Althea holding hands.

Since the grave was potentially a crime scene, a technician from the crime lab lowered himself into the hole to finish the excavation while the rest of us waited outside the iron fence once again. It took a long time, since he first laid out a grid with twine and then stopped frequently to put soil samples in baggies. The backhoe operator slumped on the seat of his machine, reading a paperback copy of a Barry Eisler thriller. Just business as usual for him, I guessed. A few clouds scudded the blue sky now and a fitful breeze kicked up dirt and blew it in our faces. Dusty grains stuck to the film of sweat on my skin. As the first shovelful of dirt plopped over the lip of the grave, we held our breaths. With each succeeding mound of dirt, the tension ratcheted up a notch until my jaw ached from clenching my teeth.

When the technician's head popped into view, hovering disembodied over the rim of the grave, Althea gasped and Lucy giggled from the sudden release of tension. He summoned Special Agent Dillon over with a wave of his hand. We crowded against the fence, trying to hear their low-voiced conversation. After a moment, Dillon straightened and returned to us.

He shook his head. "There's nothing there." His gaze, full of compassion, fell on Althea. "I'm sorry." Looking at me, he said, "It was a good idea, Grace. I'm sorry it didn't pan out." He patted my shoulder and turned to speak to the technician, who had hoisted himself out of the grave and was shucking off his gloves.

Disappointment caved in Althea's face. "I was hoping . . ."

"I'm so sorry I got your hopes up for nothing," I said. "I really thought —"

"It's okay, Grace," Althea said. "Maybe I'm not meant to know. Maybe my William is meant to lie undisturbed, wherever he is."

Her brown eyes clouded with regret. She turned her back on the cemetery and walked toward the house, moving much more stiffly than earlier. My mom caught up with her easily, and Lucy and I trailed behind, caught up in our own thoughts. I'd spent enough time in a cemetery over the last twenty-four hours to last me a lifetime.

When we got back to Mom's house late that afternoon, I phoned *The Atlanta Journal-Constitution,* using the number on Marty's card. When I asked to speak to Martin Shears, the operator transferred me. The phone rang and rang. Just when I thought I was going to end up with voice mail again, a man picked up. "Martin Shears's desk." He sounded impatient.

When I asked for Marty, he said, "Don't you read the paper, for God's sake? He was in a car accident yesterday afternoon. Coming back from the airport."

I felt my windpipe close up. "Is he — ?" I choked out.

"In the ICU," he said. "But I hear he's doing better this morning. You a friend of his?"

I said I was, and he told me what hospital Marty was in. "But I think they're only letting family visit," he warned me. "Check

353

back in a couple of days."

I hung up with trembling hands. This couldn't be coincidence, could it? I gave myself a shake. Of course it could. People had car accidents all the time, going to work, on their way to tennis lessons, coming back from the grocery store. Just because the timing was weird didn't mean anything. My logic didn't keep my skin from feeling clammy as I fished a diet root beer out of the fridge and returned to the salon.

Althea had recovered some of her usual spunk by the time I rejoined her and Mom. "I want y'all to see the design I've come up with for the label for my beauty products," she said, marching straight into the salon.

Mom and I glanced at each other but accepted her tacit request not to talk any more about William's fate.

"I'm thinking about calling my line Althea's Organic Skin Solutions," she said, plunking her purse down on the counter. "What do you think?"

"Well, it might be a little wordy," Mom said, twisting her mouth to one side.

"I like it." Feeling as badly as I did about disappointing Althea today, I'd have waxed enthusiastic if she said she wanted to call it Althea's Egg and Avocado Skin Glop. "And organic stuff is big right now . . . organic food, organic cosmetics, organic household cleansers. I've seen tons of articles about it."

Althea gave me an approving look. "You're right." She pulled a line drawing from her purse and unfolded it. "This is what I was thinking about for the label. Of course, I'll have to get a professional artist to do it up pretty, but this is the idea."

Before we could examine the drawing, the front door slammed open, setting the bell clanging and the blinds swaying. Rachel burst in, her face alight with excitement. "I saw him!"

The three of us stared at her in silence. She wore black cutoff overalls over a tank top. Her black hair bobbed in a short ponytail at the crown of her head with her bangs straggling across her forehead.

"Who?" my mom finally asked.

"Him," Rachel said. "The dude Constance argued with that day she came for her highlights."

I'd almost forgotten about the mystery man, but now my pulse quickened. "You did? Where?"

"Outside Doralynn's. I stopped in for an ice cream cone next door at the Friendly's, and I left my scooter out back 'cause they don't like it if I park it on the sidewalk.

Anyway, when I went back to the alley to get my scooter, there he was, making out with some girl."

"Did you get a good look at him?" Mom asked.

"I did better than that," Rachel said. "I took his picture." She raised her cell phone triumphantly.

"Let us see," I said.

Mom and I crowded close to Rachel while Althea folded her sketch and tucked it into her purse. Rachel flipped open her phone and skimmed a forefinger across the screen. "There," she said. She held the phone so we could see the tiny photo.

Angling the phone so glare didn't obscure the screen, I studied the image. "But that's —" I broke off, wanting to be sure before I opened my big mouth. A blond man faced the camera, eyes half closed, the bottom half of his face obscured by the head of the woman he was kissing.

"Isn't that Simone's young man?" Mom asked, peering over the top of her glasses.

"It's Greg Hutchinson," I said. I leaned back against the counter. Simone's husband had argued with her mother hours before she was murdered. And, as far as I knew, he hadn't said anything to the police or to Simone about it. To make things worse, the

356

woman he was kissing wasn't his new wife. I couldn't see enough of her to tell who it was — if it mattered — but the mass of blonde hair told me it wasn't Simone. I found myself feeling unbearably sorry for Simone, whose mother had been murdered a week ago and whose new husband was a cheating scuzzbucket . . . and maybe a murderer. Although I couldn't think of a reason for him to murder Constance. Simone was well past eighteen — Constance couldn't have kept her from marrying him, even if she'd wanted to. Maybe she'd seen him with this other woman and threatened to tell Simone about it.

"My, my," Mom said. She shook her head. "What a . . . a louse to be kissing another woman not three days after he married Simone. So many young people these days don't understand the importance of fidelity."

"Let me see this Lothario," Althea said. Rachel, pleased with the attention her discovery was getting, turned the phone so Althea could see. Althea squinted at the image. "I can't see this — it's too small. Where are my reading glasses?" she asked. She groped in her purse and pulled out the cheap magnifying glasses with the red rims. Sliding them up her nose, she peered at the photo again. She made a little choking noise and stuttered, "It can't —" before her knees buckled and she collapsed, almost bringing Mom down with her.

Mom staggered but stayed upright, catching her friend under her armpits to keep her head from knocking against the floor. Rachel sprang back, startled, and retrieved her cell phone from under the chintz chair where it had skittered when Althea dropped it.

"Help me, Grace," Mom commanded.

I didn't think we could lift Althea onto the sofa, so I got a pillow and slid it under her head. Mom dampened a cloth with cold water and laid it gently across Althea's forehead.

"Should I call 911?" Rachel asked. Worry creased her young forehead.

"I don't think we need EMTs," Mom said calmly, chafing her friend's hands. "I think she's just fainted."

Althea's eyelids fluttered and then popped open. "Do you believe in ghosts, Vi?" she asked.

I gave her a worried look, afraid she'd banged her head after all.

"Why?" Mom asked, helping Althea sit up.

"Because that's Carl Rowan, big as life,"

Althea announced, pointing at the cell
phone in Rachel's hand.

CHAPTER
TWENTY-TWO

Althea's declaration shocked us all to silence. The truth hit me after only a short moment.

"His son," I said. "Greg must be Carl Rowan's son, all grown up. Didn't he have a son who was about eleven when Carl and William disappeared?"

"I think he had a couple of kids," Althea admitted.

"This must be him. The age is about right . . . he looks to be in his mid-thirties. And I don't think he linked up with Simone by accident, do you?"

"That would be too much of a coincidence," Mom agreed.

"Let me think this through." I stood up and paced. "We know Martina Rowan moved away not long after Carl went missing. She went to Richmond, according to Marty. Then she remarried and moved to New Jersey with her new husband. Want to bet his name is Hutchinson and he adopted Greg and the other kids?" I looked around at Mom, Althea, and Rachel.

"So how did he, like, hook up with Simone?" Rachel asked. Her eyes were wide, and she had settled cross-legged on the floor, for all the world like she was listening to a campfire story. Mom and Althea were still on the floor, too, looking up at me as I pieced it together.

"The mother raised him up on stories of his father's death," Althea suggested, pulling the pillow underneath her and settling more comfortably. "She filled his mind with poison, taught him to hate the DuBoises."

"Or maybe she just told him about the property," Mom put in, "and he grew up thinking he has a right to it, that the DuBoises cheated his family out of it."

"Either way, he's got a grudge against the DuBoises, right?" I said. "Could be he tracked down the family when he got older and found out Simone was living right around the corner, as it were, in New York City."

"Why'd he wait so long?" Althea objected. "The boy's in his thirties. If he was after revenge, wouldn't he have done something sooner?"

"I don't know." I shrugged. "Maybe he

was busy earning a degree or getting his career started. There's no way to tell. The point is, he engineers a meeting with Simone, seduces her, and voilá — they're engaged. She brings him down here to meet her mom, and Constance recognizes him, like you did, Althea. Didn't you see him at the Rothemere gala?"

Althea shook her head.

Well, he was in costume, and the ball had been crowded. It wasn't too surprising that Althea hadn't run into him.

"So what?" Mom asked unexpectedly. "Why would it matter if Constance recognized him? She can hardly tell Simone that Philip Senior had Carl and William done away with, if that's what happened."

"That's what happened," Althea said grimly.

"Maybe, like Philip Junior said, she thought Greg was only interested in Simone for her money. Maybe she threatened to tell Simone that he wasn't who he appeared to be." I rethought that. "Well, he is Greg Hutchinson, but he's also the former Greg Rowan with a history in St. Elizabeth that I'll bet Simone doesn't know about."

"Didn't you tell me that Simone inherited Sea Mist Plantation when Constance died?" Mom asked.

I nodded.

"Well, then he's got what he wants — his daddy's property back again."

"But only because Constance died," Althea pointed out. "That makes him the number one suspect, in my opinion. Especially when you consider how nervy she was when she came back in here after arguing with him."

"But he doesn't really own Sea Mist, does he?" Rachel said. "It's Simone's."

We all stared at her, and a taut silence hung over the salon. A *drip-drip* from the shampoo sink's leaky faucet sounded loud in the stillness. "With that photo Rachel took of Greg playing kissy face with another woman, I'm not sure he's in this marriage for the long haul," Mom said after a long moment.

"And he'd risk losing Sea Mist in a divorce," I added.

"I think Simone's in danger," Mom said. "We need to warn her."

"I've got her cell phone number somewhere, from the committee," I said.

"We can't call her," Mom said, giving me a reproving look. "Something like this needs to be done face-to-face. She'd just hang up on us if we called and accused her new husband of being a gold-digging murderer."

"The sins of the fathers will be visited on their children," Althea said. "The DuBois family is coming by its just desserts."

"I never did think much of that particular passage," Mom said with asperity. "God's not punishing Simone because her father did something wicked a quarter century ago. That's not the way He works."

"We'd better get going, then," Althea said, pushing herself slowly to her feet. "Damn, I'm too old to be sitting on the floor. My behind's gone to sleep." She rubbed the afflicted area.

I helped her up. Rachel bounced up with the flexibility of youth and gave my mom a hand.

"We should call Special Agent Dillon," I said.

"Rachel can call him and wait here for him so he can see the photograph she took," Mom suggested. "We don't have time to fill him in on everything. We need to warn Simone *now*."

Rachel pushed her lips out in a rebellious pout. "You're not going to let me come with you, are you? You think I'm too young. Well, I'm not. I'm going to graduate, like, next year. I'm old enough to join the military and almost old enough to vote, so why can't I come?"

Momentarily distracted by the thought of goth Rachel in a military uniform, I recovered quickly as Mom said, "Rachel, honey, how would I ever explain it to your folks if something happened to you? We may be completely wrong about Mr. Hutchinson, but if we're not, and he's with Simone when we arrive, he might get angry."

"Well, like duh," Rachel said. "If you call him a two-timing murderer to his face." She rolled her eyes.

I didn't take the time to explain that accusing Greg of murder to his face wasn't our preferred approach. "We'll try to get Simone alone," I said, hatching a plan. "I'll tell her I have to talk to her about committee business."

"That's good," Althea said. "You can call her while we're driving over there. We'll take my car."

Leaving Rachel sulkily dialing police headquarters, we hustled out the side door and climbed into Althea's old Ford LTD. Formerly maroon, it had been faded by the sun to a dismal pinkish color. The car must be nearly as old as I was, I thought, thunking the heavy back door closed and fastening my seat belt. Mom had barely shut her door before Althea gunned the engine and reversed down the driveway. We bumped off the curb and onto the street with a scraping sound and sparks from the front bumper. It was wise to have your life insurance paid up when riding with Althea behind the wheel. She seemed to view traffic laws such as speed limits and stop signs as loose guidelines and had a habit of facing whoever she was talking to so the car veered from one side of the road to the other. She was exceeding the speed limit by a good twenty miles per hour, but both Mom and I knew enough not to distract her by commenting on it. At least she wasn't trying to talk, so her eyes stayed on the road.

We were three-quarters of the way to the DuBois house when a thought struck me. "Didn't Philip inherit the house?" I asked. "What if Simone and Greg aren't living there?"

"Well, now's a fine time to bring that up," Althea said, craning her head around to frown at me. The car headed for the opposite curb and a man walking two beagles. His eyes widened at the sight of death coming at him in the form of a runaway LTD.

Mom grabbed the wheel. "Althea, pay attention," she said, wrenching the car into its proper lane.

I let my breath out and realized I was gripping the seat so hard my fingers were cramping. "I'll call Philip and find out. Damn. I don't have his number."

"We're almost there now," Mom said as I dialed directory assistance. "We'll just knock and ask him."

"Yeah, he won't think that's strange," Althea muttered.

Two minutes later we pulled into the circular drive fronting the DuBois family home, a mini-mansion that looked like it belonged in the English countryside. Althea crunched over a border of Johnny-jump-ups and pink ice plant lining the oyster-shell driveway, and I leaped out of the back seat before she came to a full stop. "I'll be right back," I flung over my shoulder.

Racing up the front steps, I rang the bell and pounded on the front door.

It opened to reveal Susan DuBois, an attractive blonde whose bee-stung lips looked fuller than they had at Constance's wake. She must have had them plumped. "Grace! What on earth — ?" Her raised brows expressed her disapproval of my knocking technique.

"Hi, Susan. I need to see Simone, but I don't have her address. Can you tell me where she's staying?"

"Who's that in the car?" she asked, peering over my shoulder.

"My mom and Althea Jenkins," I said. "The address?"

Suspicion lurked in her gray-green eyes. "Why are you so all fired up about finding Simone? It's not like you were ever best friends."

"It's about the mayor's committee," I said. "I've got some data I need to give her to put in the PowerPoint presentation."

"Well, I don't see how that's such an emergency," Susan said. But she rattled off the address.

"Thanks," I yelled over my shoulder, trotting back to the car.

"Well!" Susan stared after us as the tires spewed oyster shells and Althea slewed onto the road like a moonshine smuggler trying to outrun the revenuers. I waved through the back window.

Simone and her new husband were renting a Cape Cod–style house that backed to the river at Sea Mist Plantation. It was at the west end of the Plantation, in an area just being developed. The Hutchinsons had no neighbors yet, only the framed shell of a house on the opposite side of the cul-de-sac. The construction workers had knocked off for the day, and the area hummed with crickets, owls, and other critters beginning to stir as dusk descended. The three of us were grimly silent, infected by an urgency that was hard to explain. Althea stopped the car with the passenger-side wheels on the sidewalk. We all piled out and hurried up the walkway to the glossy blue front door. When I pushed it, the doorbell ding-donged deep in the house, and we fidgeted on the small stoop. No one came. I rang again, trying to peer in the narrow windows that flanked the door. Blinds prevented me from seeing much except a strip of oak floor. Althea cut across the grass and stood on tiptoe to look into the garage. Then she walked around the side of the house and stood on tiptoe to peer over the fence.

"Car is there," she announced, rejoining us. "Can't see over the fence."

"Whose car?" Mom asked.

She shrugged. "Dark green Camry with New York plates."

Since none of us knew what Simone drove, we didn't know if it was her car, but I thought it must be, since I'd seen Greg driving a BMW when he picked her up at the town hall.

"Here, let me," Althea said, shouldering me out of the way. She banged the brass knocker hard enough to startle two squirrels chasing each other in the yard. They scampered up a dogwood sapling.

Footsteps sounded inside the house, and a man's disgruntled voice said, "Coming."

We stepped back as the door swung open and Greg Hutchinson stood in the doorway, looking casually elegant in belted khaki shorts and a crisp white shirt with the top button undone to show a spritz of chest hair. His shoulders almost filled the doorframe, and the look on his face hovered between welcoming and exasperated. When he saw me, he forced a smile. "Hello, Grace." He looked from Mom to Althea but didn't say anything.

I introduced them, worried by the look of hostility on Althea's face. "We're looking for Simone," I said. "Is she in?"

"I'm sorry. She isn't here right now. I'll tell her you came by."

He started to close the door, but I stopped it with my hand. "It's kind of important," I said with an apologetic smile. "I have some data she needs to include in the PowerPoint slide show she's making for the mayor. Do you know when she'll be back?"

"Oh." He hesitated, his hand still on the knob. "I'm not sure, exactly. She went shopping. You know how women are when they smell a sale." His grin faded as the three of us glared at him. "Look, just give me the stuff, and I'll see that she gets it when she gets back."

I scrambled for a way around his reasonable suggestion. "Uh, it's in the car."

"I'll fetch it," Mom said, taking her time about returning to the car and pretending to search the back seat. Greg tapped his foot.

"And I need to explain some of it to her," I said.

"Good thinking, baby girl," Althea murmured.

"Then leave your number, and she can call you," he said impatiently. He raked a hand through his brassy gold hair. "I'm sorry, but I'm working on a real estate deal —"

"I'll call her now and maybe we can meet up with her," I said, pulling out my cell phone. "I'm sorry we bothered you." Finding the entry for "Simone Cell," I dialed.

"Wait," Greg said, reaching for the phone.

I jerked it back out of reach as the strains of "My Way" sounded from inside the house. We all stared at Greg. Before he could react, Althea had pushed past him, saying, "Sounds like she's still here after all." She raised her voice. "Simone-honey! We've got that paperwork you needed."

"Hey," he said. "You can't —"

Greg grabbed at her shoulder, but Mom

371

and I bumped against him as we crowded into the foyer. "Simone!" we called.

The door closed hard behind us, and I heard the deadbolt shoot home. I turned to see Greg pocketing the key, an ugly look on his face. "I don't know what you think you're —" he started when Althea's voice interrupted him.

"Oh, my God!"

Ignoring Greg, Mom and I hurried in the direction of Althea's voice. We skidded to a stop where the wood floor of the hall gave way to the greenish slate tile of the kitchen. A maple table with four lyre-back chairs dominated an eating nook. The back door to the left of the table was open a crack, and the wet smell of the river drifted in. Simone lay on the floor by the door I assumed opened to the garage, Althea kneeling beside her. Peaches was licking her mistress's face and whining. Two wineglasses sat on the granite counter beside a nearly empty bottle.

"Is she — ?" Mom asked.

"She's alive," Althea said, her fingers pressed to Simone's neck. "But she needs help. You poisoned her," she said to Greg, her gaze flashing from the wineglasses to his face.

"Just a little Rohypnol," he said.

372

He herded us closer to where Althea huddled over Simone, trying to wake her by pinching her cheeks. With a growl that sounded like it came from a dog twice her size, Peaches launched herself at Greg and latched onto his ankle. "Get off, you rabid flea," he said, kicking out so hard that Peaches went flying, thumping into the pantry door and lying still.

I caught my breath at the brutality as Mom went to the little dog and stroked her, glaring at Greg.

"Rohypnol? The date rape drug?" I asked, bewildered.

"It has many uses," he said, his eyes cold. "Usually it makes women pliable. I must have given her too much," he said, staring at his wife's inanimate form.

"Call a doctor," Althea ordered. "It's not too late."

He barked out a laugh. "A doctor? That *would* mess up the plan. My poor, dear wife, distraught over her mother's death and our first marital spat, is going to have a car accident tonight." He feigned distress. "And I'll be the heart-broken husband —"

"Who inherits Sea Mist Plantation," I said.

"So you figured that out, did you?" he said, narrowing his eyes. "I knew you were getting too close when that girl from the

Records division called to say you were looking for my birth certificate." He laughed at my astonished look. "Oh, yes. I paid her twenty bucks to let me know if anyone else came around. I told her it had to do with identity theft."

"Well, aren't you the clever one," Althea said sarcastically. Simone moaned, and Althea chafed her hands.

"Not clever enough to discourage this one," he said, nodding toward me. "I thought the Molotov cocktail would scare you off, but no, you kept poking your nose in. Even when I planted the sword and egged Simone on to get the salon shut down, thinking it would distract you, you kept chasing after me."

"Well, I didn't know it was you until today," I said, "but I had nothing better to do once I didn't have a job to go to." I edged a bit away from Mom, thinking that if we were spread out, he'd find it harder to control us. Whatever his plan was, I didn't think it included letting us all walk out of here whenever we felt like it. I saw Mom eyeing the back door, probably calculating our chances of reaching it before Greg did something. She inched toward it.

"Why did you kill Constance?" I asked, trying to distract him so Mom could make a run for it.

"Why do you think?" he said roughly. "It took her a few days, but she recognized me. She suspected I was shamming it with Simone and that I was only after the money. Sea Mist, specifically, because it should have been mine. Mine! Philip DuBois cheated my father. He stole the land from him and then he killed him." His voice rose and he stepped closer, fists clenched at his sides. "I was only eleven, but I remember."

"Remember what?" Althea asked.

He looked down at her as if he'd forgotten she was there. "Him coming back from that poker game, telling my mom he was going to have it out with Philip DuBois. Him and that other guy."

"William," Althea said in a carefully controlled voice. "William Jenkins."

"Yeah, him," Greg said dismissively.

I didn't think Greg got the connection. "And . . ." I prompted.

"And when he never came home, I knew DuBois had killed him."

"Why didn't you ever say something?" Althea asked, her upper lip poking out so the lines around her mouth deepened.

"My mom," he said. "I was afraid that if I said anything, Philip DuBois would kill the rest of us, too. He came by later that week and talked to my mom. I didn't hear it all, but I heard him say we might all be safer if we moved away. He gave her an envelope."

"Money," I said.

He nodded. "To help with the moving costs, he said. She took it — she had me and my sisters to protect, you know — and we moved. She said she couldn't stay in St. Elizabeth where there were so many bad memories. But I knew the truth. And I vowed that one day I'd get back what was rightfully mine."

"Even if you had to kill someone to do it," Althea said.

"I didn't plan that," he said. He paused, as if listening.

I heard it, too. A scrape of sound out back. Special Agent Dillon! I didn't let my relief show on my face. "But you did kill Constance," I said loudly, thinking to cover up the sounds the police made as they approached.

"She was going to put an investigator on me. That's what she said that afternoon outside the salon. That she was hiring a PI. It wouldn't have taken him a day to find out I was already married. She'd tell Simone, and years of planning would go up in smoke. Not that marrying Simone was the original plan. But when I saw her name on the list of attendees for the speed-dating event my friend Bob was setting up, I knew I had to seize the opportunity. My wife agreed — she knew I had to do this. Simone and I hit it off, and things sort of snowballed. At first, I planned to marry her and divorce her, taking Sea Mist in the divorce. But then Constance . . ." He frowned, twisting the wedding ring around his finger. "After the town hall meeting, I tried to talk her out of investigating me, persuade her that I loved Simone for herself and that the money meant nothing to me, but she wasn't buying it. When she pulled that damned sword out of the car, I lost it. I grabbed it from her and . . . It was self defense."

Hm. A two-hundred-pound man couldn't defend himself against a woman half his size without running her through? I wasn't buying it and I didn't think a jury would, either.

"You're married?" Mom asked.

She had sidled much closer to the back door. Run, I urged her mentally, run.

She was too appalled by Greg's confession to make a break for it. "To someone other than Simone? You're a bigamist?"

"Not for long," a new voice said. The back door opened wider, and Amber stood there, the waitress from Doralynn's. With her blond hair slicked back into a ponytail and

377

dressed in black jeans and a hoodie, she looked older somehow. It was hard to think of her as Greg's wife. She stepped into the kitchen and closed the door with a kick of her heel. She now stood between Mom and the door, cutting off the escape route. She held something squat and black in her un-bandaged hand. A gun, I thought, with a nervous flutter in my stomach.

Chapter
Twenty-Three

"What the hell are they doing here?" Amber asked Greg.

"They just —" Greg started.

"You're Greg's other wife?" Althea asked, her whole face pursing with disapproval.

"I'm his *real* wife." Before we could guess her intent, she shoved the gun into Mom's back. It crackled and Mom yelped, trying to jump away. Amber kept the device pressed into her back for another few seconds until Mom crumpled to the floor, twitching and moaning.

"Mom!" I cried, horrified. I started toward her, but Greg grabbed my arm.

"Stun gun," Amber said, holding up the device. "She's not dead. Yet." Her cold eyes took in the scene. "This is going to be harder," she said to Greg. "Get the duct tape."

"You can't get rid of three of us," Althea said triumphantly. "You can't make three people disappear without any questions."

"Questions we can handle as long as there's no evidence," Amber said. One long stride brought her closer to Althea, and she pulled the trigger on the stun gun again. Althea's eyes rolled back in her head, and she slumped down atop Simone.

"Stop!" I yelled, tears starting to my eyes. I wrenched myself away from Greg and ran to my mother's still form. She moaned softly, and her hand spasmed. Greg yanked open a kitchen drawer and rummaged through it. He held the duct tape roll aloft, and Amber gave a satisfied nod.

"Tape their hands and feet," she said, pointing to Mom and Althea. "You can help us carry them," she said to me, nudging me away from my mother with one knee.

"Carry them? Where?" My gaze scanned the kitchen as I sought desperately for a way to keep all of us from dying.

"To the boat."

"You're going to dump the four of us at sea?" A knife block held four wicked-looking blades on the counter. Could I lunge for it and grab a knife before Amber short-circuited my nervous system with the stun gun? Unlikely.

"Not Simone," Greg said, wrapping tape efficiently around Mom's wrists. He tore the end with his teeth and started on her ankles. Her foot flicked out like she was trying to kick him, but the electrical charge had robbed her of coordination and power, and he caught the foot easily.

"We need Simone's body," Amber explained. Tearing a length of tape from the roll, she kept her eyes on me as she plastered it over Mom's mouth, her splint making her awkward. "For Greg to inherit, she needs to be declared dead. So she's going to have a car accident on that turn out by the old cemetery. Her car will skid into the water, and she'll drown. So sad." She delivered the words in the cold, unsympathetic tones of an android. "They'll find alcohol in her bloodstream" — she nodded toward the wine bottle — "and Greg will tell the cops they had a little spat, and she rushed out before he could stop her. You all, on the other hand —"

She paused, and the look in her eyes gave me the creeps. Greg stepped over Mom's trussed figure and began taping Althea's hands behind her back. When he was done, he did her ankles and slapped a piece of tape over her mouth for good measure. Althea bucked, and I could tell she was regaining some control of her muscles.

"We have to make you disappear. The

381

boat. We can put you overboard three or four miles out to sea."

"You can kill us," I said, "but you'll go to jail. Three women can't just disappear from St. Elizabeth without the police combing every inch of the town."

"You're right." A small smile curved her lips. "But you won't disappear in St. Elizabeth. Aren't you on your way to Alabama? Ruthie mentioned it. You can disappear on the road. It'll be a huge mystery. Maybe you'll even make one of those crime reenactment shows on the Discovery channel. You'll be famous." She looked at Greg. "We have to improvise. We'll stage Simone's accident first —"

"She might be found too soon, before we dispose of these three," he objected.

"You're right." Amber bit her lip, thinking. "Okay, we take the boat out and dump them first. Then we stage Simone's accident, and I drop you back here. I'll take their clunker and drive to Alabama and abandon it in a rest stop. You'll be here to play the grieving husband when the police come with the tragic news about poor Simone. I'll make my way back to New Jersey."

Amber paused again, and her eyes took on a faraway look as she calculated, "I can call Ruthie from the road somewhere and tell her I had to leave for a family emergency. You wait a decent interval after the funeral, until all the fuss dies down — maybe a couple of months — and come back to your job in New York. We won't be able to see each other or even talk on the phone while you're here, but the payoff will be worth it. Is there anything I haven't thought of?"

Didn't sound like it to me. Her scheme to leave our car in Alabama was brilliant. Lots of people knew we planned to leave today. When Aunt Flora or someone reported us missing, the search efforts would concentrate in Alabama. Our bodies would never turn up, not if Amber and Greg weighted us before tipping us into the ocean. Susan might say something about us stopping by to ask for Simone, but Greg could talk his way out of that. Sure, he'd say, we'd stopped by, but we'd left when he said Simone was out. No one would be able to prove otherwise, and it would account for our car being outside in case an alert neighbor had noticed it. Rachel had the photo, too — maybe she had even shown it to Special Agent Dillon by now — but no one could identify Amber from it, and Greg could say that's what he and Simone fought about —

his flirting with another woman. People would think he was a slimeball to be kissing another woman so soon after his marriage to Simone, but being a slimeball wasn't against the law.

Amber glanced out the window. "It's dark enough. Let's do it. Take that one's feet," she told me, nudging Althea with her toe. "You get her shoulders, Greg. Don't even think about yelling while you're outside," Amber said to me, squatting beside Mom, "or I'll scramble her brains." She pressed the stun gun against Mom's temple.

Fear flickered in Mom's eyes, and a mute appeal. Her eyes slid to the side. I followed her gaze to the knife block and nodded infinitesimally. She was telling me to try to get us out of this, even if it meant more pain for herself. Hooking my hands under Althea's ankles, I hoisted her lower half while Greg caught her under her arms and lifted her torso with a grunt. Her butt sagged toward the floor. For a medium-sized woman, she weighed a ton, and I leaned back a bit to brace myself. Greg backed toward the door and I followed. We drew abreast of Amber and Mom. Amber dug the stun gun into Mom's temple so it dented the flesh.

"Maybe there'll be another ghost story for

St. Elizabeth's ghost walk after tonight," she said with a small smile.

My arms pimpled with gooseflesh as I passed her, either from the coldness wafting off her or the hint of breeze blowing from the water. An empty expanse of grass — no potential weapons — stretched between the back door and the wooden dock. Lights glinted from across the bayou but not so close anyone would hear me if I called out. This side of the bayou lay in total darkness, with only the flitterings of fireflies providing sparks of illumination. Even though it was only twenty feet or so to the dock, my shoulders ached by the time we stepped onto the wood. The dock shifted beneath us, and the timbers groaned. The stink of a dead fish slapped at me, and I coughed, almost dropping Althea's legs.

"Here," Greg said. He lowered Althea's shoulders to the dock as we came alongside the cabin cruiser. For a moment, he was distracted and off balance, and I considered shoving him into the water. But the thought of Amber holding the stun gun to my mother's head stopped me. I didn't know if a stun gun could kill or permanently disable, but I wasn't willing to take the chance. Instead, I laid Althea's legs on the dock, giving her knee a surreptitious pat, and followed Greg back to the kitchen.

"Don't even think about trying something," Amber warned as I beat Greg to Mom's shoulders. He shrugged and hoisted her under her knees. Amber stayed by Mom's head, stun gun at the ready, as we lifted her and tromped out the door. I'd decided what I had to do and I tensed as we reached the dock. Sorry, Mom, I apologized internally, dropping her shoulders so her upper half crashed to the dock, jerking her away from the stun gun and jolting Greg off balance. In almost the same motion, I jumped at Amber, ramming my shoulders into her stomach. She gave an "oof" of pain and went sprawling, me on top of her. The stun gun skittered past Althea and lodged by a piling.

Greg dropped Mom's legs and lunged for me. He grabbed my wrist as I scrambled off Amber, perilously close to the edge.

"Get the gun," he yelled to Amber. She rolled over and scrabbled toward it on her hands and knees. As she scooted past Althea, Althea bunched her legs to her chest and shot them toward Amber, taking the younger woman by surprise and knocking her over the side.

"Hel— !" She cried before a splash drowned her words. Fury twisted Greg's face into an ugly mask, and he jerked me closer with the hand around my wrist, using his free hand to slap me.

The pain made my head ring and brought tears to my eyes. I sagged forward, and before he could react, I snapped my head up, butting him under the chin and slamming his jaw shut with a force that reverberated down my spine. Before I could jump back, both his arms came around me, and he squeezed me against his chest in a painful bear hug. My back popped, and I was afraid he was going to snap my spine. I cried out wordlessly. I did the only thing I could do. I flung myself sideways with as much force as I could muster, and we toppled off the dock toward the water.

I felt like time had slowed. Air whistled past my face and then I splatted into the water. The cool wetness seized me, and river water splashed into my open mouth. The impact broke Greg's hold, but I was beneath him, and his weight bore me down before I could gulp a breath of air. Although my eyes were open, total darkness enveloped me. Frantic, I kicked as hard as I could. My heel connected with something solid that could have been Greg or a piling. I was totally disoriented. A giant hand wrung my lungs like a sponge, and I felt myself running out of air. My ears buzzed, and I knew that in seconds I would open my mouth and suck in not life-giving air, but river water. My arms flailed in a frenzied crawl and moved me toward what I hoped was the surface. I kicked once more and exploded through the darkness, gasping.

After three quick breaths, I spun around in the water to locate Greg and Amber. Amber stood in waist-high water dockside, reaching for the stun gun. I hoped it would electrocute her if she tried to use it in the water. Splashing alerted me to Greg's presence behind me, and I turned to face him, realizing that my toes had brushed the river bottom. Paddling backward toward the bank, I found myself able to stand. Greg bared his teeth and lunged toward me, seeing escape within my reach. If I could make it to the shore . . . His hand closed around my ankle.

A shot rang out, freezing us all in place. Greg's grip loosened, and I shook my foot free. My ears ringing, I looked up to see Special Agent Dillon moving onto the dock with a phalanx of cops behind him, his gun trained squarely on Amber as she crouched on the dock as if she'd just hauled herself from the water, her good hand clutching the stun gun.

"Drop it," Dillon demanded.

She hesitated, then complied. The stun gun plopped into the water. Amber, her hair straggling wetly over her shoulders, stood slowly and raised her hands. A uniformed policeman hurried to cuff her, being careful to stay out of the line of fire.

Special Agent Dillon approached down the muddy bank and leveled the gun at Greg, beckoning to me with his left hand. "Don't move," he ordered Greg. I'd never seen him look so grim or so imposing, with the Kevlar vest strapped around him and his eyes as steely as the gun's barrel. Legs trembling, I slogged out of the river and grasped Dillon's hand. It closed tightly around mine, and he guided me behind him. "Out." He motioned with the gun for Greg to leave the water.

Greg spread his arms out, hands at shoulder height, risking a quick glance behind him.

"Don't even think about it," Dillon said.

At his tone, Greg apparently abandoned all thought of swimming away and started slowly toward the bank, where two officers searched him and cuffed him. I trotted to the dock and dropped to my knees beside Mom, ripping the tape from her mouth with a quick jerk.

"Sorry," I said as she winced, "but faster is better. At least, that's what you always said when taking off Band-Aids. And I'm so sorry I had to drop you. Are you okay?"

"Just a little shaken up. You done good, baby girl," she said, smiling at me. "Can you get this — ?" She struggled to sit up and lifted her taped wrists.

"Let me," said Hank, squatting beside her. He produced a knife and sawed through the duct tape with ruthless efficiency. His partner was reading Greg Hutchinson his rights, and a female officer I didn't know was patting down a dripping Amber, whose hands were cuffed behind her. An EMT had freed Althea and was holding a stethoscope to her chest.

"I'm fine," she said, batting his hand away.

"Thank you, Hank," my mother said, peeling the tape fragments off her wrists. "I appreciate it."

I signaled to the EMT to come have a look at Mom. She grimaced but let him examine her.

A hand on my shoulder brought me to my feet. "Are you all right, Miss Terhune?" Dillon asked. The concern in his eyes belied the formal tone.

"Wet, but alive," I said with a small smile. "I guess you are pretty handy at rescuing damsels in distress."

"Looked to me like you three butt-kicking damsels were about to win free on your own," he said, humor banishing the dark look from his eyes.

"Well, we were at least going to do a little damage," I said. I shivered at the thought of being rolled over the side of the boat, immobilized by duct tape, to drown in the dark wetness of the ocean. I had come too close as it was. "Will Simone be okay? Greg drugged her."

"Her vitals are good. She'll be fine," a paramedic assured me, as his partner rolled Simone out of the kitchen on a gurney. "Although she might not remember everything. We'll take her in for observation."

It seemed like dozens of people swarmed the house and lawn as crime scene technicians replaced the EMTs who bore Simone away. Other paramedics helped Mom and Althea to the kitchen. As the adrenaline seeped out of my system, my limbs shook and I felt shivery. I needed to get away. And get dry. As if sensing my need, Dillon took my elbow and walked me down to the end of the dock. Weak moonlight played over the river, and frogs croaked from the bank now that the action was over. The incoming tide must have floated the rotten fish free, because the noxious odor was gone. The boat that would have been our hearse tugged gently at its moorings. Dark water flowed inland, seeming peaceful and unthreatening from my vantage point on the dock. Dillon put an arm around my shoulders and squeezed me up against his side despite my wetness. The bulletproof vest was hard and unyielding, but I rested against him for a moment. "You did a very brave thing," he said softly. "Thank God you're okay."

Suddenly, I didn't feel so cold. I smiled into his shoulder. When I pulled away after a long moment, he said, "Why don't you and your mom and Mrs. Jenkins go home. I heard enough of what Hutchinson and the woman were saying to wait until tomorrow for your statements."

"Sounds good," I said, giving him a tired smile. "It's been a long day."

He grinned. "You said it. Just promise me I won't have to come out in the middle of the night because you're chasing intruders or dodging snakes in your pajamas again."

CHAPTER TWENTY-FOUR

[Wednesday]

The next few days jumbled together as we gave our statements to the police and then underwent even more grueling questions from friends, family, and the merely curious. My sister Alice Rose popped in for a day to make sure Mom and I were okay and get the scoop firsthand. Marty Shears called me from his hospital room in Atlanta to get the story. He sounded more interested in the conversation I'd overheard between Del Richardson and the man in the cemetery than in Greg and Amber Hutchinson's murderous plans, although he wrote a story about the decades-old grudge and the obsession with revenge that landed on an inside page of *The Atlanta Journal-Constitution*. (Addie McGowan had a front-page article about the murders coming out in tomorrow's *Gazette;* she'd grilled me about my part in the investigation for three hours on Tuesday.) Nailing Governor Lansky was still Marty's driving focus. Maybe someday he'd tell me why he had it in for the governor. He was convinced Richardson or Lansky or both had arranged his car accident, and he was redoubling his efforts to nail the governor. He said he'd be back in St. Elizabeth before too long and told me he'd take me to dinner, to make up for missing the Rothmere ball. Sounded good to me.

Simone DuBois stopped by the salon on Wednesday. She knocked timidly on the door and then pushed it open. I was alone. Stella had found part-time work at Chez Pierre, Rachel was at school, and Mom and Althea had gone to Jacksonville for the day to tour a personal products manufacturing facility Althea was considering to produce Althea's Organic Skin Solutions. I was using the downtime to clean out the shampoo sink, which had been draining sluggishly of late, so Simone caught me jabbing a straightened hanger into the section of PVC piping I'd loosened, prying globs of nasty gook and hair into a bucket.

"How are you feeling?" I asked when I saw who it was. I stood and wiped my hands on a towel.

Simone looked pale, her black hair seeming to suck the color out of her makeupless face. Her slacks hung loosely on her thin frame, and I thought she'd lost weight.

"It looks so empty," she said, looking around without answering.

"You had us closed down," I reminded her quietly. "Is Peaches going to be okay?" I asked when she didn't say anything.

She nodded. "Yes. She has a broken leg and some bruising. She's got a little doggy cast on one leg, but other than that she's okay. I can pick her up from the vet this afternoon." She fell silent again, moving farther into the room. Her hand traced the line of the hair dryer hanging at Mom's station. "I came to thank you," she said, looking up. "You and your mom and Althea saved my life. I still can't believe —" Tears trickled down her face.

"We all make mistakes about men," I said, trying to comfort her. "I wasted a decade on Hank Parker, for heaven's sake."

She shot me a look reminiscent of the old Simone. "My mistake got my mother killed." The stark statement hung in the air between us.

"Your dad cheating Carl Rowan out of his property set that in motion," I said. "And Greg's mother fostering his obsession and his own greedy personality. Greg killed

Constance. You are not responsible for your mother's death, Simone."

She flapped a hand as if batting away the words and the comfort that went with them.

"Anyway, thank you," she said. "I owe you. I'd like to help set this right" — she gestured to the empty salon — "if I can."

I'd already done my research with the State Board of Cosmetology and knew just how she could help. "Call Barbara Mayhew," I said, leading her to the phone. "Here's what you say." And I filled her in on my idea.

Ten minutes later, Simone hung up the phone and gave me a wry smile. "She went for it," she said.

I beamed. I couldn't wait to tell my mom.

"This doesn't mean we have to get all mushy and huggy, does it?" Simone asked with something like her old acerbity.

"I won't if you won't," I promised, thinking maybe Simone wasn't so bad after all.

"Thank you," we both said at the same time. I laughed, and Simone shrugged.

I put out my hand, and Simone shook it tentatively. "Maybe you'd like to have a drink with me and Vonda one of these nights," I heard myself saying. What was I doing? Vonda would kill me. Still, the new Simone looked like she might not be a complete witch.

"Maybe," Simone said. She pulled the door open and paused on the threshold. "Really," she said, "thank you for everything."

I nodded, and she closed the door softly behind her.

I had barely ducked under the sink to reattach the PVC when I heard the door jingle open again. "Down here," I called, thinking Simone had forgotten something.

A heavy tread approached, and I saw two feet shod in wingtips that Simone wouldn't wear if she were a bag lady and her only other option was barefoot.

"You have many talents, don't you?" an amused voice asked. "Beautician, investigator, plumber. Is there anything you don't do?"

"Brain surgery," I said, scooting out from under the sink to see Special Agent Dillon smiling down at me. "Also calf roping, surfing, and anything that requires math more sophisticated than two plus two."

He reached down a hand and helped me to my feet. A warm feeling seeped through me at his touch. "Let me see if this works," I said, pulling my hand away and turning to the sink. I twisted the taps on and stooped to look under the sink. No drips. Yay. I turned the taps off again and watched the water drain freely. Double yay.

"Want some coffee?" I asked. Dillon hadn't moved while I tested the sink, and now he was uncomfortably close in a really comfortable way.

"Sure," he said after a moment, and backed off a few steps so I could get past him.

I scooped coffee into the pot and poured in the water. The first drip hissed onto the burner before I slid the carafe beneath the stream. Watching the pot fill, I asked, "What brings you out this way?"

He propped himself against the counter and folded his arms across his chest. "I wanted to let you know we matched Amber Falstead Hutchinson's fingerprints to the ones we took off the shovel at the cemetery. She saw you leave and decided to take the opportunity to make another stab at getting rid of you. The shovel being by the grave was just serendipitous, she said."

"Yeah, that's the word I would've chosen." Being knocked into a grave by an assailant who wanted to bury me alive entitled me to a little sarcasm.

Dillon raised a brow at my tone, but kept going. "She also admits to buying the cottonmouth from some seedy character who works on the river and breakfasts at Doralynn's. She's the one who wrote the 'MYOB' note, too, although Hutchinson apparently made and threw the Molotov cocktail and broke in here to plant the sword."

"Sounds like they were made for each other," I observed. Selecting a blue earthenware mug from the cabinet, I filled it from the steaming carafe and passed it to Dillon. Our fingers brushed.

"That's too bad," he said, blowing on the coffee, "because I don't think the state goes in for his and her adjoining cells."

Special Agent Dillon had mentioned the sword; something about that still puzzled me. "How come Constance had the sword in her car that night? I was sure she'd given it to Philip for his birthday. He was my favorite suspect for a while."

"According to Philip and Simone, their mother was planning to give it to him at his birthday party, which was scheduled for Friday evening. They cancelled, of course, after Constance was murdered."

We were silent for a moment, contemplating twists of fate. At least, I was thinking about how differently things might have turned out if Constance had given Philip the sword on his actual birthday. Then it wouldn't have been in her car when Greg confronted her Wednesday night.

"What did Greg say about the night his father and William Jenkins disappeared?" I asked, hoping he had seen or heard something that might give a hint as to where Carl and William ended up.

"Nothing other than what he already told you," Dillon said. "His dad came home with William that night and announced he was going to 'have it out' with Philip DuBois about the land deal. He stomped out of the house, Jenkins following him, and that's all he knows."

I sighed. "I was really hoping he might know more. For Althea's sake."

"I know." He set his mug down on the counter.

Reluctant to let him leave for some strange reason, I asked, "What will happen to Philip DuBois and Del Richardson?"

"Nothing."

I slanted a look at him, and he shrugged. "There's no proof they did anything wrong. I know Shears is convinced they engineered his accident, and the mechanic says it looks like the brake line was cut, but there's absolutely no evidence pointing toward Richardson or DuBois, much less the governor."

"So Richardson wins." I thought with frustration of Richardson's infuriating contention that he never lost.

"I wouldn't say that," Dillon said. "The town voted against his store. Well —"

"So this is where Marshal Dillon rides off into the sunset, right? On his white horse?"

"You're thinking of the Lone Ranger," he said. "My horse is black. An Arabian named Groucho. Maybe you'd like to meet him sometime?"

"Sure," I said casually, although my heartbeat doubled. "Sounds like fun, Marsh."

"Don't you think it's time you started calling me John, Grace?"

"If you prefer, John-Grace." Hey, anybody who named his horse Groucho ought to appreciate a little "who's on first" kind of humor. I suppressed a grin.

John rolled his eyes. "Soon," he promised, and left.

Mom and Althea came bustling in half an hour later, talking knowledgeably about packaging and labels and price per unit. I had called Stella and Rachel, catching them on their lunch breaks, and the three of us were waiting for them.

"What's going on?" Althea asked, setting down a shopping bag. "If you don't look like the cat that's swallowed a couple of canaries with a mouse chaser, Grace."

Stella looked at her watch. "I've got a one o'clock client," she said, "and it's a twenty-minute drive. What's your big surprise?"

"What if I said you don't have to go back to Chez Pierre because Violetta's is reopening tomorrow?" I asked with a huge grin.

Total silence and dumbfounded expressions met my announcement.

"What do you mean?" Mom asked cautiously, blinking at me from behind her glasses.

"I mean that I've found a way to get Mrs. Mayhew to let us start doing business again," I said, "and Simone called her and she agreed."

"Simone?" Althea said suspiciously.

I nodded. "Look. I've got a Master Cosmetology license, so we can post that and legally operate the business under my license. It's still your shop, Mom," I said, forestalling the objection I saw in her face. "We don't have to change the names on the business license or anything."

"Are you thinking of cutting hair on your own while I'm at beauty school?" Mom asked, knitting her brows. "That could be a year, Grace. You'd be awfully busy."

"Nope. You don't have to go to beauty

school." I paused to let the suspense build. "State law says you can either get your license by going to an approved cosmetology school, *or* you can do three thousand hours as an apprentice. Well, you can be my apprentice, right here in your own shop! And Mrs. Mayhew has agreed, with Simone's prompting, to let us backdate a lot of the required hours, so you really only have to log hours for about six months before taking your exam."

I looked around at the stunned faces. Althea was the first to speak. "Well, hallelujah," she said, slapping her knee. "There's more than one way to skin a cat."

Rachel set her cauldron earring to swinging when she jumped up. "Well, I'll be here, like, tomorrow afternoon, right after school lets out, okay? Gotta run. I haven't studied near enough for my geometry test next period." She trotted out, ponytail bouncing.

Stella stood up next, relief on her face. She tucked a strand of auburn hair behind her ear. "Well, thank goodness. I'll give Chez Pierre my notice as soon as I get back. I guess I'll need to work out the week, if that's okay? It doesn't seem right to leave them in the lurch."

"Of course it's okay, Stel," Mom said, rising to give her a hug. "It's the right thing to do."

Stella hugged her back hard. "I can't say I really took to the folks at Chez Pierre. Oh, they're nice enough, but they're not family." And with a misty smile, she followed Rachel out the door.

"Oh, shoot," Althea said, pushing to her feet. "We're going to be late."

"Late for what?" I asked as my mom came over to hug me.

"Thank you, Grace," she said.

"I only did it so I could have a job again," I said, hugging her back.

"Late for Walter's groundbreaking," Althea said. "Come on."

"His groundbreaking?" I trailed Althea and Mom out of the shop.

"Well, the start of his demolition — whatever you want to call it. He's starting his renovation today, and we promised we'd help just to get him started. Good thing you're dressed for it," she added, eyeing the jeans and old tee shirt I'd donned for plumbing.

Great. I had better things to do with my afternoon than swing a sledge hammer, but I followed them down to Confederate Artefacts anyway. Walter greeted us at the door, atwitter with excitement. If it hadn't been

404

for the mustache, I wouldn't have recognized him. He was wearing overalls and a henley shirt instead of his Confederate uniform. The room behind him was empty of artifacts, only faded spots on the walls showing where weapons and frames had hung. Plastic sheeting covered the floor, with a wheelbarrow positioned in the middle of the room. Three sledge hammers and a large toolbox made up the rest of the room's contents.

"We're ready to start," Walter said, gesturing at the empty space. "The carpenter will be here tomorrow, so we have to complete the task today. You can't believe how much I'm saving by doing the demolition myself!"

Hm. Himself plus three unpaid slaves. I didn't really mind helping him, though, so I said, "Where do we start?"

"That wall." He pointed to the wall separating what had been the display area from the back offices. "The contractor tells me it's not load bearing, so have at it. Here, you might want these." He gave us each goggles and blue dust masks to fit over our faces. "Maybe Miss Althea should take the first swing," he said, "since it's her building."

"Oh, no," she said, shaking her head firmly. "It's your project. I might be good

405

for pulling out drywall, but I'd put myself in the hospital if I tried to swing that sledge hammer. You do the honors."

With a huge grin that made his mustache tickle his cheeks, he hefted a sledge hammer and swung at the wall. A gaping hole appeared, and a cloud of white dust filled the air. I coughed. Mom picked up one of the other sledge hammers and swung it like a croquet mallet at the wall.

"This is kind of therapeutic," she told me, her voice muffled by the mask. "Try it."

I did, slinging the sledge hammer at the far end of the wall so hard I thought it would pull my arms out of their sockets. I did it again. Mom was right; there was something freeing in the act of whacking down a wall. It was so contrary to what we're all taught to do. We build walls, or mend them, or paint them; we don't knock holes in them. I set the hammer down after only a few minutes. I was breathing heavily, and sweat was already pouring down my sides. The air was white with drifting particles, like a thick fog had seeped into the building. Althea and Mom and Walter all looked like ghosts, their clothing, hair, and exposed skin coated white. I imagined I looked the same.

"Let's get some of this debris out of here,"

Althea said practically when Walter set his sledge down. "Looks like plaster and wallboard and heaven knows what else." Trundling the wheelbarrow closer to the wall, she began picking up the biggest slabs of wall and tossing them in.

I was thinking that I should run out to get some bottled water for all of us when Althea screeched and scrambled back from the wall. She stopped ten feet from it, trembling.

The three of us rushed toward her. I was afraid she'd stepped on a rusty nail and was already planning to drive her to the urgent care clinic for a tetanus shot when Mom asked, "Althea! What's wrong?"

Althea's mouth opened and closed, but no words came out. Finally, she pointed. While Mom examined her friend, looking for cuts or nail punctures, I guessed, Walter and I stepped closer to the wall. The dust had settled somewhat, and we could see into the opening, a space about eighteen inches wide that ran the length of the wall.

"I see nothing out of the ordinary," Walter said, edging a chunk of drywall out of the way with his foot.

Something red caught my eye. I leaned forward to examine it, my head and shoulders inside the space that, up until twenty minutes ago, had been a wall. What I saw

407

made me gasp. Sliding my mask down over my chin, I drew in a deep breath. I steadied myself and looked again to be sure. The red was the tattered remains of a shirt, I thought, and it hung on the gleaming white bones of a skeleton. I knew, beyond the shadow of a doubt, that we had found William Jenkins and Carl Rowan.

"They must have gone to see Philip DuBois at the bank after the poker game," my mom said later that afternoon as we sat on the veranda, recovering with tea and snickerdoodles from another round of police interviews. "And he shot them."

The medical examiner had found a bullet hole in each skull.

"No wonder that bank was closed up for so long," Althea said. "We thought it was just because they had moved to the new building. We never suspected."

I'd thought she would be traumatized by the day's events, but she seemed calm, even peaceful.

As if she'd read my thoughts, she turned to look at me. Her familiar face with its cocoa skin and warm brown eyes was dear to me, and I blinked back tears as she said, "It was the not knowing that bothered me all these years. Now, we can lay him to rest.

He deserves to rest easy." She lapsed into silence, sipping at her tea. A fly buzzed around her head, but she ignored it.

She'd already talked to the funeral home and made arrangements for a burial at Cypress Grove Cemetery on Saturday. I knew the whole town would be there.

"I guess that's why Constance left you the building," I said, the thought suddenly hitting me. "Maybe it was her way of making reparations."

"Hmph," was all Althea said.

"Hey, y'all," a voice called from the foot of the stairs.

The three of us looked down, resigned, to see Hank Parker clomping up the stairs, a rectangular box tucked under his arm. "So, I hear you found some more bodies over at the old bank building," he said with a smile, like he was congratulating us for finding the prize in a Cracker Jack box or winning a scavenger hunt. "I wish I'd been on duty."

When we stared at him, not replying, he shuffled his feet. "Here, Grace, I brought this for you." He thrust the box at me.

Surprised, I took it. "Thank you," I said automatically, uncomfortable and irritated by a gift from Hank. So why had I said "thank you"? I pushed it back toward him. "You shouldn't be giving me gifts, Hank."

He whipped his hands behind his back so he couldn't take the box. His smile never faltered. "Now, now, Grace, it's just a little something. I remembered what you were wearing that night when the house was broken into."

I began hastily opening the box to get the man off our porch as quickly as possible.

"You should maybe wait —" Hank started uneasily.

Two pieces of purple satin trimmed with stiff black lace fell out. They lay on the veranda with four pairs of eyes fixed on them.

"Oh, my." Mom sighed, rolling her eyes up. "God grant me patience."

I struggled with emotions ranging from embarrassment to rage.

Althea, however, bent and picked up the thong, testing its stretchy elastic waistband with two fingers. " 'Bout the only thing this is good for is running off fools who don't have the sense God gave a tadpole and have tacky taste in underthings, to boot."

"Now, wait a minute, Miss Althea," Hank said, backing down two steps.

Ignoring him, she braced a forefinger against the waistband, pulled back with her other hand, and slingshot the thong toward Hank's head. It looped around his right ear, and he turned to run as she loaded the nightie top into firing position.

Hank pounded down the sidewalk as Mom said, "Ready, aim, fire!"

Althea launched the lingerie. It fell well short of Hank's fleeing figure. The three of us high-fived each other, laughing so hard we doubled over.

"I'd call that a good day's work," Althea said, wiping her eyes. "We find my husband and we run yours off with a few scraps of lace and some spandex. It doesn't get any better than that."

I had to agree.

ORGANIC SKIN-CARE RECIPES

MOISTURIZING TREATMENTS

For Normal or Oily Skin:

1 avocado, mashed

1 tsp. raspberry balsamic vinegar (white or apple cider vinegars work just as well; Althea prefers the scent of the raspberry balsamic)

3 tsps. sesame oil (you can also use olive oil or almond oil)

1 tsp. honey

1 egg white, beaten

Combine the first four ingredients, mixing to a paste. Beat egg white and add last, mixing well. Apply to face, neck, and chest (as desired). Let sit for approximately 20–30 minutes, then rinse gently with tepid water.

For Dry Skin:

1 tbsp. Greek yogurt (any plain yogurt will work — Althea likes the texture of Greek)

1 egg yolk

1/2 cup cooked oatmeal (traditional oatmeal
works better than instant or microwave)

2 tsps. honey

1–2 tsps. mint, chopped

Mix all ingredients in small bowl until well blended. Apply to face, neck, and chest (as desired). Relax for 20 minutes, then rinse with tepid water.

EXFOLIATING TREATMENT

2 tbsp. kosher salt

1 1/2 tsps. honey

1 1/2 tsps. olive oil

Juice of 1/2 lemon or 1 tsp. lemon juice
from bottle

Mix all ingredients in small bowl. Rub gently into face, elbows, heels, chest (wherever exfoliation is needed). The key word is "gently," especially on delicate facial skin. Even natural exfoliants such as salt and sugar can cause microscopic skin tears if used too roughly or too frequently. Rinse immediately with tepid water.

ABOUT THE AUTHOR

Author of the Southern Beauty Shop Mysteries, **Lila Dare** was born in Georgia and has lived in Alabama, Mississippi, and Virginia, as well as in some bastions of Yankee culture. Although she has never worked in a beauty shop, she has spent plenty of time in salons and likes to tell her stylist: "Just do what you think would look good." Maybe that's why there's no picture of her available. She currently lives west of the Mississippi with her husband, two daughters, and dog, and misses Southern manners, cooking, and friendliness, but not the humidity.

We hope you have enjoyed this Large Print book. Other Thorndike, Wheeler, Kennebec, and Chivers Press Large Print books are available at your library or directly from the publishers.

For information about current and upcoming titles, please call or write, without obligation, to:

Publisher
Thorndike Press
295 Kennedy Memorial Drive
Waterville, ME 04901
Tel. (800) 223-1244

or visit our Web site at:

http://gale.cengage.com/thorndike

OR

Chivers Large Print
published by BBC Audiobooks Ltd
St James House, The Square
Lower Bristol Road
Bath BA2 3SB
England
Tel. +44(0) 800 136919
email: bbcaudiobooks@bbc.co.uk
www.bbcaudiobooks.co.uk

All our Large Print titles are designed for easy reading, and all our books are made to last.